**Rafael Sabatini**, creator of some of the world's best-loved heroes, was born in Italy in 1875 and educated in both Portugal and Switzerland. He eventually settled in England in 1892, by which time he was fluent in a total of five languages. He chose to write in English, claiming that 'all the best stories are written in English'.

His writing career was launched in the 1890s with a collection of short stories, and it was not until 1902 that his first novel was published. His fame, however, came with *Scaramouche*, the much-loved story of the French Revolution, which became an international bestseller. *Captain Blood* followed soon after, which resulted in a renewed enthusiasm for his earlier work.

For many years a prolific writer, he was forced to abandon writing in the 1940s through illness and he eventually died in 1950.

Sabatini is best-remembered for his heroic characters and high-spirited novels, many of which have been adapted into classic films, including *Scaramouche, Captain Blood* and *The Sea Hawk* starring Errol Flynn.

# Bardelys the Magnificent

Rafael Sabatini

This edition published in 2001 by House of Stratus, an imprint of
Stratus Books Ltd., 21 Beeching Park, Kelly Bray,
Cornwall, PL17 8QS, UK.
www.houseofstratus.com

Typeset, printed and bound by House of Stratus.

A catalogue record for this book is available from the British Library
and the Library of Congress.

ISBN 07551-152-5-2

# Chapter 1

# The Wager

"Speak of the Devil," whispered La Fosse in my ear, and, moved by the words and by the significance of his glance, I turned in my chair. The door had opened, and under the lintel stood the thick-set figure of the Comte de Chatellerault. Before him a lacquey in my escutcheoned livery of red-and-gold was receiving, with back obsequiously bent, his hat and cloak.

A sudden hush fell upon the assembly where a moment ago this very man had been the subject of our talk, and silenced were the wits that but an instant since had been making free with his name and turning the Languedoc courtship – from which he was newly returned with the shame of defeat – into a subject for heartless mockery and jest. Surprise was in the air for we had heard that Chatellerault was crushed by his ill-fortune in the lists of Cupid, and we had not looked to see him joining so soon a board at which – or so at least I boasted – mirth presided.

And so for a little space the Count stood pausing on my threshold, whilst we craned our necks to contemplate him as though he had been an object for inquisitive inspection. Then a smothered laugh from the brainless La Fosse seemed to break the spell. I frowned. It was a climax of discourtesy whose impression I must at all costs efface.

I leapt to my feet, with a suddenness that sent my chair gliding a full half-yard along the glimmering parquet of the floor, and in two strides I had reached the Count and put forth my hand to bid him welcome. He took it with a leisureliness that argued sorrow. He advanced into the full blaze of the candlelight, and fetched a dismal sigh from the depths of his portly bulk.

"You are surprised to see me, Monsieur le Marquis," said he, and his tone seemed to convey an apology for his coming – for his very existence almost.

Now Nature had made my Lord of Chatellerault as proud and arrogant as Lucifer – some resemblance to which illustrious personage his downtrodden retainers were said to detect in the lineaments of his swarthy face. Environment had added to that store of insolence wherewith Nature had equipped him, and the King's favour – in which he was my rival – had gone yet further to mould the peacock attributes of his vain soul. So that this wondrous humble tone of his gave me pause; for to me it seemed that not even a courtship gone awry could account for it in such a man.

"I had not thought to find so many here," said he. And his next words contained the cause of his dejected air. "The King, Monsieur de Bardelys, has refused to see me; and when the sun is gone, we lesser bodies of the courtly firmament must needs turn for light and comfort to the moon." And he made me a sweeping bow.

"Meaning that I rule the night?" quoth I, and laughed. "The figure is more playful than exact, for whilst the moon is cold and cheerless, me you shall find ever warm and cordial. I could have wished, Monsieur de Chatellerault, that your gracing my board were due to a circumstance less untoward than His Majesty's displeasure."

"It is not for nothing that they call you the Magnificent," he answered, with a fresh bow, insensible to the sting in the tail of my honeyed words.

I laughed, and, setting compliments to rest with that, I led him to the table.

"Ganymède, a place here for Monsieur le Comte. Gilles, Antoine, see to Monsieur de Chatellerault. Basile, wine for Monsieur le Comte. Bestir there!"

In a moment he was become the centre of a very turmoil of attention.

My lacqueys flitted about him buzzing and insistent as bees about a rose. Would Monsieur taste of this capon à la casserole, or of this truffled peacock? Would a slice of this juicy ham à l'anglaise tempt Monsieur le Comte, or would he give himself the pain of trying this turkey aux olives? Here was a salad whose secret Monsieur le Marquis' cook had learnt in Italy, and here a vol-au-vent that was invented by Quelon himself.

Basile urged his wines upon him, accompanied by a page who bore a silver tray laden with beakers and flagons. Would Monsieur le Comte take white Armagnac or red Anjou? This was a Burgundy of which Monsieur le Marquis thought highly, and this a delicate Lombardy wine that His Majesty had oft commended. Or perhaps Monsieur de Chatellerault would prefer to taste the last vintage of Bardelys?

And so they plagued him and bewildered him until his choice was made; and even then a couple of them held themselves in readiness behind his chair to forestall his slightest want. Indeed, had he been the very King himself, no greater honour could we have shown him at the Hôtel de Bardelys.

But the restraint that his coming had brought with it hung still upon the company, for Chatellerault was little loved, and his presence there was much as that of the skull at an Egyptian banquet.

For of all these fair-weather friends that sat about my table – amongst whom there were few that had not felt his power – I feared there might be scarcely one would have the grace to dissemble his contempt of the fallen favourite. That he was fallen, as much his words as what already we had known, had told us.

Yet in my house I would strive that he should have no foretaste of that coldness that tomorrow all Paris would be showing him, and to this end I played the host with all the graciousness that role may bear, and overwhelmed him with my cordiality, whilst to thaw all iciness from the bearing of my other guests, I set the wines to flow more freely still. My dignity would permit no less of me, else would it have seemed that I rejoiced in a rival's downfall and took satisfaction from the circumstance that his disfavour with the King was like to result in my own further exaltation.

My efforts were not wasted. Slowly the mellowing influence of the grape pronounced itself. To this influence I added that of such wit as Heaven has graced me with, and by a word here and another there I set myself to lash their mood back into the joviality out of which his coming had for the moment driven it.

And so, presently, Good-Humour spread her mantle over us anew, and quip and jest and laughter decked our speech, until the noise of our merry-making drifting out through the open windows must have been borne upon the breeze of that August night down the rue Saint-Dominique, across the rue de l'Enfer, to the very ears perhaps of those within the Luxembourg, telling them that Bardelys and his friends kept another of those revels which were become a byword in Paris, and had contributed not a little to the sobriquet of "Magnificent" which men gave me.

But, later, as the toasts grew wild and were pledged less for the sake of the toasted than for that of the wine itself, wits grew more barbed and less restrained by caution; recklessness hung a moment, like a bird of prey, above us, then swooped abruptly down in the words of that fool La Fosse.

"Messieurs," he lisped, with that fatuousness he affected, and with his eye fixed coldly upon Chatellerault, "I have a toast for you."

He rose carefully to his feet – he had arrived at that condition in which to move with care is of the first importance. He shifted his eye from the Count to his glass, which stood half empty. He signed to a lacquey to fill it. "To the brim, gentlemen," he commanded.

Then, in the silence that ensued, he attempted to stand with one foot on the ground and one on his chair; but encountering difficulties of balance, he remained upright – safer if less picturesque.

"Messieurs, I give you the most peerless, the most beautiful, the most difficult and cold lady in all France. I drink to those her thousand graces, of which Fame has told us, and to that greatest and most vexing charm of all – her cold indifference to man. I pledge you, too, the swain whose good fortune it may be to play Endymion to this Diana.

"It will need," pursued La Fosse, who dealt much in mythology and classic lore – "it will need an Adonis in beauty, a Mars in valour, an Apollo in song, and a very Eros in love to accomplish it. And I fear me," he hiccoughed, "that it will go unaccomplished, since the one man in all France on whom we have based our hopes has failed.

"Gentlemen, to your feet! I give you the matchless Roxalanne de Lavedan!"

Such amusement as I felt was tempered by apprehension. I shot a swift glance at Chatellerault to mark how he took this pleasantry and this pledging of the lady whom the King had sent him to woo, but whom he had failed to win. He had risen with the others at La Fosse's bidding, either unsuspicious or else deeming suspicion too flimsy a thing by which to steer conduct. Yet at the mention of her name a scowl darkened his ponderous countenance. He set down his glass with such sudden force that its slender stem was snapped and a red stream of wine streaked the white tablecloth and spread around a silver flowerbowl. The sight of that stain recalled him to himself and to the manners he had allowed himself for a moment to forget.

"Bardelys, a thousand apologies for my clumsiness," he muttered.

"Spilt wine," I laughed, "is a good omen."

And for once I accepted that belief, since but for the shedding of that wine and its sudden effect upon him, it is likely we had witnessed a shedding of blood. Thus, was the ill-timed pleasantry of my feather-brained La Fosse tided over in comparative safety. But the topic being raised was not so easily abandoned. Mademoiselle de Lavédan grew to be openly discussed, and even the Count's courtship of her came to be hinted at, at first vaguely, then pointedly, with a lack of delicacy for which I can but blame the wine with which these gentlemen had made a salad of their senses.

In growing alarm I watched the Count. But he showed no further sign of irritation. He sat and listened as though no jot concerned.

There were moments when he even smiled at some lively sally, and at last he went so far as to join in that merry combat of wits, and defend himself from their attacks, which were made with a good-humour that but thinly veiled the dislike he was held in and the satisfaction that was culled from his late discomfiture.

For a while I hung back and took no share in the banter that was toward. But in the end – lured perhaps by the spirit in which I have shown that Chatellerault accepted it, and lulled by the wine which in common with my guests I may have abused – I came to utter words but for which this story never had been written.

"Chatellerault," I laughed, "abandon these defensive subterfuges; confess that you are but uttering excuses, and acknowledge that you have conducted this affair with a clumsiness unpardonable in one equipped with your advantages of courtly rearing."

A flush overspread his face, the first sign of anger since he had spilled his wine.

"Your successes, Bardelys, render you vain, and of vanity is presumption born," he replied contemptuously.

"See!" I cried, appealing to the company. "Observe how he seeks to evade replying! Nay, but you shall confess your clumsiness."

"A clumsiness," murmured La Fosse drowsily, "as signal as that which attended Pan's wooing of the Queen of Lydia."

"I have no clumsiness to confess," he answered hotly, raising his voice. "It is a fine thing to sit here in Paris, among the languid, dull, and nerveless beauties of the Court, whose favours are easily won because they look on dalliance as the best pastime offered them, and are eager for such opportunities of it as you fleering coxcombs will afford them. But this Mademoiselle de Lavédan is of a vastly different mettle. She is a woman; not a doll. She is flesh and blood; not sawdust, powder, and vermilion. She has a heart and a will; not a spirit corrupted by vanity and licence."

La Fosse burst into a laugh.

"Hark! O, hark!" he cried, "to the apostle of the chaste!"

"Saint Gris!" exclaimed another. "This good Chatellerault has lost both heart and head to her."

Chatellerault glanced at the speaker with an eye in which anger smouldered.

"You have said it," I agreed. "He has fallen her victim, and so his vanity translates her into a compound of perfections. Does such a woman as you have described exist, Comte? Bah! In a lover's mind, perhaps, or in the pages of some crack-brained poet's fancies; but nowhere else in this dull world of ours."

He made a gesture of impatience.

"You have been clumsy, Chatellerault," I insisted. "You have lacked address. The woman does not live that is not to be won by any man who sets his mind to do it, if only he be of her station and have the means to maintain her in it or raise her to a better. A woman's love, sir, is a tree whose root is vanity. Your attentions flatter her, and predispose her to capitulate.

"Then, if you but wisely-choose your time to deliver the attack, and do so with the necessary adroitness – nor is overmuch demanded – the battle is won with ease, and she surrenders. Believe me, Chatellerault, I am a younger man than you by full five years, yet in experience I am a generation older, and I talk of what I know."

He sneered heavily. "If to have begun your career of dalliance at the age of eighteen with an amour that resulted in a scandal be your title to experience, I agree," said he. "But for the rest, Bardelys, for all your fine talk of conquering women, believe me when I tell you that in all your life you have never met a woman, for I deny the claim of these Court creatures to that title. If you would know a woman, go to Lavédan, Monsieur le Marquis. If you would have your army of amorous wiles suffer a defeat at last, go employ it against the citadel of Roxalanne de Lavédan's heart. If you would be humbled in your pride, betake yourself to Lavédan."

"A challenge!" roared a dozen voices. "A challenge, Bardelys!"

"Mais voyons," I deprecated, with a laugh, "would you have me journey into Languedoc and play at wooing this embodiment of all the marvels of womanhood for the sake of making good my argument? Of your charity, gentlemen, insist no further."

"The never-failing excuse of the boaster," sneered Chatellerault, "when desired to make good his boast."

"Monsieur conceives that I have made a boast?" quoth I, keeping my temper.

"Your words suggested one – else I do not know the meaning of words. They suggested that where I have failed you could succeed, if you had a mind to try. I have challenged you, Bardelys. I challenge you again. Go about this wooing as you will; dazzle the lady with your wealth and your magnificence, with your servants, your horses, your equipages, and all the splendours you can command; yet I make bold to say that not a year of your scented attentions and most insidious wiles will bear you fruit. Are you sufficiently challenged?"

"But this is rank frenzy!" I protested. "Why should I undertake this thing?"

"To prove me wrong," he taunted me. "To prove me clumsy. Come, Bardelys, what of your spirit?"

"I confess I would do much to afford you the proof you ask. But to take a wife! Pardieu! That is much indeed!"

"Bah!" he sneered. "You do well to draw back. You are wise to avoid discomfiture. This lady is not for you. When she is won, it will be by some bold and gallant gentleman, and by no mincing squire of dames, no courtly coxcomb, no fop of the Luxembourg, be his experiences of dalliance never so vast."

"Po' Cap de Dieu!" growled Cazalet, who was a Gascon captain in the Guards, and who swore strange, southern oaths. "Up, Bardelys! Afoot! Prove your boldness and your gallantry, or be forever shamed; a squire of dames, a courtly coxcomb, a fop of the Luxembourg! Mordemondieu! I have given a man a bellyful of steel for the half of those titles!"

I heeded him little, and as little the other noisy babblers, who now on their feet – those that could stand – were spurring me excitedly to accept the challenge, until from being one of the baiters it seemed that of a sudden the tables were turned and I was become the baited. I sat in thought, revolving the business in my mind, and frankly liking it but little. Doubts of the issue, were I to undertake it, I had none.

My views of the other sex were neither more nor less than my words to the Count had been calculated to convey. It may be – I know now – that it was that the women I had known fitted Chatellerault's description, and were not over-difficult to win. Hence, such successes as I had had with them in such comedies of love as I had been engaged upon had given me a false impression. But such at least was not my opinion that night. I was satisfied that Chatellerault talked wildly, and that no such woman lived as he depicted. Cynical and soured you may account me. Such I know I was accounted in Paris; a man satiated with all that wealth and youth and the King's favour could give him; stripped of illusions, of faith and of zest, the very magnificence – so envied – of my existence affording me more disgust than satisfaction, since already I had gauged its shallows.

Is it strange, therefore, that in this challenge flung at me with such insistence, a business that at first I disliked grew presently to beckon me with its novelty and its promise of new sensations?

"Is your spirit dead, Monsieur de Bardelys?" Chatellerault was gibing, when my silence had endured some moments. "Is the cock that lately crowed so lustily now dumb? Look you, Monsieur le Marquis, you are accounted here a reckless gamester. Will a wager induce you to this undertaking?"

I leapt to my feet at that. His derision cut me like a whip. If what I did was the act of a braggart, yet it almost seems I could do no less to bolster up my former boasting – or what into boasting they had translated.

"You'll lay a wager, will you, Chatellerault?" I cried, giving him back defiance for defiance. A breathless silence fell. "Then have it so. Listen, gentlemen, that you may be witnesses. I do here pledge my castle of Bardelys, and my estates in Picardy, with every stick and stone and blade of grass that stands upon them, that I shall woo and

9

win Roxalanne de Lavédan to be the Marquise of Bardelys. Does the stake satisfy you, Monsieur le Comte? You may set all you have against it," I added coarsely, "and yet, I swear, the odds will be heavily in your favour."

I remember it was Mironsac who first found his tongue, and sought even at that late hour to set restraint upon us and to bring judgment to our aid.

"Messieurs, messieurs!" he besought us. "In Heaven's name, bethink you what you do. Bardelys, your wager is a madness. Monsieur de Chatellerault, you'll not accept it. You'll – "

"Be silent," I rebuked him, with some asperity. "What has Monsieur de Chatellerault to say?"

He was staring at the tablecloth and the stain of the wine that he had spilled when first Mademoiselle de Lavédan's name was mentioned.

His head had been bent so that his long black hair had tumbled forward and partly veiled his face. At my question he suddenly looked up. The ghost of a smile hung on his sensuous lips, for all that excitement had paled his countenance beyond its habit.

"Monsieur le Marquis," said he rising, "I take your wager, and I pledge my lands in Normandy against yours of Bardelys. Should you lose, they will no longer call you the Magnificent; should I lose – I shall be a beggar. It is a momentous wager, Bardelys, and spells ruin for one of us."

"A madness!" groaned Mironsac.

"Mordieux!" swore Cazalet. Whilst La Fosse, who had been the original cause of all this trouble, vented his excitement in a gibber of imbecile laughter.

"How long do you give me, Chatellerault?" I asked, as quietly as I might.

"What time shall you require?"

"I should prefer that you name the limit," I answered.

He pondered a moment. Then, "Will three months suffice you?" he asked.

"If it is not done in three months, I will pay," said I.

And then Chatellerault did what after all was, I suppose, the only thing that a gentleman might do under the circumstances. He rose to his feet, and, bidding the company charge their glasses, he gave them a parting toast.

"Messieurs, drink with me to Monsieur le Marquis de Bardelys' safe journey into Languedoc, and to the prospering of his undertaking."

In answer, a great shout went up from throats that suspense had lately held in leash. Men leapt on to their chairs, and, holding their glasses on high, they acclaimed me as thunderously as though I had been the hero of some noble exploit, instead of the main figure in a somewhat questionable wager.

"Bardelys!" was the shout with which the house re-echoed. "Bardelys! Bardelys the Magnificent! Vive Bardelys!"

# Chapter 2

## The Warning

It was daybreak ere the last of them had left me, for a dozen or so had lingered to play lansquenet after the others had departed. With those that remained my wager had soon faded into insignificance, as their minds became engrossed in the fluctuations of their own fortunes.

I did not play myself; I was not in the mood, and for one night, at least, of sufficient weight already I thought the game upon which I was launched.

I was out on the balcony as the first lines of dawn were scoring the east, and in a moody, thoughtful condition I had riveted my eyes upon the palace of the Luxembourg, which loomed a black pile against the lightening sky, when Mironsac came out to join me. A gentle, lovable lad was Mironsac, not twenty years of age, and with the face and manners of a woman. That he was attached to me I knew.

"Monsieur le Marquis," said he softly, "I am desolated at this wager into which they have forced you."

"Forced me?" I echoed. "No, no; they did not force me. And yet," I reflected, with a sigh, "perhaps they did."

"I have been thinking, monsieur, that if the King were to hear of it the evil might be mended."

"But the King must not hear of it, Armand," I answered quickly. "Even if he did, matters would be no better – much worse, possibly."

"But, monsieur, this thing done in the heat of wine – "

"Is none the less done, Armand," I concluded. "And I for one do not wish it undone."

"But have you no thought for the lady?" he cried.

I laughed at him. "Were I still eighteen, boy, the thought might trouble me. Had I my illusions, I might imagine that my wife must be some woman of whom I should be enamoured. As it is, I have grown to the age of twenty-eight unwed. Marriage becomes desirable. I must think of an heir to all the wealth of Bardelys. And so I go to Languedoc. If the lady be but half the saint that fool Chatellerault has painted her, so much the better for my children; if not, so much the worse. There is the dawn, Mironsac, and it is time we were abed. Let us drive these plaguy gamesters home."

When the last of them had staggered down my steps, and I had bidden a drowsy lacquey extinguish the candles, I called Ganymède to light me to bed and aid me to undress. His true name was Rodenard; but my friend La Fosse, of mythological fancy, had named him Ganymède, after the cup-bearer of the gods, and the name had clung to him.

He was a man of some forty years of age, born into my father's service, and since become my intendant, factotum, major-domo, and generalissimo of my regiment of servants and my establishments both in Paris and at Bardelys.

We had been to the wars together ere I had cut my wisdom teeth, and thus had he come to love me. There was nothing this invaluable servant could not do. At baiting or shoeing a horse, at healing a wound, at roasting a capon, or at mending a doublet, he was alike a master, besides possessing a score of other accomplishments that do not now occur to me, which in his campaigning he had acquired.

Of late the easy life in Paris had made him incline to corpulency, and his face was of a pale, unhealthy fullness. Tonight, as he assisted me to undress, it wore an expression of supreme woe.

"Monseigneur is going into Languedoc?" he inquired sorrowfully.

He always called me his "seigneur", as did the other of my servants born at Bardelys.

"Knave, you have been listening," said I.

"But, monseigneur," he explained, "when Monsieur le Comte de Chatellerault laid his wager – "

"And have I not told you, Ganymède, that when you chance to be among my friends you should hear nothing but the words addressed to you, see nothing but the glasses that need replenishing? But, there! We are going into Languedoc. What of it?"

"They say that war may break out at any moment," he groaned; "that Monsieur le Duc de Montmorency is receiving reinforcements from Spain, and that he intends to uphold the standard of Monsieur and the rights of the province against the encroachments of His Eminence the Cardinal."

"So! We are becoming politicians, eh, Ganymède? And how shall all this concern us? Had you listened more attentively, you had learnt that we go to Languedoc to seek a wife, and not to concern ourselves with Cardinals and Dukes. Now let me sleep ere the sun rises."

On the morrow I attended the levee, and I applied to His Majesty for leave to absent myself. But upon hearing that it was into Languedoc I went, he frowned inquiry. Trouble enough was his brother already making in that province. I explained that I went to seek a wife, and deeming all subterfuge dangerous, since it might only serve to provoke him when later he came to learn the lady's name, I told him – withholding yet all mention of the wager – that I fostered the hope of making Mademoiselle de Lavédan my marquise.

Deeper came the line between his brows at that, and blacker grew the scowl. He was not wont to bestow on me such looks as I now met in his weary eyes, for Louis XIII had much affection for me.

"You know this lady?" he demanded sharply.

"Only by name, Your Majesty."

At that his brows went up in astonishment.

"Only by name? And you would wed her? But, Marcel, my friend, you are a rich man, one of the richest in France. You cannot be a fortune hunter."

"Sire," I answered, "Fame sings loudly the praises of this lady, her beauty and her virtue – praises that lead me to opine she would make me an excellent chatelaine. I am come to an age when it is well to wed; indeed, Your Majesty has often told me so. And it seems to me that all France does not hold a lady more desirable. Heaven send she will agree to my suit!"

In that tired way of his that was so pathetic: "Do you love me a little, Marcel?" he asked.

"Sire," I exclaimed, wondering whither all this was leading us, "need I protest it?"

"No," he answered dryly, "you can prove it. Prove it by abandoning this Languedoc quest. I have motives – sound motives, motives of political import. I desire another wedding for Mademoiselle de Lavédan. I wish it so, Bardelys, and I look to be obeyed."

For a moment temptation had me by the throat. Here was an unlooked-for chance to shake from me a business which reflection was already rendering odious. I had but to call together my friends of yesternight, and with them the Comte de Chatellerault, and inform them that by the King was I forbidden to go awooing Roxalanne de Lavédan. So should my wager be dissolved. And then in a flash I saw how they would sneer one and all, and how they would think that I had caught avidly at this opportunity of freeing myself from an undertaking into which a boastful mood had lured me. The fear of that swept aside my momentary hesitation.

"Sire," I answered, bending my head contritely, "I am desolated that my inclinations should run counter to your wishes, but to your wonted kindness and clemency I must look for forgiveness if these same inclinations drive me so relentlessly that I may not now turn back."

He caught me viciously by the arm and looked sharply into my face.

"You defy me, Bardelys?" he asked, in a voice of anger.

"God forbid, Sire!" I answered quickly. "I do but pursue my destiny."

He took a turn in silence, like a man who is mastering himself before he will speak. Many an eye, I knew, was upon us, and not a few may have been marvelling whether already Bardelys were about to share the fate that yesterday had overtaken his rival Chatellerault. At last he halted at my side again.

"Marcel," said he, but though he used that name his voice was harsh, "go home and ponder what I have said. If you value my favour, if you desire my love, you will abandon this journey and the suit you contemplate. If, on the other hand, you persist in going – you need not return. The Court of France has no room for gentlemen who are but lip-servers, no place for courtiers who disobey their King."

That was his last word. He waited for no reply, but swung round on his heel, and an instant later I beheld him deep in conversation with the Duke of Saint-Simon. Of such a quality is the love of princes – vain, capricious, and wilful. Indulge it ever and at any cost, else you forfeit it.

I turned away with a sigh, for in spite of all his weaknesses and meannesses I loved this cardinal-ridden king, and would have died for him had the need occurred, as well he knew. But in this matter – well, I accounted my honour involved, and there was now no turning back save by the payment of my wager and the acknowledgment of defeat.

# Chapter 3

## *René de Lesperon*

That very day I set out. For since the King was opposed to the affair, and knowing the drastic measures by which he was wont to enforce what he desired, I realized that did I linger he might find a way definitely to prevent my going.

I travelled in a coach, attended by two lacqueys and a score of men-at-arms in my own livery, all commanded by Ganymède. My intendant himself came in another coach with my wardrobe and travelling necessaries. We were a fine and almost regal cortège as we passed down the rue de l'Enfer and quitted Paris by the Orléans gate, taking the road south. So fine a cortège, indeed, that it entered my mind His Majesty would come to hear of it, and, knowing my destination, send after me to bring me back. To evade such a possibility, I ordered a divergence to be made, and we struck east and into Touraine. At Pont-le-Duc, near Tours, I had a cousin in the Vicomte d'Amaral, and at his chateau I arrived on the third day after quitting Paris.

Since that was the last place where they would seek me, if to seek me they were inclined, I elected to remain my cousin's guest for fifteen days. And whilst I was there we had news of trouble in the South and of a rising in Languedoc under the Duc de Montmorency.

Thus was it that when I came to take my leave of Amaral, he, knowing that Languedoc was my destination, sought ardently to keep me with him until we should learn that peace and order were restored in the province. But I held the trouble lightly, and insisted upon going.

Resolutely, then, if by slow stages, we pursued our journey, and came at last to Montauban. There we lay a night at the Auberge de Navarre, intending to push on to Lavédan upon the morrow. My father had been on more than friendly terms with the Vicomte de Lavédan, and upon this I built my hopes of a cordial welcome and an invitation to delay for a few days the journey to Toulouse, upon which I should represent myself as bound.

Thus, then, stood my plans. And they remained unaltered for all that upon the morrow there were wild rumours in the air of Montauban.

There were tellings of a battle fought the day before at Castelnaudary, of the defeat of Monsieur's partisans, of the utter rout of Gonzalo de Cordova's Spanish tatterdemalions, and of the capture of Montmorency, who was sorely wounded – some said with twenty and some with thirty wounds – and little like to live.

Sorrow and discontent stalked abroad in Languedoc that day, for they believed that it was against the Cardinal, who sought to strip them of so many privileges, that Gaston d'Orléans had set up his standard.

That those rumours of battle and defeat were true we had ample proof some few hours later, when a company of dragoons in buff and steel rode into the courtyard of the Auberge de Navarre, headed by a young spark of an officer, who confirmed the rumour and set the number of Montmorency's wounds at seventeen. He was lying, the officer told us, at Castelnaudary, and his duchess was hastening to him from Beziers. Poor woman! She was destined to nurse him back to life and vigour only that he might take his trial at Toulouse and pay with his head the price of his rebellion.

Ganymède who, through the luxurious habits of his more recent years had – for all his fine swagger – developed a marked distaste for warfare and excitement, besought me to take thought for my safety and to lie quietly at Montauban until the province should be more settled.

"The place is a hotbed of rebellion," he urged. "If these Chouans but learn that we are from Paris and of the King's party, we shall have our throats slit, as I live. There is not a peasant in all this countryside, indeed, scarce a man of any sort but is a red-hot Orléanist, anti-Cardinalist, and friend of the Devil. Bethink you, monseigneur, to push on at the present is to court murder."

"Why, then, we will court murder," said I coldly. "Give the word to saddle."

I asked him at the moment of setting out did he know the road to Lavédan, to which the lying poltroon made answer that he did. In his youth he may have known it, and the countryside may have undergone since then such changes as bewildered him. Or it may be that fear dulled his wits, and lured him into taking what may have seemed the safer rather than the likelier road. But this I know, that as night was falling my carriage halted with a lurch, and as I put forth my head I was confronted by my trembling intendant, his great fat face gleaming whitely in the gloom above the lawn collar on his doublet.

"Why do we halt, Ganymède?" quoth I.

"Monseigneur," he faltered, his trembling increasing as he spoke, and his eyes meeting mine in a look of pitiful contrition, "I fear we are lost."

"Lost?" I echoed. "Of what do you talk? Am I to sleep in the coach?"

"Alas, monseigneur, I have done my best – "

"Why, then, God keep us from your worst," I snapped. "Open me this door."

I stepped down and looked about me, and, by my faith, a more desolate spot to lose us in my henchman could not have contrived had he been at pains to do so. A bleak, barren landscape – such as I could hardly have credited was to be found in all that fair province – unfolded itself, looking now more bleak, perhaps, by virtue of the dim evening mist that hovered over it. Yonder, to the right, a dull russet patch of sky marked the west, and then in front of us I made out the hazy outline of the Pyrenees. At sight of them, I swung round and gripped my henchman by the shoulder.

"A fine trusty servant thou!" I cried. "Boaster! Had you told us that age and fat living had so stunted your wits as to have extinguished memory, I had taken a guide at Montauban to show us the way. Yet, here, with the sun and the Pyrenees to guide you, even had you no other knowledge, you lose yourself!"

"Monseigneur," he whimpered, "I was choosing my way by the sun and the mountains, and it was thus that I came to this impasse. For you may see, yourself, that the road ends here abruptly."

"Ganymède," said I slowly, "when we return to Paris – if you do not die of fright 'twixt this and then – I'll find a place for you in the kitchens. God send you may make a better scullion than a follower!" Then, vaulting over the wall, "Attend me, some half-dozen of you," I commanded, and stepped out briskly towards the barn.

As the weather-beaten old door creaked upon its rusty hinges, we were greeted by a groan from within, and with it the soft rustle of straw that is being moved. Surprised, I halted, and waited whilst one of my men kindled a light in the lanthorn that he carried.

By its rays we beheld a pitiable sight in a corner of that building. A man, quite young and of a tall and vigorous frame, lay stretched upon the straw. He was fully dressed even to his great riding-boots, and from the loose manner in which his back-and-breast hung now upon him, it would seem as if he had been making shift to divest himself of his armour, but had lacked the strength to complete the task.

Beside him lay a feathered headpiece and a sword attached to a richly broidered baldrick. All about him the straw was clotted with brown, viscous patches of blood. The doublet, which had been of sky-blue velvet, was all sodden and stained, and inspection showed us that he had been wounded in the right side, between the straps of his breastplate.

As we stood about him now, a silent, pitying group, appearing fantastic, perhaps, by the dim light of that single lanthorn, he attempted to raise his head, and then with a groan he dropped it back upon the straw that pillowed it. From out of a face white, as in death, and drawn with haggard lines of pain, a pair of great lustrous blue eyes were turned upon us, abject and pitiful as the gaze of a dumb beast that is stricken mortally.

It needed no acuteness to apprehend that we had before us one of yesterday's defeated warriors; one who had spent his last strength in creeping hither to get his dying done in peace. Lest our presence should add fear to the agony already upon him, I knelt beside him in the blood-smeared straw, and, raising his head, I pillowed it upon my arm.

"Have no fear," said I reassuringly. "We are friends. Do you understand?"

The faint smile that played for a second on his lips and lighted his countenance would have told me that he understood, even had I not caught his words, faint as a sigh, "Merci, monsieur." He nestled his head into the crook of my arm. "Water – for the love of God!" he gasped, to add in a groan, "Je me meurs, monsieur."

Assisted by a couple of knaves, Ganymède went about attending to the rebel at once. Handling him as carefully as might be, to avoid giving him unnecessary pain, they removed his back-and-breast, which was flung with a clatter into one of the corners of the barn. Then, whilst one of them gently drew off his boots, Rodenard, with the lanthorn close beside him, cut away the fellow's doublet, and laid bare the oozing sword-wound that gaped in his mangled side. He whispered an order to Gilles, who went swiftly off to the coach in quest of something that he had asked for; then he sat on his heels and waited, his hand upon the man's pulse, his eyes on his face.

I stooped until my lips were on a level with my intendant's ear.

"How is it with him?" I inquired.

"Dying," whispered Rodenard in answer. "He has lost too much blood, and he is probably bleeding inwardly as well. There is no hope of his life, but he may linger thus some little while, sinking gradually, and we can at least mitigate the suffering of his last moments."

When presently the men returned with the things that Ganymède had asked for, he mixed some pungent liquid with water, and, whilst a servant held the bowl, he carefully sponged the rebel's wound. This and a cordial that he had given him to drink seemed to revive him and to afford him ease. His breathing was no longer marked by any rasping sound, and his eyes seemed to burn more intelligently.

"I am dying – is it not so?" he asked, and Ganymède bowed his head in silence. The poor fellow sighed. "Raise me," he begged, and when this service had been done him, his eyes wandered round until they found me. Then, "Monsieur," he said, "will you do me a last favour?"

"Assuredly, my poor friend," I answered, going down on my knees beside him.

"You – you were not for the Duke?" he inquired, eyeing me more keenly.

"No, monsieur. But do not let that disturb you; I have no interest in this rising and I have taken no side. I am from Paris, on a journey of – of pleasure. My name is Bardelys – Marcel de Bardelys."

"Bardelys the Magnificent?" he questioned, and I could not repress a smile.

"I am that overrated man."

"But then you are for the King!" And a note of disappointment crept into his voice. Before I could make him any answer, he had resumed.

"No matter; Marcel de Bardelys is a gentleman, and party signifies little when a man is dying. I am René de Lesperon, of Lesperon in Gascony," he pursued. "Will you send word to my sister afterwards?"

I bowed my head without speaking.

"She is the only relative I have, monsieur. But" – and his tone grew wistful – "there is one other to whom I would have you bear a message." He raised his hand by a painful effort to the level of his breast. Strength failed him, and he sank back. "I cannot, monsieur," he said in a tone of pathetic apology. "See; there is a chain about my neck with a locket. Take it from me. Take it now, monsieur. There are some papers also, monsieur. Take all. I want to see them safely in your keeping."

I did his bidding, and from the breast of his doublet I drew some loose letters and a locket which held the miniature of a woman's face.

"I want you to deliver all to her, monsieur."

"It shall be done," I answered, deeply moved.

"Hold it – hold it up," he begged, his voice weakening. "Let me behold the face."

Long his eyes rested on the likeness I held before him. At last, as one in a dream –

"Well-beloved," he sighed. "Bien aimée!" And down his grey, haggard cheeks the tears came slowly. "Forgive this weakness, monsieur," he whispered brokenly. "We were to have been wed in a month, had I lived." He ended with a sob, and when next he spoke it was more labouredly, as though that sob had robbed him of the half of what vitality remained. "Tell her, monsieur, that my dying thoughts were of her. Tell – tell her – I – "

"Her name?" I cried, fearing he would sink before I learned it. "Tell me her name."

He looked at me with eyes that were growing glassy and vacant. Then he seemed to brace himself and to rally for a second.

"Her name?" he mused, in a far-off manner. "She is – Ma-de-moiselle de – "

His head rolled on the suddenly relaxed neck. He collapsed into Rodenard's arms.

"Is he dead?" I asked.

Rodenard nodded in silence.

# Chapter 4

## Moonlight

I do not know whether it was the influence of that thing lying in a corner of the barn under the cloak that Rodenard had flung over it, or whether other influences of destiny were at work to impel me to rise at the end of a half-hour and announce my determination to set out on horseback and find myself quarters more congenial.

"Tomorrow," I instructed Ganymède, as I stood ready to mount, "you will retrace your steps with the others, and, finding the road to Lavédan, you will follow me to the chateau."

"But you cannot hope to reach it tonight, monseigneur, through a country that is unknown to you," he protested.

"I do not hope to reach it tonight. I will ride south until I come upon some hamlet that will afford me shelter and, in the morning, direction."

I left him with that, and set out at a brisk trot. Night had now fallen, but the sky was clear, and a crescent moon came opportunely if feebly to dispel the gloom.

I quitted the field, and went back until I gained a crossroad, where, turning to the right, I set my face to the Pyrenees, and rode briskly amain. That I had chosen wisely was proved when some twenty minutes later I clattered into the hamlet of Mirepoix, and drew up before an inn flaunting the sign of a peacock – as if in irony of its humbleness, for it was no better than a wayside tavern. Neither

24

stable boy nor ostler was here, and the unclean, overgrown urchin to whom I entrusted my horse could not say whether indeed Père Abdon the landlord would be able to find me a room to sleep in. I thirsted, however; and so I determined to alight, if it were only to drink a can of wine and obtain information of my whereabouts.

As I was entering the hostelry there was a clatter of hoofs in the street, and four dragoons headed by a sergeant rode up and halted at the door of the Paon. They seemed to have ridden hard and some distance, for their horses were jaded almost to the last point of endurance.

Within, I called the host, and having obtained a flagon of the best vintage – Heaven fortify those that must be content with his worst! – I passed on to make inquiries touching my whereabouts and the way to Lavédan. This I learnt was but some three or four miles distant.

About the other table – there were but two within the room – stood the dragoons in a whispered consultation, of which it had been well had I taken heed, for it concerned me more closely than I could have dreamt.

"He answers the description," said the sergeant, and though I heard the words I took no thought that it was of me they spoke.

"Pardieu," swore one of his companions, "I'll wager it is our man."

And then, just as I was noticing that Master Abdon, who had also overheard the conversation, was eyeing me curiously, the sergeant stepped up to me, and –

"What is your name, monsieur?" quoth he.

I vouchsafed him a stare of surprise before asking in my turn "How may that concern you?"

"Your pardon, my master, but we are on the King's business."

I remembered then that he had said I answered some description. With that it flashed through my mind that they had been sent after me by His Majesty to enforce my obedience to his wishes and to hinder me from reaching Lavédan. At once came the dominant desire to conceal my identity that I might go unhindered. The first name that occurred to me was that of the poor wretch I had left in the barn half an hour ago, and so –

"I am," said I, "Monsieur de Lesperon, at your service."

Too late I saw the mistake that I had made. I own it was a blunder that no man of ordinary intelligence should have permitted himself to have committed. Remembering the unrest of the province, I should rather have concluded that their business was more like to be in that connection.

"He is bold, at least," cried one of the troopers, with a burst of laughter. Then came the sergeant's voice, cold and formal, "In the King's name, Monsieur de Lesperon, I arrest you."

He had whipped out his sword, and the point was within an inch of my breast. But his arm, I observed, was stretched to its fullest extent, which forbade his making a sudden thrust. To hamper him in the lunge there was the table between us.

So, my mind working quickly in this desperate situation, and realizing how dire and urgent the need to attempt an escape, I leapt suddenly back to find myself in the arms of his followers.

But in moving I had caught up by one of its legs the stool on which I had been sitting. As I raised it, I eluded the pinioning grip of the troopers. I twisted in their grasp, and brought the stool down upon the head of one of them with a force that drove him to his knees. Up went that three-legged stool again, to descend like a thunderbolt upon the head of another. That freed me. The sergeant was coming up behind, but another flourish of my improvised battle-axe sent the two remaining soldiers apart to look to their swords. Ere they could draw, I had darted like a hare between them and out into the street. The sergeant, cursing them with horrid volubility, followed closely upon my heels.

Leaping as far into the roadway as I could, I turned to meet the fellow's onslaught. Using the stool as a buckler, I caught his thrust upon it. So violently was it delivered that the point buried itself in the wood and the blade snapped, leaving him a hilt and a stump of steel. I wasted no time in thought. Charging him wildly, I knocked him over just as the two unhurt dragoons came stumbling out of the tavern.

I gained my horse and vaulted into the saddle. Tearing the reins from the urchin that held them, and driving my spurs into the beast's flanks, I went careering down the street at a gallop, gripping tightly with my knees, whilst the stirrups, which I had had no time to step into, flew wildly about my legs.

A pistol cracked behind me; then another, and a sharp, stinging pain in the shoulder warned me that I was hit. But I took no heed of it then. The wound could not be serious, else I had already been out of the saddle, and it would be time enough to look to it when I had outdistanced my pursuers. I say my pursuers, for already there were hoofbeats behind me, and I knew that those gentlemen had taken to their horses. But, as you may recall, I had on their arrival noted the jaded condition of their cattle, whilst I bestrode a horse that was comparatively fresh, so that pursuit had but small terrors for me. Nevertheless, they held out longer, and gave me more to do than I had imagined would be the case. For nigh upon a half-hour I rode, before I could be said to have got clear of them, and then for aught I knew they were still following, resolved to hound me down by the aid of such information as they might cull upon their way.

I was come by then to the Garonne. I drew rein beside the swiftly flowing stream, winding itself like a flood of glittering silver between the black shadows of its banks. A little while I sat there listening, and surveying the stately, turreted chateau that loomed, a grey, noble pile, beyond the water. I speculated what demesne this might be, and I realized that it was probably Lavédan.

I pondered what I had best do, and in the end I took the resolve to swim the river and knock at the gates. If it were indeed Lavédan, I had but to announce myself, and to one of my name surely its hospitalities would be spread. If it were some other household, even then the name of Marcel de Bardelys should suffice to ensure me a welcome.

By spurring and coaxing, I lured my steed into the river. There is a proverb having it that though you may lead a horse to the water you cannot make him drink. It would have now applied to my case, for although I had brought mine to the water I could not make him swim; or, at least, I could not make him breast the rush of the stream. Vainly did I urge him and try to hold him; he plunged frantically, snorted, coughed, and struggled gamely, but the current was bearing us swiftly away, and his efforts brought us no nearer to the opposite shore. At last I slipped from his back, and set myself to swim beside him, leading him by the bridle. But even thus he proved unequal to the task of resisting the current, so that in the end I let him go, and swam ashore alone, hoping that he would land farther down, and that I might then recapture him. When, however, I had reached the opposite bank, and stood under the shadow of the chateau, I discovered that the cowardly beast had turned back, and, having scrambled out, was now trotting away along the path by which we had come. Having no mind to go after him, I resigned myself to the loss, and turned my attention to the mansion now before me.

Some two hundred yards from the river it raised its great square bulk against the background of black, star-flecked sky. From the façade before me down to the spot where I stood by the water came a flight of half a dozen terraces, each balustraded in white marble, ending in square, flat-topped pillars of Florentine design. What moon there was revealed the quaint architecture of that stately edifice and glittered upon the mullioned windows. But within nothing stirred; no yellow glimmer came to clash with the white purity of the moonlight; no sound of man or beast broke the stillness of the night, for all that the hour was early. The air of the place was as that of some gigantic sepulchre. A little daunted by this all-enveloping stillness, I skirted the terraces and approached the house on the eastern side. Here I found an old-world drawbridge – now naturally in disuse – spanning a ditch fed from the main river for the erstwhile purposes of a moat. I crossed the bridge, and entered an imposing courtyard. Within this quadrangle the same silence dwelt, and there was the same obscurity in the windows that overlooked it. I paused, at a loss how to proceed, and I leaned against a buttress of the portcullis, what time I considered.

I was weak from fasting, worn with hard riding, and faint from the wound in my shoulder, which had been the cause at least of my losing some blood. In addition to all this, I was shivering with the cold of my wet garments, and generally I must have looked as little like that Bardelys they called the Magnificent as you might well conceive. How, then, if I were to knock, should I prevail in persuading these people – whoever they might be – of my identity?

Infinitely more had I the air of some fugitive rebel, and it was more than probable that I should be kept in durance to be handed over to my friends the dragoons, if later they came to ride that way. I was separated from those who knew me, and as things now stood – unless this were, indeed, Lavédan – it might be days before they found me again.

I was beginning to deplore my folly at having cut myself adrift from my followers in the first place, and having embroiled myself with the soldiers in the second; I was beginning to contemplate the wisdom of seeking some outhouse of this mansion wherein to lie until morning, when of a sudden a broad shaft of light, coming from one of the windows on the first floor, fell athwart the courtyard.

Instinctively I crouched back into the shadow of my friendly buttress, and looked up.

That sudden shaft of light resulted from the withdrawal of the curtains that masked a window. At this window, which opened outward on to a balcony, I now beheld – and to me it was as the vision of Beatrice may have been to Dante – the white figure of a woman. The moonlight bathed her, as in her white robe she leaned upon the parapet gazing upward into the empyrean. A sweet, delicate face I saw, not endowed, perhaps, with that exquisite balance and proportion of feature wherein they tell us beauty lies, but blessed with a wondrously dainty beauty all its own; a beauty, perhaps, as much of expression as of form; for in that gentle countenance was mirrored every tender grace of girlhood, all that is fresh and pure and virginal.

I held my breath, I think, as I stood in ravished contemplation of that white vision. If this were Lavédan, and that the cold Roxalanne who had sent my bold Chatellerault back to Paris empty-handed, then were my task a very welcome one.

How little it had weighed with me that I was come to Languedoc to woo a woman bearing the name of Roxalanne de Lavédan I have already shown. But here in this same Languedoc I beheld tonight a woman whom it seemed I might have loved, for not in ten years – not, indeed, in all my life – had any face so wrought upon me and called to my nature with so strong a voice.

I gazed at that child, and I thought of the women that I had known – the bold, bedizened beauties of a Court said to be the first in Europe. And then it came to me that this was no demoiselle of Lavédan, no demoiselle at all in fact, for the noblesse of France owned no such faces. Candour and purity were not to be looked for in the high-bred countenances of our great families; they were sometimes found in the faces of the children of their retainers.

Yes; I had it now. This child was the daughter of some custodian of the demesne before me.

Suddenly, as she stood there in the moonlight, a song, sung at half-voice, floated down on the calm air. It was a ditty of old Provence, a melody I knew and loved, and if aught had been wanting to heighten the enchantment that already ravished me, that soft melodious voice had done it. Singing still, she turned and re-entered the room, leaving wide the windows, so that faintly, as from a distance, her voice still reached me after she was gone from sight.

It was in that hour that it came to me to cast myself upon this fair creature's mercy. Surely one so sweet and saintly to behold would take compassion on an unfortunate! Haply my wound and all the rest that I had that night endured made me dull-witted and warped my reason.

With what strength I still possessed I went to work to scale her balcony. The task was easy even for one in my spent condition. The wall was thick with ivy, and, moreover, a window beneath afforded some support, for by standing on the heavy coping I could with my fingers touch the sill of the balcony above. Thus I hoisted myself, and presently I threw an arm over the parapet. Already I was astride of that same parapet before she became aware of my presence.

The song died suddenly on her lips, and her eyes, blue as forget-me-nots, were wide now with the fear that the sight of me occasioned. Another second and there had been an outcry that would have brought the house about our ears, when, stepping to the threshold of the room, "Mademoiselle," I entreated, "for the love of God, be silent! I mean you no harm. I am a fugitive. I am pursued."

This was no considered speech. There had been no preparing of words; I had uttered them mechanically almost – perhaps by inspiration, for they were surely the best calculated to enlist this lady's sympathy.

And so far as went the words themselves, they were rigorously true.

With eyes wide open still, she confronted me, and I now observed that she was not so tall as from below I had imagined. She was, in fact, of a short stature rather, but of proportions so exquisite that she conveyed an impression of some height. In her hand she held a taper by whose light she had been surveying herself in her mirror at the moment of my advent. Her unbound hair of brown fell like a mantle about her shoulders, and this fact it was drew me to notice that she was in her night-rail, and that this room to which I had penetrated was her chamber.

"Who are you?" she asked breathlessly, as though in such a pass my identity were a thing that signified.

I had almost answered her, as I had answered the troopers at Mirepoix, that I was Lesperon. Then, bethinking me that there was no need for such equivocation here, I was on the point of giving her my name.

But noting my hesitation, and misconstruing it, she forestalled me.

31

"I understand, monsieur," said she more composedly. "And you need have no fear. You are among friends."

Her eyes had travelled over my sodden clothes, the haggard pallor of my face, and the blood that stained my doublet from the shoulder downward. From all this she had drawn her conclusions that I was a hunted rebel. She drew me into the room, and, closing the window, she dragged the heavy curtain across it, thereby giving me a proof of confidence that smote me hard – impostor that I was.

"I crave your pardon, mademoiselle, for having startled you by the rude manner of my coming," said I, and never in my life had I felt less at ease than then. "But I was exhausted and desperate. I am wounded, I have ridden hard, and I swam the river."

The latter piece of information was vastly unnecessary, seeing that the water from my clothes was forming a pool about my feet. "I saw you from below, mademoiselle, and surely, I thought, so sweet a lady would have pity on an unfortunate." She observed that my eyes were upon her, and in an act of instinctive maidenliness she bore her hand to her throat to draw the draperies together and screen the beauties of her neck from my unwarranted glance, as though her daily gown did not reveal as much and more of them.

That act, however, served to arouse me to a sense of my position. What did I there? It was a profanity – a defiling, I swore; from which you'll see, that Bardelys was grown of a sudden very nice.

"Monsieur," she was saying, "you are exhausted."

"But that I rode hard," I laughed, "it is likely they had taken me to Toulouse, where I might have lost my head before my friends could have found and claimed me. I hope you'll see it is too comely a head to be so lightly parted with."

"For that," said she, half seriously, half whimsically, "the ugliest head would be too comely."

I laughed softly, amusedly; then of a sudden, without warning, a faintness took me, and I was forced to brace myself against the wall, breathing heavily the while. At that she gave a little cry of alarm.

"Monsieur, I beseech you to be seated. I will summon my father, and we will find a bed for you. You must not retain those clothes."

"Angel of goodness!" I muttered gratefully, and being still half dazed, I brought some of my Court tricks into that chamber by taking her hand and carrying it towards my lips. But ere I had imprinted the intended kiss upon her fingers – and by some miracle they were not withdrawn – my eyes encountered hers again. I paused as one may pause who contemplates a sacrilege. For a moment she held my glance with hers; then I fell abashed, and released her hand.

The innocence peeping out of that child's eyes it was that had in that moment daunted me, and made me tremble to think of being found there, and of the vile thing it would be to have her name coupled with mine. That thought lent me strength. I cast my weariness from me as though it were a garment, and, straightening myself, I stepped of a sudden to the window. Without a word, I made shift to draw back the curtain when her hand, falling on my sodden sleeve, arrested me.

"What will you do, monsieur?" she cried in alarm. "You may be seen."

My mind was now possessed by the thing I should have thought of before. I climbed to her balcony, and my one resolve was to get me thence as quickly as might be.

"I had not the right to enter here," I muttered. "I –" I stopped short; to explain would only be to sully, and so, "Good-night! Adieu!" I ended brusquely.

"But, monsieur – " she began.

"Let me go," I commanded almost roughly, as I shook my arm free of her grasp.

"Bethink you that you are exhausted. If you go forth now, monsieur, you will assuredly be taken. You must not go."

I laughed softly, and with some bitterness, too, for I was angry with myself.

"Hush, child," I said. "Better so, if it is to be."

And with that I drew aside the curtains and pushed the leaves of the window apart. She remained standing in the room, watching me, her face pale, and hex eyes pained and puzzled.

One last glance I gave her as I bestrode the rail of her balcony.

Then I lowered myself as I had ascended. I was hanging by my hands, seeking with my foot for the coping of the window beneath me, when, suddenly, there came a buzzing in my ears. I had a fleeting vision of a white figure leaning on the balcony above me; then a veil seemed drawn over my eyes; there came a sense of falling; a rush as of a tempestuous wind; then – nothing.

# Chapter 5

## The Vicomte de Lavédan

When next I awakened, it was to find myself abed in an elegant apartment, spacious and sunlit, that was utterly strange to me.

For some seconds I was content to lie and take no count of my whereabouts. My eyes travelled idly over the handsome furnishings of that choicely appointed chamber, and rested at last upon the lean, crooked figure of a man whose back was towards me and who was busy with some phials at a table not far distant. Then recollection awakened also in me, and I set my wits to work to grapple with my surroundings. I looked through the open window, but from my position on the bed no more was visible than the blue sky and a faint haze of distant hills.

I taxed my memory, and the events of yesternight recurred to me.

I remembered the girl, the balcony, and my flight ending in my giddiness and my fall. Had they brought me into that same chateau, or – or what? No other possibility came to suggest itself, and, seeing scant need to tax my brains with speculation, since there was one there of whom I might ask the question –

"Hola, my master!" I called to him, and as I did so I essayed to move. The act wrung a sharp cry of pain from me. My left shoulder was numb and sore, but in my right foot that sudden movement had roused a sharper pang.

At my cry that little wizened old man swung suddenly round. He had the face of a bird of prey, yellow as a louis d'or with a great hooked nose, and a pair of beady black eyes that observed me solemnly.

The mouth alone was the redeeming feature in a countenance that had otherwise been evil; it was instinct with good-humour. But I had small leisure to observe him then, for simultaneously with his turning there had been another movement at my bedside, which drew my eyes elsewhere. A gentleman, richly dressed, and of an imposing height, approached me.

"You are awake, monsieur?" he said in a half interrogative tone.

"Will you do me the favour to tell me where I am, monsieur?" quoth I.

"You do not know? You are at Lavédan. I am the Vicomte de Lavédan – at your service."

Although it was no more than I might have expected, yet a dull wonder filled me, to which presently I gave expression by asking stupidly, "At Lavédan? But how came I hither?"

"How you came is more than I can tell," he laughed. "But I'll swear the King's dragoons were not far behind you. We found you in the courtyard last night; in a swoon of exhaustion, wounded in the shoulder, and with a sprained foot. It was my daughter who gave the alarm and called us to your assistance. You were lying under her window." Then, seeing the growing wonder in my eyes and misconstruing it into alarm: "Nay, have no fear, monsieur," he cried. "You were very well advised in coming to us. You have fallen among friends.

"We are Orléanists too, at Lavédan, for all that I was not in the fight at Castelnaudary. That was no fault of mine. His Grace's messenger reached me overlate, and for all that I set out with a company of my men, I put back when I had reached Lautrec upon hearing that already a decisive battle had been fought and that our side had suffered a crushing defeat." He uttered a weary sigh.

"God help us, monsieur! Monseigneur de Richelieu is likely to have his way with us. But let that be for the present. You are here, and you are safe. As yet no suspicion rests on Lavédan. I was, as I have said, too late for the fight, and so I came quietly back to save my skin, that I might serve the Cause in whatever other way might offer still. In sheltering you I am serving Gaston d'Orléans, and, that I may continue so to do, I pray that suspicion may continue to ignore me. If they were to learn of it at Toulouse or of how with money and in other ways I have helped this rebellion – I make no doubt that my head would be the forfeit I should be asked to pay."

I was aghast at the freedom of treasonable speech with which this very debonnaire gentleman ventured to address an utter stranger.

"But tell me, Monsieur de Lesperon," resumed my host, "how is it with you?"

I started in fresh astonishment.

"How – how do you know that I am Lesperon?" I asked.

"Ma foi!" he laughed, "do you imagine I had spoken so unreservedly to a man of whom I knew nothing? Think better of me, monsieur, I beseech you. I found these letters in your pocket last night, and their superscription gave me your identity. Your name is well known to me," he added. "My friend Monsieur de Marsac has often spoken of you and of your devotion to the Cause, and it affords me no little satisfaction to be of some service to one whom by repute I have already learned to esteem."

I lay back on my pillows, and I groaned. Here was a predicament!

Mistaking me for that miserable rebel I had succoured at Mirepoix, and whose letters I bore upon me that I might restore them to someone whose name he had failed to give me at the last moment, the Vicomte de Lavédan had poured the damning story of his treason into my ears.

What if I were now to enlighten him? What if I were to tell him that I was not Lesperon – no rebel at all, in fact – but Marcel de Bardelys, the King's favourite? That he would account me a spy I hardly thought; but assuredly he would see that my life must be a danger to his own; he must fear betrayal from me; and to protect himself he would be justified in taking extreme measures. Rebels were not addicted to an excess of niceness in their methods, and it was more likely that I should rise no more from the luxurious bed on which his hospitality had laid me. But even if I had exaggerated matters, and the Vicomte were not quite so bloodthirsty as was usual with his order, even if he chose to accept my promise that I would forget what he had said, he must nevertheless – in view of his indiscretion – demand my instant withdrawal from Lavédan. And what, then, of my wager with Chatellerault?

Then, in thinking of my wager, I came to think of Roxalanne herself – that dainty, sweet-faced child into whose chamber I had penetrated on the previous night. And would you believe it that I – the satiated, cynical, unbelieving Bardelys – experienced dismay at the very thought of leaving Lavédan for no other reason than because it involved seeing no more of that provincial damsel?

My unwillingness to be driven from her presence determined me to stay. I had come to Lavédan as Lesperon, a fugitive rebel. In that character I had all but announced myself last night to Mademoiselle.

In that character I had been welcomed by her father. In that character, then, I must remain, that I might be near her, that I might woo and win her, and thus – though this, I swear, had now become a minor consideration with me – make good my boast and win the wager that must otherwise involve my ruin.

As I lay back with closed eyes and gave myself over to pondering the situation, I took a pleasure oddly sweet in the prospect of urging my suit under such circumstances. Chatellerault had given me a free hand. I was to go about the wooing of Mademoiselle de Lavédan as I chose. But he had cast it at me in defiance that not with all my magnificence, not with all my retinue and all my state to dazzle her, should I succeed in melting the coldest heart in France.

And now, behold! I had cast from me all these outward embellishments; I came without pomp, denuded of every emblem of wealth, of every sign of power; as a poor fugitive gentleman, I came, hunted, proscribed, and penniless – for Lesperon's estate would assuredly suffer sequestration. To win her thus would, by my faith, be an exploit I might take pride in, a worthy achievement to encompass.

And so I left things as they were, and since I offered no denial to the identity that was thrust upon me, as Lesperon I continued to be known to the Vicomte and to his family.

Presently he called the old man to my bedside and I heard them talking of my condition.

"You think, then, Anatole," he said in the end, "that in three or four days Monsieur de Lesperon may be able to rise?"

"I am assured of it," replied the old servant.

Whereupon, turning to me, "Be therefore of good courage, monsieur," said Lavédan, "for your hurt is none so grievous after all."

I was muttering my thanks and my assurances that I was in excellent spirits, when we were suddenly disturbed by a rumbling noise as of distant thunder.

"Mort Dieu!" swore the Vicomte, a look of alarm coming into his face. With a bent head, he stood in a listening attitude.

"What is it?" I inquired.

"Horsemen – on the drawbridge," he answered shortly. "A troop, by the sound."

And then, in confirmation of these words, followed a stamping and rattle of hoofs on the flags of the courtyard below. The old servant stood wringing his hands in helpless terror, and wailing, "Monsieur, monsieur!"

But the Vicomte crossed rapidly to the window and looked out. Then he laughed with intense relief; and in a wondering voice "They are not troopers," he announced. "They have more the air of a company of servants in private livery; and there is a carriage – pardieu, two carriages!"

At once the memory of Rodenard and my followers occurred to me, and I thanked Heaven that I was abed where he might not see me, and that thus he would probably be sent forth empty-handed with the news that his master was neither arrived nor expected.

But in that surmise I went too fast. Ganymède was of a tenacious mettle, and of this he now afforded proof. Upon learning that naught was known of the Marquis de Bardelys at Lavédan, my faithful henchman announced his intention to remain there and await me, since that was, he assured the Vicomte, my destination.

"My first impulse," said Lavédan, when later he came to tell me of it, "was incontinently to order his departure. But upon considering the matter and remembering how high in power and in the King's favour stands that monstrous libertine Bardelys, I deemed it wiser to afford shelter to this outrageous retinue. His steward – a flabby, insolent creature – says that Bardelys left them last night near Mirepoix, to ride hither, bidding them follow today. Curious that we should have no news of him! That he should have fallen into the Garonne and drowned himself were too great a good fortune to be hoped for."

The bitterness with which he spoke of me afforded me ample cause for congratulation that I had resolved to accept the role of Lesperon.

Yet, remembering that my father and he had been good friends, his manner left me nonplussed. What cause could he have for this animosity to the son? Could it be merely my position at Court that made me seem in his rebel eyes a natural enemy?

"You are acquainted with this Bardelys?" I inquired, by way of drawing him.

"I knew his father," he answered gruffly. "An honest, upright gentleman."

"And the son," I inquired timidly, "has he none of these virtues?"

"I know not what virtues he may have; his vices are known to all the world. He is a libertine, a gambler, a rake, a spendthrift. They say he is one of the King's favourites, and that his monstrous extravagances have earned for him the title of 'Magnificent'."

He uttered a short laugh. "A fit servant for such a master as Louis the Just!"

"Monsieur le Vicomte," said I, warming in my own defence, "I swear you do him injustice. He is extravagant, but then he is rich; he is a libertine, but then he is young, and he has been reared among libertines; he is a gamester, but punctiliously honourable at play. Believe me, monsieur, I have some acquaintance with Marcel de Bardelys, and his vices are hardly so black as is generally believed; whilst in his favour I think the same may be said that you have just said of his father – he is an honest, upright gentleman."

"And that disgraceful affair with the Duchesse de Bourgogne?" inquired Lavédan, with the air of a man setting an unanswerable question.

"Mon Dieu!" I cried, "will the world never forget that indiscretion? An indiscretion of youth, no doubt much exaggerated outside Court circles."

The Vicomte eyed me in some astonishment for a moment.

"Monsieur de Lesperon," he said at length, "you appear to hold this Bardelys in high esteem. He has a staunch supporter in you and a stout advocate. Yet me you cannot convince." And he shook his head solemnly. "Even if I did not hold him to be such a man as I have pronounced him, but were to account him a paragon of all the virtues, his coming hither remains an act that I must resent."

"But why, Monsieur le Vicomte?"

"Because I know the errand that brings him to Lavédan. He comes to woo my daughter."

Had he flung a bomb into my bed he could not more effectively have startled me.

"It astonishes you, eh?" he laughed bitterly. "But I can assure you that it is so. A month ago I was visited by the Comte de Chatellerault – another of His Majesty's fine favourites. He came unbidden; offered no reason for his coming, save that he was making a tour of the province for his amusement. His acquaintance with me was of the slightest, and I had no desire that it should increase; yet here he installed himself with a couple of servants, and bade fair to take a long stay.

"I was surprised, but on the morrow I had an explanation. A courier, arriving from an old friend of mine at Court, bore me a letter with the information that Monsieur de Chatellerault was come to

Lavédan at the King's instigation to sue for my daughter's hand in marriage.

"The reasons were not far to seek. The King, who loves him, would enrich him; the easiest way is by a wealthy alliance, and Roxalanne is accounted an heiress. In addition to that, my own power in the province is known, whilst my defection from the Cardinalist party is feared. What better link wherewith to attach me again to the fortunes of the Crown – for Crown and Mitre have grown to be synonymous in this topsy-turvy France – than to wed my daughter to one of the King's favourites?

"But for that timely warning, God knows what mischief had been wrought. As it was, Monsieur de Chatellerault had but seen my daughter upon two occasions. On the very day that I received the tidings I speak of, I sent her to Auch to the care of some relatives of her mother's. Chatellerault remained a week. Then, growing restive, he asked when my daughter would return. 'When you depart, monsieur,' I answered him, and, being pressed for reasons, I dealt so frankly with him that within twenty-four hours he was on his way back to Paris."

The Vicomte paused and took a turn in the apartment, whilst I pondered his words, which were bringing me a curious revelation.

Presently he resumed.

"And now, Chatellerault having failed in his purpose, the King chooses a more dangerous person for the gratifying of his desires. He sends the Marquis, Marcel de Bardelys to Lavédan on the same business. No doubt he attributes Chatellerault's failure to clumsiness, and he has decided this time to choose a man famed for courtly address and gifted with such arts of dalliance that he cannot fail but enmesh my daughter in them. It is a great compliment that he pays us in sending hither the handsomest and most accomplished gentleman of all his Court – so fame has it – yet it is a compliment of whose flattery I am not sensible. Bardelys goes hence as empty-handed as went Chatellerault. Let him but show his face, and my daughter journeys to Auch again. Am I not well advised, Monsieur de Lesperon?"

"Why, yes," I answered slowly, after the manner of one who deliberates, "if you are persuaded that your conclusions touching Bardelys are correct."

"I am more than persuaded. What other business could bring him to Lavédan?"

It was a question that I did not attempt to answer. Haply he did not expect me to answer it. He left me free to ponder another issue of this same business of which my mind was become very full.

Chatellerault had not dealt fairly with me. Often, since I had left Paris, had I marvelled that he came to be so rash as to risk his fortune upon a matter that turned upon a woman's whim. That I possessed undeniable advantages of person, of birth, and of wealth, Chatellerault could not have disregarded. Yet these, and the possibility that they might suffice to engage this lady's affections, he appeared to have set at naught when he plunged into that rash wager.

He must have realized that because he had failed was no reason to presume that I must also fail. There was no consequence in such an argument, and often, as I have said, had I marvelled during the past days at the readiness with which Chatellerault had flung down the gage. Now I held the explanation of it. He counted upon the Vicomte de Lavédan to reason precisely as he was reasoning, and he was confident that no opportunities would be afforded me of so much as seeing this beautiful and cold Roxalanne.

It was a wily trap he had set me, worthy only of a trickster.

Fate, however, had taken a hand in the game, and the cards were redealt since I had left Paris. The terms of the wager permitted me to choose any line of action that I considered desirable; but Destiny, it seemed, had chosen for me, and set me in a line that should at least suffice to overcome the parental resistance – that breastwork upon which Chatellerault had so confidently depended.

As the rebel René de Lesperon I was sheltered at Lavédan and made welcome by my fellow-rebel the Vicomte, who already seemed much taken with me, and who had esteemed me before seeing me from the much that Monsieur de Marsac – whoever he might be – had told him of me. As René de Lesperon I must remain, and turn to best account my sojourn, praying God meanwhile that this same Monsieur de Marsac might be pleased to refrain from visiting Lavédan whilst I was there.

# Chapter 6

## Convalescence

Of the week that followed my coming to Lavédan I find some difficulty in writing. It was for me a time very crowded with events – events that appeared to be moulding my character anew and making of me a person different, indeed, from that Marcel de Bardelys whom in Paris they called the Magnificent. Yet these events, although significant in their total, were of so vague and slight a nature in their detail, that when I come to write of them I find really little that I may set down.

Rodenard and his companions remained for two days at the chateau, and to me his sojourn there was a source of perpetual anxiety, for I knew not how far the fool might see fit to prolong it. It was well for me that this anxiety of mine was shared by Monsieur de Lavédan, who disliked at such a time the presence of men attached to one who was so notoriously of the King's party. He came at last to consult me as to what measures might be taken to remove them, and I – nothing loath to conspire with him to so desirable an end – bade him suggest to Rodenard that perhaps evil had befallen Monsieur de Bardelys, and that, instead of wasting his time at Lavédan, he were better advised to be searching the province for his master.

This counsel the Vicomte adopted, and with such excellent results that that very day – within the hour, in fact – Ganymède, aroused to a sense of his proper duty, set out in quest of me, not a little disturbed in mind – for with all his shortcomings the rascal loved me very faithfully.

That was on the third day of my sojourn at Lavédan. On the morrow I rose, my foot being sufficiently recovered to permit it. I felt a little weak from loss of blood, but Anatole – who, for all his evil countenance, was a kindly and gentle servant – was confident that a few days – a week at most – would see me completely restored.

Of leaving Lavédan I said nothing. But the Vicomte, who was one of the most generous and noble hearted men that it has ever been my good fortune to meet, forestalled any mention of my departure by urging that I should remain at the chateau until my recovery were completed, and, for that matter, as long thereafter as should suit my inclinations.

"At Lavédan you will be safe, my friend," he assured me; "for, as I have told you, we are under no suspicion. Let me urge you to remain until the King shall have desisted from further persecuting us."

And when I protested and spoke of trespassing, he waived the point with a brusqueness that amounted almost to anger.

"Believe, monsieur, that I am pleased and honoured at serving one who has so stoutly served the Cause and sacrificed so much to it."

At that, being not altogether dead to shame, I winced, and told myself that my behaviour was unworthy, and that I was practising a detestable deception. Yet some indulgence I may justly claim in consideration of how far I was victim of circumstance. Did I tell him that I was Bardelys, I was convinced that I should never leave the chateau alive. Very noble-hearted was the Vicomte, and no man have I known more averse to bloodthirstiness, but he had told me much during the days that I had lain abed, and many lives would be jeopardized did I proclaim what I had learned from him. Hence I argued that any disclosure of my identity must perforce drive him to extreme measures for the sake of the friends he had unwittingly betrayed.

On the day after Rodenard's departure I dined with the family, and met again Mademoiselle de Lavédan, whom I had not seen since the balcony adventure of some nights ago. The Vicomtesse was also present, a lady of very austere and noble appearance – lean as a pike and with a most formidable nose – but, as I was soon to discover, with a mind inclining overmuch to scandal and the high-seasoned talk of the Courts in which her girlhood had been spent.

From her lips I heard that day the old, scandalous story of Monseigneur de Richelieu's early passion for Anne of Austria. With much unction did she tell us how the Queen had lured His Eminence to dress himself in the motley of a jester that she might make a mock of him in the eyes of the courtiers she had concealed behind the arras of her chamber.

This anecdote she gave us with much wealth of discreditable detail and scant regard for either her daughter's presence or for the blushes that suffused the poor child's cheeks. In every way she was a pattern of the class of women amongst whom my youth had been spent, a class which had done so much towards shattering my faith and lowering my estimate of her sex. Lavédan had married her and brought her into Languedoc, and here she spent her years lamenting the scenes of her youth, and prone, it would seem, to make them matter for conversation whenever a newcomer chanced to present himself at the chateau.

Looking from her to her daughter, I thanked Heaven that Roxalanne was no reproduction of the mother. She had inherited as little of her character as of her appearance. Both in feature and in soul Mademoiselle de Lavédan was a copy of that noble, gallant gentleman, her father.

One other was present at that meal, of whom I shall have more to say hereafter. This was a young man of good presence, save, perhaps, a too obtrusive foppishness, whom Monsieur de Lavédan presented to me as a distant kinsman of theirs, one Chevalier de Saint-Eustache.

He was very tall – of fully my own height – and of an excellent shape, although extremely young. But his head if anything was too small for his body, and his good-natured mouth was of a weakness that was confirmed by the significance of his chin, whilst his eyes were too closely set to augur frankness.

He was a pleasant fellow, seemingly of that negative pleasantness that lies in inoffensiveness, but otherwise dull and of an untutored mind – rustic, as might be expected in one the greater part of whose life had been spent in his native province, and of a rusticity rendered all the more flagrant by the very efforts he exerted to dissemble it.

It was after Madame had related that unsavoury anecdote touching the Cardinal that he turned to ask me whether I was well acquainted with the Court. I was near to committing the egregious blunder of laughing in his face, but, recollecting myself betimes, I answered vaguely that I had some knowledge of it, whereupon he all but caused me to bound from my chair by asking me had I ever met the Magnificent Bardelys.

"I – I am acquainted with him," I answered warily. "Why do you ask?"

"I was reminded of him by the fact that his servants have been here for two days. You were expecting the Marquis himself, were you not, Monsieur le Vicomte?"

Lavédan raised his head suddenly, after the manner of a man who has received an affront.

"I was not, Chevalier," he answered, with emphasis. "His intendant, an insolent knave of the name of Rodenard, informed me that this Bardelys projected visiting me. He has not come, and I devoutly hope that he may not come. Trouble enough had I to rid myself of his servants, and but for Monsieur de Lesperon's well-conceived suggestion they might still be here."

"You have never met him, monsieur?" inquired the Chevalier.

"Never," replied our host in such a way that any but a fool must have understood that he desired nothing less than such a meeting.

"A delightful fellow," murmured Saint-Eustache – "a brilliant, dazzling personality."

"You – you are acquainted with him?" I asked.

"Acquainted?" echoed that boastful liar. "We were as brothers."

"How you interest me! And why have you never told us?" quoth Madame, her eyes turned enviously upon the young man – as enviously as were Lavédan's turned in disgust. "It is a thousand pities that Monsieur de Bardelys has altered his plans and is no longer coming to us. To meet such a man is to breathe again the air of the grand monde.

"You remember, Monsieur de Lesperon, that affair with the Duchesse de Bourgogne?" And she smiled wickedly in my direction.

"I have some recollection of it," I answered coldly. "But I think that rumour exaggerates. When tongues wag, a little rivulet is often described as a mountain torrent."

"You would not say so did you but know what I know," she informed me roguishly. "Often, I confess, rumour may swell the importance of such an affaire, but in this case I do not think that rumour does it justice."

I made a deprecatory gesture, and I would have had the subject changed, but ere I could make an effort to that end, the fool Saint-Eustache was babbling again.

"You remember the duel that was fought in consequence, Monsieur de Lesperon?"

"Yes," I assented wearily.

"And in which a poor young fellow lost his life," growled the Vicomte. "It was practically a murder."

"Nay, monsieur," I cried, with a sudden heat that set them staring at me; "there you do him wrong. Monsieur de Bardelys was opposed to the best blade in France. The man's reputation as a swordsman was of such a quality that for a twelvemonth he had been living upon it, doing all manner of unseemly things immune from punishment by the fear in which he was universally held. His behaviour in the unfortunate affair we are discussing was of a particularly shameful character. Oh, I know the details, messieurs, I can assure you. He thought to impose his reputation upon Bardelys as he had imposed it upon a hundred others, but Bardelys was over-tough for his teeth.

"He sent that notorious young gentleman a challenge, and on the following morning he left him dead in the horsemarket behind the Hôtel Vendôme. But far from a murder, monsieur, it was an act of justice, and the most richly earned punishment with which ever man was visited."

"Even if so," cried the Vicomte in some surprise, "why all this heat to defend a brawler?"

"A brawler?" I repeated after him. "Oh, no. That is a charge his worst enemies cannot make against Bardelys. He is no brawler. The duel in question was his first affair of the kind, and it has been his last, for unto him has clung the reputation that had belonged until then to La Vertoile, and there is none in France bold enough to send a challenge to him." And, seeing what surprise I was provoking, I thought it well to involve another with me in his defence. So, turning to the Chevalier, "I am sure," said I, "that Monsieur de Saint-Eustache will confirm my words."

Thereupon, his vanity being all aroused, the Chevalier set himself to paraphrase all that I had said with a heat that cast mine into a miserable insignificance.

"At least," laughed the Vicomte at length, "he lacks not for champions. For my own part, I am content to pray Heaven that he come not to Lavédan, as he intended."

"Mais voyons, Gaston," the Vicomtesse protested, "why harbour prejudice? Wait at least until you have seen him, that you may judge him for yourself."

"Already have I judged him; I pray that I may never see him."

"They tell me he is a very handsome man," said she, appealing to me for confirmation. Lavédan shot her a sudden glance of alarm, at which I could have laughed. Hitherto his sole concern had been his daughter, but it suddenly occurred to him that perhaps not even her years might set the Vicomtesse in safety from imprudences with this devourer of hearts, should he still chance to come that way.

"Madame," I answered, "he is accounted not ill-favoured." And with a deprecatory smile I added, "I am said somewhat to resemble him."

"Say you so?" she exclaimed, raising her eyebrows, and looking at me more closely than hitherto. And then it seemed to me that into her face crept a shade of disappointment. If this Bardelys were not more beautiful than I, then he was not nearly so beautiful a man as she had imagined. She turned to Saint-Eustache.

"It is indeed so, Chevalier?" she inquired. "Do you note the resemblance?"

"Vanitas, vanitate," murmured the youth, who had some scraps of Latin and a taste for airing them. "I can see no likeness – no trace of one. Monsieur de Lesperon is well enough, I should say. But Bardelys!" He cast his eyes to the ceiling. "There is but one Bardelys in France."

"Enfin," I laughed, "you are no doubt well qualified to judge, Chevalier. I had flattered myself that some likeness did exist, but probably you have seen the Marquis more frequently than have I, and probably you know him better. Nevertheless, should he come his way, I will ask you to look at us side by side and be the judge of the resemblance."

"Should I happen to be here," he said, with a sudden constraint not difficult to understand, "I shall be happy to act as arbiter."

"Should you happen to be here?" I echoed questioningly. "But surely, should you hear that Monsieur de Bardelys is about to arrive, you will postpone any departure you may be on the point of making, so that you may renew this great friendship that you tell us you do the Marquis the honour of entertaining for him?"

The Chevalier eyed me with the air of a man looking down from a great height upon another. The Vicomte smiled quietly to himself as he combed his fair beard with his forefinger in a meditative fashion, whilst even Roxalanne – who had sat silently listening to a conversation that she was at times mercifully spared from following too minutely – flashed me a humorous glance. To the Vicomtesse alone – who in common with women of her type was of a singular obtuseness – was the situation without significance.

Saint-Eustache, to defend himself against my delicate imputation, and to show how well acquainted he was with Bardelys, plunged at once into a thousand details of that gentleman's magnificence. He described his suppers, his retinue, his equipages, his houses, his chateaux, his favour with the King, his successes with the fair sex, and I know not what besides – in all of which I confess that even to me there was a certain degree of novelty. Roxalanne listened with an air of amusement that showed how well she read him. Later, when I found myself alone with her by the river, whither we had gone after the repast and the Chevalier's reminiscences were at an end, she reverted to that conversation.

"Is not my cousin a great fanfaron, monsieur," she asked.

"Surely you know your cousin better than I," I answered cautiously. "Why question me upon his character?"

"I was hardly questioning; I was commenting. He spent a fortnight in Paris once, and he accounts himself, or would have us account him, intimate with every courtier at the Luxembourg. Oh, he is very amusing, this good cousin, but tiresome too." She laughed, and there was the faintest note of scorn in her amusement. "Now, touching this Marquis de Bardelys, it is very plain that the Chevalier boasted when he said that they were as brothers – he and the Marquis – is it not? He grew ill at ease when you reminded him of the possibility of the Marquis' visit to Lavédan." And she laughed quaintly to herself. "Do you think that he so much as knows Bardelys?" she asked me suddenly.

"Not so much as by sight," I answered. "He is full of information concerning that unworthy gentleman, but it is only information that the meanest scullion in Paris might afford you, and just as inaccurate."

"Why do you speak of him as unworthy? Are you of the same opinion as my father?"

"Aye, and with better cause."

"You know him well?"

"Know him? Pardieu, he is my worst enemy. A worn-out libertine; a sneering, cynical misogynist; a nauseated reveller; a hateful egotist. There is no more unworthy person, I'll swear, in all France. Peste! The very memory of the fellow makes me sick. Let us talk of other things."

But although I urged it with the best will and the best intentions in the world, I was not to have my way. The air became suddenly heavy with the scent of musk, and the Chevalier de Saint-Eustache stood before us, and forced the conversation once more upon the odious topic of Monsieur de Bardelys.

The poor fool came with a plan of campaign carefully considered, bent now upon overthrowing me with the knowledge he would exhibit, and whereby he looked to encompass my humiliation before his cousin.

"Speaking of Bardelys, Monsieur de Lesperon – "

"My dear Chevalier, we were no longer speaking of him."

He smiled darkly. "Let us speak of him, then."

"But are there not a thousand more interesting things that we might speak of?"

This he took for a fresh sign of fear, and so he pressed what he accounted his advantage.

"Yet have patience; there is a point on which perhaps you can give me some information."

"Impossible," said I.

"Are you acquainted with the Duchesse de Bourgogne?"

"I was," I answered casually, and as casually I added, "Are you?"

"Excellently well," he replied unhesitatingly. "I was in Paris at the time of the scandal with Bardelys."

I looked up quickly.

"Was it then that you met her?" I inquired in an idle sort of way.

"Yes. I was in the confidence of Bardelys, and one night after we had supped at his hotel – one of those suppers graced by every wit in Paris – he asked me if I were minded to accompany him to the Louvre. We went. A masque was in progress."

"Ah," said I, after the manner of one who suddenly takes in the entire situation; "and it was at this masque that you met the Duchesse?"

"You have guessed it. Ah, monsieur, if I were to tell you of the things that I witnessed that night, they would amaze you," said he, with a great air and a casual glance at Mademoiselle to see into what depth of wonder these glimpses into his wicked past were plunging her.

"I doubt it not," said I, thinking that if his imagination were as fertile in that connection as it had been in mine he was likely, indeed, to have some amazing things to tell. "But do I understand you to say that that was the time of the scandal you have touched upon?"

"The scandal burst three days after that masque. It came as a surprise to most people. As for me – from what Bardelys had told me – I expected nothing less."

"Pardon, Chevalier, but how old do you happen to be?"

"A curious question that," said he, knitting his brows.

"Perhaps. But will you not answer it?"

"I am twenty-one," said he. "What of it?"

"You are twenty, mon cousin," Roxalanne corrected him.

He looked at her a second with an injured air.

"Why, true – twenty! That is so," he acquiesced; and again, "what of it?" he demanded.

"What of it, monsieur?" I echoed. "Will you forgive me if I express amazement at your precocity, and congratulate you upon it?"

His brows went if possible closer together and his face grew very red. He knew that somewhere a pitfall awaited him, yet hardly where.

"I do not understand you."

"Bethink you, Chevalier. Ten years have flown since this scandal you refer to. So that at the time of your supping with Bardelys and the wits of Paris, at the time of his making a confidant of you and carrying you off to a masque at the Louvre, at the time of his presenting you to the Duchesse de Bourgogne, you were just ten years of age. I never had cause to think over-well of Bardelys, but had you not told me yourself, I should have hesitated to believe him so vile a despoiler of innocence, such a perverter of youth."

He crimsoned to the very roots of his hair.

Roxalanne broke into a laugh. "My cousin, my cousin," she cried, "they that would become masters should begin early, is it not so?"

"Monsieur de Lesperon," said he, in a very formal voice, "do you wish me to apprehend that you have put me through this catechism for the purpose of casting a doubt upon what I have said?"

"But have I done that? Have I cast a doubt?" I asked, with the utmost meekness.

"So I apprehend."

"Then you apprehend amiss. Your words, I assure you, admit of no doubt whatever. And now, monsieur, if you will have mercy upon me, we will talk of other things. I am so weary of this unfortunate Bardelys and his affairs. He may be the fashion of Paris and at Court, but down here his very name befouls the air. Mademoiselle," I said, turning to Roxalanne, "you promised me a lesson in the lore of flowers."

"Come, then," said she, and, being an exceedingly wise child, she plunged straightway into the history of the shrubs about us.

Thus did we avert a storm that for a moment was very imminent. Yet some mischief was done, and some good, too, perhaps. For if I made an enemy of the Chevalier de Saint-Eustache by humbling him in the eyes of the one woman before whom he sought to shine, I established a bond 'twixt Roxalanne and myself by that same humiliation of a foolish coxcomb, whose boastfulness had long wearied her.

# Chapter 7

## *The Hostility of Saint-Eustache*

In the days that followed I saw much of the Chevalier de Saint-Eustache. He was a very constant visitor at Lavédan, and the reason of it was not far to seek. For my own part, I disliked him – I had done so from the moment when first I had set eyes on him – and since hatred, like affection, is often a matter of reciprocity, the Chevalier was not slow to return my dislike. Our manner gradually, by almost imperceptible stages, grew more distant, until by the end of a week it had become so hostile that Lavédan found occasion to comment upon it.

"Beware of Saint-Eustache," he warned me. "You are becoming very manifestly distasteful to each other, and I would urge you to have a care. I don't trust him. His attachment to our Cause is of a lukewarm character, and he gives me uneasiness, for he may do much harm if he is so inclined. It is on this account that I tolerate his presence at Lavédan. Frankly, I fear him, and I would counsel you to do no less. The man is a liar, even if but a boastful liar and liars are never long out of mischief."

The wisdom of the words was unquestionable, but the advice in them was not easily followed, particularly by one whose position was so peculiar as my own. In a way I had little cause to fear the harm the Chevalier might do me, but I was impelled to consider the harm that at the same time he might do the Vicomte.

Despite our growing enmity, the Chevalier and I were very frequently thrown together. The reason for this was, of course, that wherever Roxalanne was to be found there, generally, were we both to be found also. Yet had I advantages that must have gone to swell a rancour based as much upon jealousy as any other sentiment, for whilst he was but a daily visitor at Lavédan, I was established there indefinitely.

Of the use that I made of that time I find it difficult to speak.

From the first moment that I had beheld Roxalanne I had realized the truth of Chatellerault's assertion that I had never known a woman. He was right. Those that I had met and by whom I had judged the sex had, by contrast with this child, little claim to the title. Virtue I had accounted a shadow without substance; innocence, a synonym for ignorance; love, a fable, a fairy tale for the delectation of overgrown children.

In the company of Roxalanne de Lavédan all those old, cynical beliefs, built up upon a youth of undesirable experiences, were shattered and the error of them exposed. Swiftly was I becoming a convert to the faith which so long I had sneered at, and as lovesick as any unfledged youth in his first amour.

Damn! It was something for a man who had lived as I had lived to have his pulses quicken and his colour change at a maid's approach; to find himself colouring under her smile and paling under her disdain; to have his mind running on rhymes, and his soul so enslaved that, if she is not to be won, chagrin will dislodge it from his body.

Here was a fine mood for a man who had entered upon his business by pledging himself to win and wed this girl in cold and supreme indifference to her personality. And that pledge, how I cursed it during those days at Lavédan! How I cursed Chatellerault, cunning, subtle trickster that he was! How I cursed myself for my lack of chivalry and honour in having been lured so easily into so damnable a business! For when the memory of that wager rose before me it brought despair in its train. Had I found Roxalanne the sort of woman that I had looked to find – the only sort that I had ever known – then matters had been easy. I had set myself in cold blood, and by such wiles as I knew, to win such affection as might be hers to bestow; and I would have married her in much the same spirit as a man performs any other of the necessary acts of his lifetime and station. I would have told her that I was Bardelys, and to the woman that I had expected to find there had been no difficulty in making the confession. But to Roxalanne! Had there been no wager, I might have confessed my identity. As it was, I found it impossible to avow the one without the other. For the sweet innocence that invested her gentle, trusting soul must have given pause to any but the most abandoned of men before committing a vileness in connection with her.

We were much together during that week, and just as day by day, hour by hour, my passion grew and grew until it absorbed me utterly, so, too, did it seem to me that it awakened in her a responsive note.

There was an odd light at times in her soft eyes; I came upon her more than once with snatches of love-songs on her lips, and when she smiled upon me there was a sweet tenderness in her smile, which, had things been different, would have gladdened my soul beyond all else; but which, things being as they were, was rather wont to heighten my despair. I was no coxcomb; I had had experiences, and I knew these signs. But something, too, I guessed of the heart of such a one as Roxalanne. To the full I realized the pain and shame I should inflict upon her when my confession came; I realized, too, how the love of this dear child, so honourable and high of mind, must turn to contempt and scorn when I plucked away my mask, and let her see how poor a countenance I wore beneath.

And yet I drifted with the tide of things. It was my habit so to drift, and the habit of a lifetime is not to be set at naught in a day by a resolve, however firm. A score of times was I reminded that an evil is but increased by being ignored. A score of times confession trembled on my lips, and I burned to tell her everything from its inception – the environment that had erstwhile warped me, the honesty by which I was now inspired – and so cast myself upon the mercy of her belief.

She might accept my story, and, attaching credit to it, forgive me the deception I had practised, and recognize the great truth that must ring out in the avowal of my love. But, on the other hand, she might not accept it; she might deem my confession a shrewd part of my scheme, and the dread of that kept me silent day by day.

Fully did I see how with every hour that sped confession became more and more difficult. The sooner the thing were done, the greater the likelihood of my being believed; the later I left it, the more probable was it that I should be discredited. Alas! Bardelys, it seemed, had added cowardice to his other short-comings.

As for the coldness of Roxalanne, that was a pretty fable of Chatellerault's; or else no more than an assumption, an invention of the imaginative La Fosse. Far, indeed, from it, I found no arrogance or coldness in her. All unversed in the artifices of her sex, all unacquainted with the wiles of coquetry, she was the very incarnation of naturalness and maidenly simplicity. To the tales that – with many expurgations – I told her of Court life, to the pictures that I drew of Paris, the Luxembourg, the Louvre, the Palais Cardinal, and the courtiers that thronged those historic palaces, she listened avidly and enthralled; and much as Othello won the heart of Desdemona by a recital of the perils he had endured, so it seemed to me was I winning the heart of Roxalanne by telling her of the things that I had seen.

Once or twice she expressed wonder at the depth and intimacy of the knowledge of such matters exhibited by a simple Gascon gentleman, whereupon I would urge, in explanation, the appointment in the Guards that Lesperon had held some few years ago, a position that will reveal much to an observant man.

The Vicomte noted our growing intimacy, yet set no restraint upon it.

Down in his heart I believe that noble gentleman would have been well pleased had matters gone to extremes between us, for however impoverished he might deem me; Lesperon's estates in Gascony being, as I have said, likely to suffer sequestration in view of his treason – he remembered the causes of this and the deep devotion of the man I impersonated to the affairs of Gaston d'Orléans.

Again, he feared the very obvious courtship of the Chevalier de Saint-Eustache, and he would have welcomed a turn of events that would effectually have frustrated it. That he did not himself interfere so far as the Chevalier's wooing was concerned, I could but set down to the mistrust of Saint-Eustache – amounting almost to fear – of which he had spoken.

As for the Vicomtesse, the same causes that had won me some of the daughter's regard gained me also no little of the mother's.

She had been attached to the Chevalier until my coming. But what did the Chevalier know of the great world compared with what I could tell? Her love of scandal drew her to me with inquiries upon this person and that person, many of them but names to her.

My knowledge and wealth of detail – for all that I curbed it lest I should seem to know too much – delighted her prurient soul. Had she been more motherly, this same knowledge that I exhibited should have made her ponder what manner of life I had led, and should have inspired her to account me no fit companion for her daughter. But a selfish woman, little inclined to be plagued by the concerns of another – even when that other was her daughter – she left things to the destructive course that they were shaping.

And so everything – if we except perhaps the Chevalier de Saint-Eustache – conspired to the advancement of my suit, in a manner that must have made Chatellerault grind his teeth in rage if he could have witnessed it, but which made me grind mine in despair when I pondered the situation in detail.

One evening – I had been ten days at the chateau – we went a half-league or so up the Garonne in a boat, she and I. As we were returning, drifting with the stream, the oars idle in my hand, I spoke of leaving Lavédan.

She looked up quickly; her expression was almost of alarm, and her eyes dilated as they met mine – for, as I have said, she was all unversed in the ways of her sex, and by nature too guileless to attempt to disguise her feelings or dissemble them.

"But why must you go so soon?" she asked. "You are safe at Lavédan, and abroad you may be in danger. It was but two days ago that they took a poor young gentleman of these parts at Pau; so that you see the persecution is not yet ended. Are you" – and her voice trembled ever so slightly – "are you weary of us, monsieur?"

I shook my head at that, and smiled wistfully.

"Weary?" I echoed. "Surely, mademoiselle, you do not think it? Surely your heart must tell you something very different?"

She dropped her eyes before the passion of my gaze. And when presently she answered me, there was no guile in her words; there were the dictates of the intuitions of her sex, and nothing more.

"But it is possible, monsieur. You are accustomed to the great world – "

"The great world of Lesperon, in Gascony?" I interrupted.

"No, no; the great world you have inhabited at Paris and elsewhere. I can understand that at Lavédan you should find little of interest, and – and that your inactivity should render you impatient to be gone."

"If there were so little to interest me then it might be as you say. But, oh, mademoiselle – " I ceased abruptly. Fool! I had almost fallen a prey to the seductions that the time afforded me. The balmy, languorous eventide, the broad, smooth river down which we glided, the foliage, the shadows on the water, her presence, and our isolation amid such surroundings, had almost blotted out the matter of the wager and of my duplicity.

She laughed a little nervous laugh, and – maybe to ease the tension that my sudden silence had begotten – "You see," she said, "how your imagination deserts you when you seek to draw upon it for proof of what you protest. You were about to tell me of – of the interests that hold you at Lavédan, and when you come to ponder them, you find that you can think of nothing. Is it – is it not so?" She put the question very timidly, as if half afraid of the answer she might provoke.

61

"No; it is not so," I said.

I paused a moment, and in that moment I wrestled with myself.

Confession and avowal – confession of what I had undertaken, and avowal of the love that had so unexpectedly come to me – trembled upon my lips, to be driven shuddering away in fear.

Have I not said that this Bardelys was become a coward? Then my cowardice suggested a course to me – flight. I would leave Lavédan.

I would return to Paris and to Chatellerault, owning defeat and paying my wager. It was the only course open to me. My honour, so tardily aroused, demanded no less. Yet, not so much because of that as because it was suddenly revealed to me as the easier course, did I determine to pursue it. What thereafter might become of me I did not know, nor in that hour of my heart's agony did it seem to matter overmuch.

"There is much, mademoiselle, much, indeed, to hold me firmly at Lavédan," I pursued at last. "But my – my obligations demand of me that I depart."

"You mean the Cause," she cried. "But, believe me, you can do nothing. To sacrifice yourself cannot profit it. Infinitely better you can serve the Duke by waiting until the time is ripe for another blow. And how can you better preserve your life than by remaining at Lavédan until the persecutions are at an end?"

"I was not thinking of the Cause, mademoiselle, but of myself alone – of my own personal honour. I would that I could explain; but I am afraid," I ended lamely.

"Afraid?" she echoed, now raising her eyes in wonder.

"Aye, afraid. Afraid of your contempt, of your scorn."

The wonder in her glance increased and asked a question that I could not answer. I stretched forward, and caught one of the hands lying idle in her lap.

"Roxalanne," I murmured very gently, and my tone, my touch, and the use of her name drove her eyes for refuge behind their lids again.

A flush spread upon the ivory pallor of her face, to fade as swiftly, leaving it very white. Her bosom rose and fell in agitation, and the little hand I held trembled in my grasp. There was a moment's silence. Not that I had need to think or choose my words. But there was a lump in my throat – aye, I take no shame in confessing it, for this was the first time that a good and true emotion had been vouchsafed me since the Duchesse de Bourgogne had shattered my illusions ten years ago.

"Roxalanne," I resumed presently, when I was more master of myself, "we have been good friends, you and I, since that night when I climbed for shelter to your chamber, have we not?"

"But yes, monsieur," she faltered.

"Ten days ago it is. Think of it – no more than ten days. And it seems as if I had been months at Lavédan, so well have we become acquainted. In these ten days we have formed opinions of each other. But with this difference, that whilst mine are right, yours are wrong. I have come to know you for the sweetest, gentlest saint in all this world. Would to God I had known you earlier! It might have been very different; I might have been – I would have been – different, and I would not have done what I have done. You have come to know me for an unfortunate but honest gentleman. Such am I not. I am under false colours here, mademoiselle. Unfortunate I may be – at least, of late I seem to have become so. Honest I am not – I have not been. There, child, I can tell you no more. I am too great a coward. But when later you shall come to hear the truth – when, after I am gone, they may tell you a strange story touching this fellow Lesperon who sought the hospitality of your father's house – bethink you of my restraint in this hour; bethink you of my departure. You will understand these things perhaps afterwards. But bethink you of them, and you will unriddle them for yourself, perhaps. Be merciful upon me then; judge me not over-harshly."

I paused, and for a moment we were silent. Then suddenly she looked up; her fingers tightened upon mine.

"Monsieur de Lesperon," she pleaded, "of what do you speak? You are torturing me, monsieur."

"Look in my face, Roxalanne. Can you see nothing there of how I am torturing myself?"

"Then tell me, monsieur," she begged, her voice a very caress of suppliant softness, "tell me what vexes you and sets a curb upon your tongue. You exaggerate, I am assured. You could do nothing dishonourable, nothing vile."

"Child," I cried, "I thank God that you are right! I cannot do what is dishonourable, and I will not, for all that a month ago I pledged myself to do it!"

A sudden horror, a doubt, a suspicion flashed into her glance.

"You – you do not mean that you are a spy?" she asked; and from my heart a prayer of thanks went up to Heaven that this at least it was mine frankly to deny.

"No, no – not that. I am no spy."

Her face cleared again, and she sighed.

"It is, I think, the only thing I could not forgive. Since it is not that, will you not tell me what it is?"

For a moment the temptation to confess, to tell her everything, was again upon me. But the futility of it appalled me.

"Don't ask me," I besought her; "you will learn it soon enough."

For I was confident that once my wager was paid, the news of it and of the ruin of Bardelys would spread across the face of France like a ripple over water. Presently –

"Forgive me for having come into your life, Roxalanne!" I implored her, and then I sighed again. "Hélas! Had I but known you earlier! I did not dream such women lived in this worn-out France."

"I will not pry, monsieur, since your resolve appears to be so firm. But if – if after I have heard this thing you speak of," she said presently, speaking with averted eyes, "and if, having heard it, I judge you more mercifully than you judge yourself, and I send for you, will you – will you come back to Lavédan?"

My heart gave a great bound – a great, a sudden throb of hope. But as sudden and as great was the rebound into despair.

"You will not send for me, be assured of that," I said with finality; and we spoke no more.

I took the oars and plied them vigorously. I was in haste to end the situation. Tomorrow I must think of my departure, and, as I rowed, I pondered the words that had passed between us. Not one word of love had there been, and yet, in the very omission of it, avowal had lain on either side. A strange wooing had been mine – a wooing that precluded the possibility of winning, and yet a wooing that had won. Aye, it had won; but it might not take. I made fine distinctions and quaint paradoxes as I tugged at my oars, for the human mind is a curiously complex thing, and with some of us there is no such spur to humour as the sting of pain.

Roxalanne sat white and very thoughtful, but with veiled eyes, so that I might guess nothing of what passed within her mind.

At last we reached the chateau, and as I brought the boat to the terrace steps, it was Saint-Eustache who came forward to offer his wrist to Mademoiselle.

He noted the pallor of her face, and darted me a quick, suspicion-laden glance. As we were walking towards the chateau –

"Monsieur de Lesperon," said he in a curious tone, "do you know that a rumour of your death is current in the province?"

"I had hoped that such a rumour might get abroad when I disappeared," I answered calmly.

"And you have taken no single step to contradict it?"

"Why should I, since in that rumour may be said to lie my safety?"

"Nevertheless, monsieur, voyons. Surely you might at least relieve the anxieties, the affliction, I might almost say – of those who are mourning you."

"Ah!" said I. "And who may these be?"

He shrugged his shoulders and pursed his lips in a curiously deprecatory smile. With a sidelong glance at Mademoiselle –

"Do you need that I name Mademoiselle de Marsac?" he sneered.

I stood still, my wits busily working, my face impassive under his scrutinizing glance. In a flash it came to me that this must be the writer of some of the letters Lesperon had given me, the original of the miniature I carried.

As I was silent, I grew suddenly conscious of another pair of eyes observing me, Mademoiselle's. She remembered what I had said, she may have remembered how I had cried out the wish that I had met her earlier, and she may not have been slow to find an interpretation for my words. I could have groaned in my rage at such a misinterpretation. I could have taken the Chevalier round to the other side of the chateau and killed him with the greatest relish in the world. But I restrained myself, I resigned myself to be misunderstood. What choice had I?

"Monsieur de Saint-Eustache," said I very coldly, and looking him straight between his close-set eyes, "I have permitted you many liberties, but there is one that I cannot permit anyone – and, much as I honour you, I can make no exception in your favour. That is to interfere in my concerns and presume to dictate to me the manner in which I shall conduct them. Be good enough to bear that in your memory."

In a moment he was all servility. The sneer passed out of his face, the arrogance out of his demeanour. He became as full of smiles and capers as the meanest sycophant.

"You will forgive me, monsieur!" he cried, spreading his hands, and with the humblest smile in the world. "I perceive that I have taken a great liberty; yet you have misunderstood its purport. I sought to sound you touching the wisdom of a step upon which I have ventured."

"That is, monsieur?" I asked, throwing back my head, with the scent of danger breast high.

"I took it upon myself today to mention the fact that you are alive and well to one who had a right, I thought, to know of it, and who is coming hither tomorrow."

"That was a presumption you may regret," said I between my teeth. "To whom did you impart this information?"

"To your friend, Monsieur de Marsac," he answered, and through his mask of humility the sneer was again growing apparent. "He will be here tomorrow," he repeated.

Marsac was that friend of Lesperon's to whose warm commendation of the Gascon rebel I owed the courtesy and kindness that the Vicomte de Lavédan had meted out to me since my coming.

Is it wonderful that I stood as if frozen, my wits refusing to work and my countenance wearing, I doubt not, a very stricken look? Here was one coming to Lavédan who knew Lesperon – one who would unmask me and say that I was an impostor. What would happen then? A spy they would of a certainty account me, and that they would make short work of me I never doubted. But that was something that troubled me less than the opinion Mademoiselle must form. How would she interpret what I had said that day? In what light would she view me hereafter?

Such questions sped like swift arrows through my mind, and in their train came a dull anger with myself that I had not told her everything that afternoon. It was too late now. The confession would come no longer of my own free will, as it might have done an hour ago, but would be forced from me by the circumstances that impended. Thus it would no longer have any virtue to recommend it to her mercy.

"The news seems hardly welcome, Monsieur de Lesperon," said Roxalanne in a voice that was inscrutable. Her tone stirred me, for it betokened suspicion already. Something might yet chance to aid me, and in the meanwhile I might spoil all did I yield to this dread of the morrow. By an effort I mastered myself, and in tones calm and level, that betrayed nothing of the tempest in my soul –

"It is not welcome, mademoiselle," I answered. "I have excellent reasons for not desiring to meet Monsieur de Marsac."

"Excellent, indeed, are they!" lisped Saint-Eustache, with an ugly droop at the corners of his mouth. "I doubt not you'll find it hard to offer a plausible reason for having left him and his sister without news that you were alive."

"Monsieur," said I at random, "why will you drag in his sister's name?"

"Why?" he echoed, and he eyed me with undisguised amusement. He was standing erect, his head thrown back, his right arm outstretched from the shoulder, and his hand resting lightly upon the gold mount of his beribboned cane. He let his eyes wander from me to Roxalanne, then back again to me. At last: "Is it wonderful that I should drag in the name of your betrothed?" said he. "But perhaps you will deny that Mademoiselle de Marsac is that to you?" he suggested.

And I, forgetting for the moment the part I played and the man whose identity I had put on, made answer hotly: "I do deny it."

"Why, then, you lie," said he, and shrugged his shoulders with insolent contempt.

In all my life I do not think it could be said of me that I had ever given way to rage. Rude, untutored minds may fall a prey to passion, but a gentleman, I hold, is never angry. Nor was I then, so far as the outward signs of anger count. I doffed my hat with a sweep to Roxalanne, who stood by with fear and wonder blending in her glance.

"Mademoiselle, you will forgive that I find it necessary to birch this babbling schoolboy in your presence."

Then, with the pleasantest manner in the world, I stepped aside, and plucked the cane from the Chevalier's hand before he had so much as guessed what I was about. I bowed before him with the utmost politeness, as if craving his leave and tolerance for what I was about to do, and then, before he had recovered from his astonishment, I had laid that cane three times in quick succession across his shoulders. With a cry at once of pain and of mortification, he sprang back, and his hand dropped to his hilt.

"Monsieur," Roxalanne cried to him, "do you not see that he is unarmed?"

But he saw nothing, or, if he saw, thanked Heaven that things were in such case, and got his sword out. Thereupon Roxalanne would have stepped between us, but with arm outstretched I restrained her.

"Have no fear, mademoiselle," said I very quietly; for if the wrist that had overcome La Vertoile were not with a stick a match for a couple of such swords as this coxcomb's, then was I forever shamed.

He bore down upon me furiously, his point coming straight for my throat. I took the blade on the cane; then, as he disengaged and came at me lower, I made counter-parry, and pursuing the circle after I had caught his steel, I carried it out of his hand. It whirled an instant, a shimmering wheel of light, then it clattered against the marble balustrade half a dozen yards away. With his sword it seemed that his courage, too, departed, and he stood at my mercy, a curious picture of foolishness, surprise, and fear.

Now the Chevalier de Saint-Eustache was a young man, and in the young we can forgive much. But to forgive such an act as he had been guilty of – that of drawing his sword upon a man who carried no weapons – would have been not only a ridiculous toleration, but an utter neglect of duty. As an older man it behoved me to read the Chevalier a lesson in manners and gentlemanly feeling. So, quite dispassionately, and purely for his own future good, I went about the task, and administered him a thrashing that for thoroughness it would be hard to better. I was not discriminating. I brought my cane down with a rhythmical precision, and whether it took him on the head, the back, or the shoulders, I held to be more his affair than mine. I had a moral to inculcate, and the injuries he might receive in the course of it were inconsiderable details so that the lesson was borne in upon his soul. Two or three times he sought to close with me, but I eluded him; I had no mind to descend to a vulgar exchange of blows. My object was not to brawl, but to administer chastisement, and this object I may claim to have accomplished with a fair degree of success.

At last Roxalanne interfered; but only when one blow a little more violent, perhaps, than its precursors resulted in the sudden snapping of the cane and Monsieur de Saint-Eustache's utter collapse into a moaning heap.

"I deplore, mademoiselle, to have offended your sight with such a spectacle, but unless these lessons are administered upon the instant their effect is not half so salutary."

"He deserved it, monsieur," said she, with a note almost of fierceness in her voice. And of such poor mettle are we that her resentment against that groaning mass of fopperies and wheals sent a thrill of pleasure through me. I walked over to the spot where his sword had fallen, and picked it up.

"Monsieur de Saint-Eustache," said I, "you have so dishonoured this blade that I do not think you would care to wear it again." Saying which, I snapped it across my knee, and flung it far out into the river, for all that the hilt was a costly one, richly wrought in bronze and gold.

He raised his livid countenance, and his eyes blazed impotent fury.

"Par la mort Dieu!" he cried hoarsely, "you shall give me satisfaction for this!"

"If you account yourself still unsatisfied, I am at your service when you will," said I courteously.

Then, before more could be said, I saw Monsieur de Lavédan and the Vicomtesse approaching hurriedly across the parterre. The Vicomte's brow was black with what might have appeared anger, but which I rightly construed into apprehension.

"What has taken place? What have you done?" he asked of me.

"He has brutally assaulted the Chevalier," cried Madame shrilly, her eyes malevolently set upon me. "He is only a child, this poor Saint-Eustache," she reproached me. "I saw it all from my window, Monsieur de Lesperon. It was brutal; it was cowardly. So to beat a boy! Shame! If you had a quarrel with him, are there not prescribed methods for their adjustment between gentlemen? Pardieu, could you not have given him proper satisfaction?"

"If madame will give herself the trouble of attentively examining this poor Saint-Eustache," said I, with a sarcasm which her virulence prompted, "you will agree, I think, that I have given him very proper and very thorough satisfaction. I would have met him sword in hand, but the Chevalier has the fault of the very young – he is precipitate; he was in too great a haste, and he could not wait until I got a sword. So I was forced to do what I could with a cane."

"But you provoked him," she flashed back.

"Whoever told you so has misinformed you, madame. On the contrary, he provoked me. He gave me the lie. I struck him – could I do less? – and he drew. I defended myself, and I supplemented my defence by a caning, so that this poor Saint-Eustache might realize the unworthiness of what he had done. That is all, madame."

But she was not so easily to be appeased, not even when Mademoiselle and the Vicomte joined their voices to mine in extenuation of my conduct. It was like Lavédan. For all that he was full of dread of the result and of the vengeance Saint-Eustache might wreak – boy though he was – he expressed himself freely touching the Chevalier's behaviour and the fittingness of the punishment that had overtaken him.

The Vicomtesse stood in small awe of her husband, but his judgment upon a point of honour was a matter that she would not dare contest.

She was ministering to the still prostrate Chevalier who, I think, remained prostrate now that he might continue to make appeal to her sympathy – when suddenly she cut in upon Roxalanne's defence of me.

"Where have you been?" she demanded suddenly.

"When, my mother?"

"This afternoon," answered the Vicomtesse impatiently. "The Chevalier was waiting two hours for you."

Roxalanne coloured to the roots of her hair. The Vicomte frowned.

"Waiting for me, my mother? But why for me?"

"Answer my question – where have you been?"

"I was with Monsieur de Lesperon," she answered simply.

"Alone?" the Vicomtesse almost shrieked.

"But yes." The poor child's tones were laden with wonder at this catechism.

"God's death!" she snapped. "It seems that my daughter is no better than – "

Heaven knows what may have been coming, for she had the most virulent, scandalous tongue that I have ever known in a woman's head – which is much for one who has lived at Court to say. But the Vicomte, sharing my fears, perhaps, and wishing to spare the child's ears, interposed quickly, "Come, madame, what airs are these? What sudden assumption of graces that we do not affect? We are not in Paris. This is not the Luxembourg. En province comme en province, and here we are simple folk – "

"Simple folk?" she interrupted, gasping. "By God, am I married to a ploughman? Am I Vicomtesse of Lavédan, or the wife of a boor of the countryside? And is the honour of your daughter a matter – "

"The honour of my daughter is not in question, madame," he interrupted in his turn, and with a sudden sternness that spent the fire of her indignation as a spark that is trampled underfoot.

Then, in a calm, level voice: "Ah, here are the servants," said he. "Permit them, madame, to take charge of Monsieur de Saint-Eustache. Anatole, you had better order the carriage for Monsieur le Chevalier. I do not think that he will be able to ride home."

Anatole peered at the pale young gentleman on the ground, then he turned his little wizened face upon me, and grinned in a singularly solemn fashion. Monsieur de Saint-Eustache was little loved, it seemed.

Leaning heavily upon the arm of one of the lacqueys, the Chevalier moved painfully towards the courtyard, where the carriage was being prepared for him. At the last moment he turned and beckoned the Vicomte to his side.

"As God lives, Monsieur de Lavédan," he swore, breathing heavily in the fury that beset him, "you shall bitterly regret having taken sides today with that Gascon bully. Remember me, both of you, when you are journeying to Toulouse."

The Vicomte stood beside him, impassive and unmoved by that grim threat, for all that to him it must have sounded like a death-sentence.

"Adieu, monsieur – a speedy recovery," was all he answered.

But I stepped up to them. "Do you not think, Vicomte, that it were better to detain him?" I asked.

"Pshaw!" he ejaculated. "Let him go."

The Chevalier's eyes met mine in a look of terror. Perhaps already that young man repented him of his menace, and he realized the folly of threatening one in whose power he still chanced to be.

"Bethink you, monsieur," I cried. "Yours is a noble and useful life. Mine is not without value, either. Shall we suffer these lives – aye, and the happiness of your wife and daughter – to be destroyed by this vermin?"

"Let him go, monsieur; let him go. I am not afraid."

I bowed and stepped back, motioning to the lacquey to take the fellow away, much as I should have motioned him to remove some uncleanness from before me.

The Vicomtesse withdrew in high dudgeon to her chamber, and I did not see her again that evening. Mademoiselle I saw once, for a moment, and she employed that moment to question me touching the origin of my quarrel with Saint-Eustache.

"Did he really lie, Monsieur de Lesperon?" she asked.

"Upon my honour, mademoiselle," I answered solemnly, "I have plighted my troth to no living woman." Then my chin sank to my breast as I bethought me of how tomorrow she must opine me the vilest liar living – for I was resolved to be gone before Marsac arrived – since the real Lesperon I did not doubt was, indeed, betrothed to Mademoiselle de Marsac.

"I shall leave Lavédan betimes tomorrow, mademoiselle," I pursued presently. "What has happened today makes my departure all the more urgent. Delay may have its dangers. You will hear strange things of me, as already I have warned you. But be merciful. Much will be true, much false; yet the truth itself is very vile and – "

I stopped short, in despair of explaining or even tempering what had to come. I shrugged my shoulders in my abandonment of hope, and I turned towards the window. She crossed the room and came to stand beside me.

73

"Will you not tell me? Have you no faith in me? Ah, Monsieur de Lesperon – "

"Sh! child, I cannot. It is too late to tell you now."

"Oh, not too late! From what you say they will tell me, I should think, perhaps, worse of you than you deserve. What is this thing you hide? What is this mystery? Tell me, monsieur. Tell me."

Did ever woman more plainly tell a man she loved him, and that loving him she would find all excuses for him? Was ever woman in better case to hear a confession from the man that loved her, and of whose love she was assured by every instinct that her sex possesses in such matters? Those two questions leapt into my mind, and in resolving them I all but determined to speak even now in the eleventh hour.

And then – I know not how – a fresh barrier seemed to arise. It was not merely a matter of telling her of the wager I was embarked upon; not merely a matter of telling her of the duplicity that I had practised, of the impostures by which I had gained admittance to her father's confidence and trust; not merely a matter of confessing that I was not Lesperon. There would still be the necessity of saying who I was. Even if she forgave all else, could she forgive me for being Bardelys, the notorious Bardelys, the libertine, the rake, some of whose exploits she had heard of from her mother, painted a hundred times blacker than they really were?

Might she not shrink from me when I told her I was that man? In her pure innocence she deemed, no doubt, that the life of every man who accounted himself a gentleman was moderately clean. She would not see in me – as did her mother – no more than a type of the best class in France, and having no more than the vices of my order. As a monster of profligacy might she behold me, and that – ah, Dieu! – I could not endure that she should do whilst I was by.

It may be – indeed, now, as I look back, I know that I exaggerated my case. I imagined she would see it as I saw it then. For would you credit it? With this great love that was now come to me, it seemed the ideals of my boyhood were returned, and I abhorred the man that I had been. The life I had led now filled me with disgust and loathing; the notions I had formed seemed to me now all vicious and distorted, my cynicism shallow and unjust.

"Monsieur de Lesperon," she called softly to me, noting my silence.

I turned to her. I set my hand lightly upon her arm; I let my gaze encounter the upward glance of her eyes – blue as forget-me-nots.

"You suffer!" she murmured, with sweet compassion.

"Worse, Roxalanne! I have sown in your heart, too, the seed of suffering. Oh, I am too unworthy!" I cried out; "and when you come to discover how unworthy it will hurt you; it will sting your pride to think how kind you were to me." She smiled incredulously, in denial of my words. "No, child; I cannot tell you."

She sighed, and then before more could be said there was a sound at the door, and we started away from each other. The Vicomte entered, and my last chance of confessing, of perhaps averting much of what followed, was lost to me.

# Chapter 8

## The Portrait

Into the mind of every thoughtful man must come at times with bitterness the reflection of how utterly we are at the mercy of Fate, the victims of her every whim and caprice. We may set out with the loftiest, the sternest resolutions to steer our lives along a well-considered course, yet the slightest of fortuitous circumstances will suffice to force us into a direction that we had no thought of taking.

Now, had it pleased Monsieur de Marsac to have come to Lavédan at any reasonable hour of the day, I should have been already upon the road to Paris, intent to own defeat and pay my wager. A night of thought, besides strengthening my determination to follow such a course, had brought the reflection that I might thereafter return to Roxalanne, a poor man, it is true, but one at least whose intentions might not be misconstrued.

And so, when at last I sank into sleep, my mind was happier than it had been for many days. Of Roxalanne's love I was assured, and it seemed that I might win her, after all, once I removed the barrier of shame that now deterred me. It may be that those thoughts kept me awake until a late hour, and that to this I owe it that when on the morrow I awakened the morning was well advanced.

The sun was flooding my chamber, and at my bedside stood Anatole.

"What's o'clock?" I inquired, sitting bolt upright.

"Past ten," said he, with stern disapproval.

"And you have let me sleep?" I cried.

"We do little else at Lavédan even when we are awake," he grumbled.

"There was no reason why monsieur should rise." Then, holding out a paper, "Monsieur Stanislas de Marsac was here betimes this morning with Mademoiselle his sister. He left this letter for you, monsieur."

Amaze and apprehension were quickly followed by relief, since Anatole's words suggested that Marsac had not remained. I took the letter, nevertheless, with some misgivings, and whilst I turned it over in my hands I questioned the old servant.

"He stayed an hour at the chateau, monsieur," Anatole informed me.

"Monsieur le Vicomte would have had you roused, but he would not hear of it. 'If what Monsieur de Saint-Eustache has told me touching your guest should prove to be true,' said he, 'I would prefer not to meet him under your roof, monsieur.' 'Monsieur de Saint-Eustache,' my master replied, 'is not a person whose word should have weight with any man of honour.' But in spite of that, Monsieur de Marsac held to his resolve, and although he would offer no explanation in answer to my master's many questions, you were not aroused.

"At the end of a half-hour his sister entered with Mademoiselle. They had been walking together on the terrace, and Mademoiselle de Marsac appeared very angry. 'Affairs are exactly as Monsieur de Saint-Eustache has represented them,' said she to her brother. At that he swore a most villainous oath, and called for writing materials. At the moment of his departure he desired me to deliver this letter to you, and then rode away in a fury, and, seemingly, not on the best of terms with Monsieur le Vicomte."

"And his sister?" I asked quickly.

"She went with him. A fine pair, as I live!" he added, casting his eyes to the ceiling.

At least I could breathe freely. They were gone, and whatever damage they may have done to the character of poor René de Lesperon ere they departed, they were not there, at all events, to denounce me for an impostor. With a mental apology to the shade of the departed Lesperon for all the discredit I was bringing down upon his name, I broke the seal of that momentous epistle, which enclosed a length of some thirty-two inches of string.

"Monsieur," [I read], "wherever I may chance to meet you it shall be my duty to kill you."

A rich beginning, in all faith! If he could but maintain that uncompromising dramatic flavour to the end, his epistle should be worth the trouble of deciphering, for he penned a vile scrawl of pothooks.

"It is because of this," [the letter proceeded], "that I have refrained from coming face to face with you this morning. The times are too troublous and the province is in too dangerous a condition to admit of an act that might draw the eyes of the Keeper of the Seals upon Lavédan. To my respect, then, to Monsieur le Vicomte and to my own devotion to the Cause we mutually serve do you owe it that you still live. I am on my way to Spain to seek shelter there from the King's vengeance. To save myself is a duty that I owe as much to myself as to the Cause. But there is another duty, one that I owe my sister, whom you have so outrageously slighted, and this duty, by God's grace, I will perform before I leave. Of your honour, monsieur, we will not speak, for reasons into which I need not enter, and I make no appeal to it. But if you have a spark of manhood left, if you are not an utter craven as well as a knave, I shall expect you on the day after tomorrow, at any hour before noon, at the *Auberge de la Couronne* at Grenade. There, monsieur, if you please, we will adjust our differences. That you may come prepared, and so that no time need be wasted when we meet, I send you the length of my sword."

Thus ended that angry, fire-breathing epistle. I refolded it thoughtfully, then, having taken my resolve, I leapt from the bed and desired Anatole to assist me to dress.

I found the Vicomte much exercised in mind as to the meaning of Marsac's extraordinary behaviour, and I was relieved to see that he, at least, could conjecture no cause for it. In reply to the questions with which he very naturally assailed me, I assured him that it was no more than a matter of a misunderstanding; that Monsieur de Marsac had asked me to meet him at Grenade in two days' time, and that I should then, no doubt, be able to make all clear.

Meanwhile, I regretted the incident, since it necessitated my remaining and encroaching for two days longer upon the Vicomte's hospitality. To all this, however, he made the reply that I expected, concluding with the remark that for the present at least it would seem as if the Chevalier de Saint-Eustache had been satisfied with creating this trouble betwixt myself and Marsac.

From what Anatole had said, I had already concluded that Marsac had exercised the greatest reticence. But the interview between his sister and Roxalanne filled me with the gravest anxiety. Women are not wont to practise the restraint of men under such circumstances, and for all that Mademoiselle de Marsac may not have expressed it in so many words that I was her faithless lover, yet women are quick to detect and interpret the signs of disorders springing from such causes, and I had every fear that Roxalanne was come to the conclusion that I had lied to her yesternight. With an uneasy spirit, then, I went in quest of her, and I found her walking in the old rose garden behind the chateau.

She did not at first remark my approach, and I had leisure for some moments to observe her and to note the sadness that dwelt in her profile and the listlessness of her movements. This, then, was my work – mine, and that of Monsieur de Chatellerault, and those other merry gentlemen who had sat at my table in Paris nigh upon a month ago.

I moved, and the gravel crunched under my foot, whereupon she turned, and, at sight of me advancing towards her, she started. The blood mounted to her face, to ebb again upon the instant, leaving it paler than it had been. She made as if to depart; then she appeared to check herself, and stood immovable and outwardly calm, awaiting my approach.

But her eyes were averted, and her bosom rose and fell too swiftly to lend colour to that mask of indifference she hurriedly put on.

Yet, as I drew nigh, she was the first to speak, and the triviality of her words came as a shock to me, and for all my knowledge of woman's way caused me to doubt for a moment whether perhaps her calm were not real, after all.

"You are a laggard this morning, Monsieur de Lesperon." And, with a half laugh, she turned aside to break a rose from its stem.

"True," I answered stupidly; "I slept over-late."

"A thousand pities, since thus you missed seeing Mademoiselle de Marsac. Have they told you that she was here?"

"Yes, mademoiselle. Stanislas de Marsac left a letter for me."

"You will regret not having seen them, no doubt?" quoth she.

I evaded the interrogative note in her voice. "That is their fault. They appear to have preferred to avoid me."

"Is it matter for wonder?" she flashed, with a sudden gleam of fury which she as suddenly controlled. With the old indifference, she added, "You do not seem perturbed, monsieur?"

"On the contrary, mademoiselle; I am very deeply perturbed."

"At not having seen your betrothed?" she asked, and now for the first time her eyes were raised, and they met mine with a look that was a stab.

"Mademoiselle, I had the honour of telling you yesterday that I had plighted my troth to no living woman."

At that reminder of yesterday she winced, and I was sorry that I had uttered it, for it must have set the wound in her pride a-bleeding again. Yesterday I had as much as told her that I loved her, and yesterday she had as much as answered me that she loved me, for yesterday I had sworn that Saint-Eustache's story of my betrothal was a lie. Today she had had assurance of the truth from the very woman to whom Lesperon's faith was plighted, and I could imagine something of her shame.

"Yesterday, monsieur," she answered contemptuously, "you lied in many things."

"Nay, I spoke the truth in all. Oh, God in Heaven, mademoiselle," I exclaimed in sudden passion, "will you not believe me? Will you not accept my word for what I say, and have a little patience until I shall have discharged such obligations as will permit me to explain?"

"Explain?" quoth she, with withering disdain.

"There is a hideous misunderstanding in all this. I am the victim of a miserable chain of circumstances. Oh, I can say no more! These Marsacs I shall easily pacify. I am to meet Monsieur de Marsac at Grenade on the day after tomorrow. In my pocket I have a letter from this living sword-blade, in which he tells me that he will give himself the pleasure of killing me then. Yet— "

"I hope he does, monsieur!" she cut in, with a fierceness before which I fell dumb and left my sentence unfinished. "I shall pray God that he may!" she added. "You deserve it as no man deserved it yet!"

For a moment I stood stricken, indeed, by her words. Then, my reason grasping the motive of that fierceness, a sudden joy pervaded me. It was a fierceness breathing that hatred that is a part of love, than which, it is true, no hatred can be more deadly. And yet so eloquently did it tell me of those very feelings which she sought jealously to conceal, that, moved by a sudden impulse, I stepped close up to her.

"Roxalanne," I said fervently, "you do not hope for it. What would your life be if I were dead? Child, child, you love me even as I love you." I caught her suddenly to me with infinite tenderness, with reverence almost. "Can you lend no ear to the voice of this love? Can you not have faith in me a little? Can you not think that if I were quite as unworthy as you make-believe to your very self, this love could have no place?"

"It has no place!" she cried. "You lie – as in all things else. I do not love you. I hate you. Dieu! How I hate you!"

She had lain in my arms until then, with upturned face and piteous, frightened eyes – like a bird that feels itself within the toils of a snake, yet whose horror is blent with a certain fascination. Now, as she spoke, her will seemed to reassert itself, and she struggled to break from me. But as her fierceness of hatred grew, so did my fierceness of resolve gain strength, and I held her tightly.

"Why do you hate me?" I asked steadily. "Ask yourself, Roxalanne, and tell me what answer your heart makes. Does it not answer that indeed you do not hate me – that you love me?"

"Oh, God, to be so insulted!" she cried out. "Will you not release me, miserable? Must I call for help? Oh, you shall suffer for this! As there is a Heaven, you shall be punished!"

But in my passion I held her, despite entreaties, threats, and struggles. I was brutal, if you will. Yet think of what was in my soul at being so misjudged, at finding myself in this position, and deal not over harshly with me. The courage to confess which I had lacked for days, came to me then. I must tell her. Let the result be what it might, it could not be worse than this, and this I could endure no longer.

"Listen, Roxalanne!"

"I will not listen! Enough of insults have I heard already. Let me go!"

"Nay, but you shall hear me. I am not René de Lesperon. Had these Marsacs been less impetuous and foolish, had they waited to have seen me this morning, they would have told you so."

She paused for a second in her struggles to regard me. Then, with a sudden contemptuous laugh, she renewed her efforts more vigorously than before.

"What fresh lies do you offer me? Release me, I will hear no more!"

"As Heaven is my witness, I have told you the truth. I know how wild a sound it has, and that is partly why I did not tell you earlier. But your disdain I cannot suffer. That you should deem me a liar in professing to love you – "

Her struggles were grown so frantic that I was forced to relax my grip. But this I did with a suddenness that threw her out of balance, and she was in danger of falling backwards. To save herself, she caught at my doublet, which was torn open under the strain.

We stood some few feet apart, and, white and palpitating in her anger, she confronted me. Her eyes lashed me with their scorn, but under my steady, unflinching gaze they fell at last. When next she raised them there was a smile of quiet but unutterable contempt upon her lips.

"Will you swear," said she, "that you are not René de Lesperon? That Mademoiselle de Marsac is not your betrothed?"

"Yes – by my every hope of Heaven!" I cried passionately.

She continued to survey me with that quiet smile of mocking scorn.

"I have heard it said," quoth she, "that the greatest liars are ever those that are readiest to take oath." Then, with a sudden gasp of loathing, "I think you have dropped something, monsieur," said she, pointing to the ground. And without waiting for more, she swung round and left me.

Face upwards at my feet lay the miniature that poor Lesperon had entrusted to me in his dying moments. It had dropped from my doublet in the struggle, and I never doubted now but that the picture it contained was that of Mademoiselle de Marsac.

# Chapter 9

## The Night Alarm

I was returning that same afternoon from a long walk that I had taken – for my mood was of that unenviable sort that impels a man to be moving – when I found a travelling-chaise drawn up in the quadrangle as if ready for a journey. As I mounted the steps of the chateau I came face to face with Mademoiselle, descending. I drew aside that she might pass; and this she did with her chin in the air, and her petticoat drawn to her that it might not touch me.

I would have spoken to her, but her eyes looked straight before her with a glance that was too forbidding; besides which there was the gaze of a half-dozen grooms upon us. So, bowing before her – the plume of my doffed hat sweeping the ground – I let her go. Yet I remained standing where she had passed me, and watched her enter the coach. I looked after the vehicle as it wheeled round and rattled out over the drawbridge, to raise a cloud of dust on the white, dry road beyond.

In that hour I experienced a sense of desolation and a pain to which I find it difficult to give expression. It seemed to me as if she had gone out of my life for all time – as if no reparation that I could ever make would suffice to win her back after what had passed between us that morning. Already wounded in her pride by what Mademoiselle de Marsac had told her of our relations, my behaviour in the rose garden had completed the work of turning into hatred the tender feelings that but yesterday she had all but confessed for me. That she hated me now, I was well assured. My reflections as I walked had borne it in upon me how rash, how mad had been my desperate action, and with bitterness I realized that I had destroyed the last chance of ever mending matters.

Not even the payment of my wager and my return in my true character could avail me now. The payment of my wager, forsooth! Even that lost what virtue it might have contained. Where was the heroism of such an act? Had I not failed, indeed? And was not, therefore, the payment of my wager become inevitable?

Fool! fool! Why had I not profited that gentle mood of hers when we had drifted down the stream together? Why had I not told her then of the whole business from its ugly inception down to the pass to which things were come, adding that to repair the evil I was going back to Paris to pay my wager, and that when that was done, I would return to ask her to become my wife? That was the course a man of sense would have adopted. He would have seen the dangers that beset him in my false position, and would have been quick to have forestalled them in the only manner possible.

Heigh-ho! It was done. The game was at an end, and I had bungled my part of it like any fool. One task remained me – that of meeting Marsac at Grenade and doing justice to the memory of poor Lesperon.

What might betide thereafter mattered little. I should be ruined when I had settled with Chatellerault, and Marcel de Saint-Pol de Bardelys, that brilliant star in the firmament of the Court of France, would suffer an abrupt eclipse, would be quenched for all time. But this weighed little with me then. I had lost everything that I might have valued – everything that might have brought fresh zest to a jaded, satiated life.

Later that day I was told by the Vicomte that there was a rumour current to the effect that the Marquis de Bardelys was dead. Idly I inquired how the rumour had been spread, and he told me that a riderless horse, which had been captured a few days ago by some peasants, had been recognized by Monsieur de Bardelys' servants as belonging to their master, and that as nothing had been seen or heard of him for a fortnight, it was believed that he must have met with some mischance. Not even that piece of information served to arouse my interest. Let them believe me dead if they would. To him that is suffering worse than death to be accounted dead is a small matter.

The next day passed without incident. Mademoiselle's absence continued and I would have questioned the Vicomte concerning it, but a not unnatural hesitancy beset me, and I refrained.

On the morrow I was to leave Lavédan, but there were no preparations to be made, no packing to be done, for during my sojourn there I had been indebted to the generous hospitality of the Vicomte for my very apparel. We supped quietly together that night the Vicomte and I – for the Vicomtesse was keeping her room.

I withdrew early to my chamber, and long I lay awake, revolving a gloomy future in my mind. I had given no thought to what I should do after having offered my explanation to Monsieur de Marsac on the morrow, nor could I now bring myself to consider it with any degree of interest. I would communicate with Chatellerault to inform him that I accounted my wager lost. I would send him my note of hand, making over to him my Picardy estates, and I would request him to pay off and disband my servants both in Paris and at Bardelys.

As for myself, I did not know, and, as I have hinted, I cared but little, in what places my future life might lie. I had still a little property by Beaugency, but scant inclination to withdraw to it. To Paris I would not return; that much I was determined upon; but upon no more. I had thoughts of going to Spain. Yet that course seemed no less futile than any other of which I could bethink me. I fell asleep at last, vowing that it would be a mercy and a fine solution to the puzzle of how to dispose of the future if I were to awaken no more.

I was, however, destined to be roused again just as the veil of night was being lifted and the chill breath of dawn was upon the world. There was a loud knocking at the gates of Lavédan, confused noises of voices, of pattering feet, of doors opening and closing within the chateau.

There was a rapping at my chamber door, and when I went to open, I found the Vicomte on the threshold, nightcapped, in his shirt, and bearing a lighted taper.

"There are troopers at the gate!" he exclaimed as he entered the room. "That dog Saint-Eustache has already been at work!"

For all the agitation that must have been besetting him, his manner was serene as ever. "What are we to do?" he asked.

"You are admitting them – naturally?" said I, inquiry in my voice.

"Why, yes;" and he shrugged his shoulders. "What could it avail us to resist them? Even had I been prepared for it, it would be futile to attempt to suffer a siege."

I wrapped a dressing-gown about me, for the morning air was chill.

"Monsieur le Vicomte," said I gravely, "I heartily deplore that Monsieur de Marsac's affairs should have detained me here. But for him, I had left Lavédan two days ago. As it is, I tremble for you, but we may at least hope that my being taken in your house will draw down no ill results upon you. I shall never forgive myself if through my having taken refuge here I should have encompassed your destruction."

"There is no question of that," he replied, with the quick generosity characteristic of the man. "This is the work of Saint-Eustache. Sooner or later I always feared that it would happen, for sooner or later he and I must have come to enmity over my daughter. That knave had me in his power. He knew – being himself outwardly one of us – to what extent I was involved in the late rebellion, and I knew enough of him to be assured that if some day he should wish to do me ill, he would never scruple to turn traitor. I am afraid, Monsieur de Lesperon, that it is not for you alone – perhaps not for you at all – that the soldiers have come, but for me."

Then, before I could answer him, the door was flung wide, and into the room, in nightcap and hastily donned robe – looking a very mégère in that disfiguring déshabillé – swept the Vicomtesse.

"See," she cried to her husband, her strident voice raised in reproach – "see to what a pass you have brought us!"

"Anne, Anne!" he exclaimed, approaching her and seeking to soothe her; "be calm, my poor child, and be brave."

But, evading him, she towered, lean and malevolent as a fury.

"Calm?" she echoed contemptuously. "Brave?" Then a short laugh broke from her – a despairing, mocking, mirthless expression of anger. "By God, do you add effrontery to your other failings? Dare you bid me be calm and brave in such an hour? Have I been warning you fruitlessly these twelve months past, that, after disregarding me and deriding my warnings, you should bid me be calm now that my fears are realized?"

There was a sound of creaking gates below. The Vicomte heard it.

"Madame," he said, putting aside his erstwhile tender manner, and speaking with a lofty dignity, "the troopers have been admitted. Let me entreat you to retire. It is not befitting our station – "

"What is our station?" she interrupted harshly. "Rebels – proscribed, houseless beggars. That is our station, thanks to you and your insane meddling with treason. What is to become of us, fool? What is to become of Roxalanne and me when they shall have hanged you and have driven us from Lavédan? By God's death, a fine season this to talk of the dignity of our station! Did I not warn you, malheureux, to leave party faction alone? You laughed at me."

"Madame, your memory does me an injustice," he answered in a strangled voice. "I never laughed at you in all my life."

"You did as much, at least. Did you not bid me busy myself with women's affairs? Did you not bid me leave you to follow your own judgment? You have followed it – to a pretty purpose, as God lives! These gentlemen of the King's will cause you to follow it a little farther," she pursued, with heartless, loathsome sarcasm. "You will follow it as far as the scaffold at Toulouse. That, you will tell me, is your own affair. But what provision have you made for your wife and daughter? Did you marry me and get her to leave us to perish of starvation? Or are we to turn kitchen wenches or sempstresses for our livelihood?"

With a groan, the Vicomte sank down upon the bed, and covered his face with his hands.

"God pity me!" he cried, in a voice of agony – an agony such as the fear of death could never have infused into his brave soul; an agony born of the heartlessness of this woman who for twenty years had shared his bed and board, and who now in the hour of his adversity failed him so cruelly – so tragically.

"Aye," she mocked in her bitterness, "call upon God to pity you, for I shall not."

She paced the room now, like a caged lioness, her face livid with the fury that possessed her. She no longer asked questions; she no longer addressed him; oath followed oath from her thin lips, and the hideousness of this woman's blasphemy made me shudder. At last there were heavy steps upon the stairs, and, moved by a sudden impulse, "Madame," I cried, "let me prevail upon you to restrain yourself."

She swung round to face me, her close-set eyes ablaze with anger.

"Sangdieu! By what right do you –" she began but this was no time to let a woman's tongue go babbling on; no time for ceremony; no season for making a leg and addressing her with a simper. I caught her viciously by the wrist, and with my face close up to hers, "Folle!" I cried, and I'll swear no man had ever used the word to her before.

She gasped and choked in her surprise and rage.

Then lowering my voice lest it should reach the approaching soldiers: "Would you ruin the Vicomte and yourself?" I muttered. Her eyes asked me a question, and I answered it. "How do you know that the soldiers have come for your husband? It may be that they are seeking me – and only me. They may know nothing of the Vicomte's defection. Shall you, then, be the one to inform them of it by your unbridled rantings and your accusations?"

Her jaw fell open in astonishment. This was a side of the question she had not considered.

"Let me prevail upon you, madame, to withdraw and to be of

good courage. It is more than likely that you alarm yourself without cause."

She continued to stare at me in her amazement and the confusion that was congenital with it, and if there was not time for her to withdraw, at least the possibility I had suggested acted as a timely warning.

In that moment the door opened again, and on the threshold appeared a young man in a plumed hat and corselet, carrying a naked sword in one hand and a lanthorn in the other. Behind him I caught the gleam of steel from the troopers at his heels.

"Which of you is Monsieur René de Lesperon?" he inquired politely, his utterance flavoured by a strong Gascon accent.

I stood forward. "I am known by that name, Monsieur le Capitaine," said I.

He looked at me wistfully, apologetically almost, then, "In the King's name, Monsieur de Lesperon, I call upon you to yield!" said he.

"I have been expecting you. My sword is yonder, monsieur," I replied suavely. "If you will allow me to dress, I shall be ready to accompany you in a few minutes."

He bowed, and it at once became clear that his business at Lavédan was – as I had suggested to the Vicomtesse might be possible – with me alone.

"I am grateful for the readiness of your submission," said this very polite gentleman. He was a comely lad, with blue eyes and a good-humoured mouth, to which a pair of bristling moustaches sought vainly to impart an expression of ferocity.

"Before you proceed to dress, monsieur, I have another duty to discharge."

"Discharge your duty, monsieur," I answered. Whereupon he made a sign to his men, and in a moment they were ransacking my garments and effects. While this was taking place, he turned to the Vicomte and Vicomtesse, and offered them a thousand apologies for having interrupted their slumbers, and for so rudely depriving them of their guest. He advanced in his excuse the troublous nature of the times, and threw in a bunch of malisons at the circumstances which forced upon soldiers the odious duties of the tipstaff, hoping that we would think him none the less a gentleman for the unsavoury business upon which he was engaged.

From my clothes they took the letters addressed to Lesperon which that poor gentleman had entrusted to me on the night of his death; and among these there was one from the Duc d'Orléans himself, which would alone have sufficed to have hanged a regiment. Besides these, they took Monsieur de Marsac's letter of two days ago, and the locket containing the picture of Mademoiselle de Marsac.

The papers and the portrait they delivered to the Captain, who took them with the same air of deprecation tainted with disgust that coloured all his actions in connection with my arrest.

To this same repugnance for his catchpoll work do I owe it that at the moment of setting out he offered to let me ride without the annoyance of an escort if I would pass him my parole not to attempt an escape.

We were standing, then, in the hall of the chateau. His men were already in the courtyard, and there were only present Monsieur le Vicomte and Anatole – the latter reflecting the look of sorrow that haunted his master's face. The Captain's generosity was certainly leading him beyond the bounds of his authority, and it touched me.

"Monsieur is very generous," said I.

He shrugged his shoulders impatiently.

"Cap de Dieu!" he cried – he had a way of swearing that reminded me of my friend Cazalet. "It is no generosity, monsieur. It is a desire to make this obscene work more congenial to the spirit of a gentleman, which, devil take me, I cannot stifle, not for the King himself. And then, Monsieur de Lesperon, are we not fellow-countrymen? Are we not Gascons both? Pardieu, there is no more respected a name in the whole of Gascony than that of Lesperon, and that you belong to so honourable a family is alone more than sufficient to warrant such slight favours as it may be in my power to show you."

"You have my parole that I will attempt no escape, Monsieur le

Capitaine," I answered, bowing my acknowledgment of his compliments.

"I am Mironsac de Castelroux, of Chateau Rouge in Gascony," he informed me, returning my bow. My faith, had he not made a pretty soldier he would have made an admirable master of deportment.

My leave-taking of Monsieur de Lavédan was brief but cordial; apologetic on my part, intensely sympathetic on his. And so I went out alone with Castelroux upon the road to Toulouse, his men being ordered to follow in half an hour's time and to travel at their leisure.

As we cantered along – Castelroux and I – we talked of many things, and I found him an amusing and agreeable companion. Had my mood been other than despairing, the news he gave me might have occasioned me some concern; for it seemed that prisoners arraigned for treason and participation in the late rising were being very summarily treated. Many were never so much as heard in their own defence, the evidence collected of their defection being submitted to the Tribunal, and judgment being forthwith passed upon them by judges who had no ears for anything they might advance in their own favour.

The evidence of my identity was complete: there was my own admission to Castelroux; the evidence of the treason of Lesperon was none the less complete; in fact, it was notorious; and there was the Duke's letter found amongst my effects. If the judges refused to lend an ear to my assurances that I was not Lesperon at all, but the missing Bardelys, my troubles would likely to receive a very summary solution.

The fear of it, however, weighed not over-heavily upon me. I was supremely indifferent. Life was at an end so far as I was concerned.

I had ruined the one chance of real happiness that had ever been held out to me, and if the gentlemen of the courts of Toulouse were pleased to send me unheeded to the scaffold, what should it signify?

But there was another matter that did interest me, and that was my interview with Marsac. Touching this, I spoke to my captor.

"There is a gentleman I wish to see at Grenade this morning. You have amongst the papers taken from me a letter making this assignation, Monsieur le Capitaine, and I should be indeed grateful if you would determine that we shall break our fast there, so that I may have an opportunity of seeing him. The matter is to me of the highest importance."

"It concerns – ?" he asked.

"A lady," I answered.

"Ah, yes! But the letter is of the nature of a challenge, is it not? Naturally, I cannot permit you to endanger your life."

"Lest we disappoint the headsman at Toulouse?" I laughed. "Have no fear. There shall be no duel!"

"Then I am content, monsieur, and you shall see your friend."

I thanked him, and we talked of other things thereafter as we rode in the early morning along the Toulouse road. Our conversation found its way, I scarce know how, to the topic of Paris and the Court, and when I casually mentioned, in passing, that I was well acquainted with the Luxembourg, he inquired whether I had ever chanced to meet a young spark of the name of Mironsac.

"Mironsac?" I echoed. "Why, yes." And I was on the point of adding that I knew the youth intimately, and what a kindness I had for him, when, deeming it imprudent, I contented myself with asking, "You know him?"

"Pardieu!" he swore. "The fellow is my cousin. We are both Mironsacs; he is Mironsac of Castelvert, whilst I, as you may remember I told you, am Mironsac of Castelroux. To distinguish us, he is always known as Mironsac, and I as Castelroux. Peste! It is not the only distinction, for while he basks in the sunshine of the great world of Paris – they are wealthy, the Mironsacs of Castelvert – I, a poor devil of a Gascony cadet, am playing the catchpoll in Languedoc!"

I looked at him with fresh interest, for the mention of that dear lad Mironsac brought back to my mind the night in Paris on which my ill-starred wager had been laid, and I was reminded of how that high-minded youth had sought – when it was too late – to reason me out of the undertaking by alluding to the dishonour with which in his honest eyes it must be fraught.

We spoke of his cousin – Castelroux and I – and I went so far now as to confess that I had some love for the youth, whom I praised in unmistakable terms. This inclined to increase the friendliness which my young Captain had manifested since my arrest, and I was presently emboldened by it to beg of him to add to the many favours that I already owed him by returning to me the portrait which his men had subtracted from my pocket. It was my wish to return this to Marsac, whilst at the same time it would afford corroboration of my story.

To this Castelroux made no difficulty.

"Why, yes," said he, and he produced it. "I crave your pardon for not having done the thing of my own accord. What can the Keeper of the Seals want with that picture?"

I thanked him, and pocketed the locket.

"Poor lady!" he sighed, a note of compassion in his voice. "By my soul, Monsieur de Lesperon, fine work this for soldiers, is it not? Diable! It is enough to turn a gentleman's stomach sour for life, and make him go hide himself from the eyes of honest men. Had I known that soldiering meant such business, I had thought twice before I adopted it as a career for a man of honour. I had remained in Gascony and tilled the earth sooner than have lent myself to this!"

"My good young friend," I laughed, "what you do, you do in the King's name."

"So does every tipstaff," he answered impatiently, his moustaches bristling as the result of the scornful twist he gave his lips. "To think that I should have a hand in bringing tears to the eyes of that sweet lady! Quelle besogne! Bon Dieu, quelle besogne!"

I laughed at the distress vented in that whimsical Gascon tongue of his, whereupon he eyed me in a wonder that was tempered with admiration. For to his brave soul a gentleman so stoical as to laugh under such parlous circumstances was very properly a gentleman to be admired.

# Chapter 10

## The Risen Dead

It was close upon ten o'clock as we rode into the yard of the imposing Hôtel de la Couronne at Grenade.

Castelroux engaged a private room on the first floor – a handsome chamber overlooking the courtyard – and in answer to the inquiries that I made I was informed by the landlord that Monsieur de Marsac was not yet arrived.

"My assignation was 'before noon', Monsieur de Castelroux," said I. "With your permission, I would wait until noon."

He made no difficulty. Two hours were of no account. We had all risen very early, and he was, himself, he said, entitled to some rest.

Whilst I stood by the window it came to pass that a very tall, indifferently apparelled gentleman issued from the hostelry and halted for some moments in conversation with the ostler below. He walked with an enfeebled step, and leaned heavily for support upon a stout cane. As he turned to re-enter the inn I had a glimpse of a face woefully pale, about which, as about the man's whole figure, there was a something that was familiar – a something that puzzled me, and on which my mind was still dwelling when presently I sat down to breakfast with Castelroux.

It may have been a half-hour later, and, our meal being at an end, we were sitting talking – I growing impatient the while that this Monsieur de Marsac should keep me waiting so – when of a sudden the rattle of hoofs drew me once more to the window. A gentleman, riding very recklessly, had just dashed through the porte-cochère, and was in the act of pulling up his horse. He was a lean, active man, very richly dressed, and with a face that by its swarthiness of skin and the sable hue of beard and hair looked almost black.

"Ah, you are there!" he cried, with something between a snarl and a laugh, and addressing somebody within the shelter of the porch. "Par la mort Dieu, I had hardly looked to find you!"

From the recess of the doorway I heard a gasp of amazement and a cry of, "Marsac! You here?"

So this was the gentleman I was to see! A stable boy had taken his reins, and he leapt nimbly to the ground. Into my range of vision hobbled now the enfeebled gentleman whom earlier I had noticed.

"My dear Stanislas!" he cried, "I cannot tell you how rejoiced I am to see you!" and he approached Marsac with arms that were opened as if to embrace him.

The newcomer surveyed him a moment in wonder, with eyes grown dull.

Then abruptly raising his hand, he struck the fellow on the breast, and thrust him back so violently that but for the stable boy's intervention he had of a certainty fallen. With a look of startled amazement on his haggard face, the invalid regarded his assailant.

As for Marsac, he stepped close up to him.

"What is this?" he cried harshly. "What is this make-believe feebleness? That you are pale, poltroon, I do not wonder! But why these tottering limbs? Why this assumption of weakness? Do you look to trick me by these signs?"

"Have you taken leave of your senses?" exclaimed the other, a note of responsive anger sounding in his voice. "Have you gone mad, Stanislas?"

"Abandon this pretence," was the contemptuous answer. "Two days ago at Lavédan, my friend, they informed me how complete was your recovery; from what they told us, it was easy to guess why you tarried there and left us without news of you. That was my reason, as you may have surmised, for writing to you. My sister has mourned you for dead – was mourning you for dead whilst you sat at the feet of your Roxalanne and made love to her among the roses of Lavédan."

"Lavédan?" echoed the other slowly. Then, raising his voice, "What the devil are you saying?" he blazed. "What do I know of Lavédan?"

In a flash it had come to me who that enfeebled gentleman was.

Rodenard, the blunderer, had been at fault when he had said that Lesperon had expired. Clearly he could have no more than swooned; for here, in the flesh, was Lesperon himself, the man I had left for dead in that barn by Mirepoix.

How or where he had recovered were things that at the moment did not exercise my mind – nor have I since been at any pains to unravel the mystery of it; but there he was, and for the moment that fact was all-sufficing. What complications would come of his presence Heaven alone could foretell.

"Put an end to this play-acting!" roared the savage Marsac. "It will avail you nothing. My sister's tears may have weighed lightly with you, but you shall pay the price of them, and of the slight you have put upon her."

"My God, Marsac!" cried the other, roused to an equal fierceness. "Will you explain?"

"Aye," snarled Marsac, and his sword flashed from his scabbard, "I'll explain. As God lives, I'll explain – with this!" And he whirled his blade under the eyes of the invalid. "Come, my master, the comedy's played out. Cast aside that crutch and draw; draw, man, or, sangdieu, I'll run you through as you stand!"

There was a commotion below. The landlord and a posse of his satellites – waiters, ostlers, and stable boys – rushed between them, and sought to restrain the bloodthirsty Marsac. But he shook them off as a bull shakes off a pack of dogs, and like an angry bull, too, did he stand his ground and bellow. In a moment his sweeping sword had cleared a circle about him. In its lightning dartings hither and thither at random, it had stung a waiter in the calf, and when the fellow saw the blood staining his hose, he added to the general din his shrieks that he was murdered.

Marsac swore and threatened in a breath, and a kitchen wench, from a point of vantage on the steps, called shame upon him and abused him roundly for a cowardly assassin to assail a poor sufferer who could hardly stand upright.

"Po' Cap de Dieu!" swore Castelroux at my elbow. "Saw you ever such an ado? What has chanced?"

But I never stayed to answer him. Unless I acted quickly blood would assuredly be shed. I was the one man who could explain matters, and it was a mercy for Lesperon that I should have been at hand in the hour of his meeting that fire-eater Marsac. I forgot the circumstances in which I stood to Castelroux; I forgot everything but the imminent necessity that I should intervene.

Some seven feet below our window was the roof of the porch; from that to the ground it might be some eight feet more. Before my Gascon captain knew what I was about, I had swung myself down from the window on to the projecting porch. A second later, I created a diversion by landing in the midst of the courtyard fray, with the alarmed Castelroux – who imagined that I was escaping – following by the same unusual road, and shouting as he came "Monsieur de Lesperon! Hi! Monsieur de Lesperon! Mordieu! Remember your parole, Monsieur de Lesperon!"

Nothing could have been better calculated to stem Marsac's fury; nothing could have so predisposed him to lend an ear to what I had to say, for it was very evident that Castelroux's words were addressed to me, and that it was I whom he called by the name of Lesperon. In an instant I was at Marsac's side. But before I could utter a word, "What the devil does this mean?" he asked, eyeing me with fierce suspicion.

"It means, monsieur, that there are more Lesperons than one in France. I am the Lesperon who was at Lavédan. If you doubt me, ask this gentleman, who arrested me there last night. Ask him, too, why we have halted here. Ask him, if you will, to show you the letter that you left at Lavédan making an assignation here before noon today, which letter I received."

The suspicion faded from Marsac's eyes, and they grew round with wonder as he listened to this prodigious array of evidence.

Lesperon looked on in no less amazement, yet I am sure from the manner of his glance that he did not recognize in me the man that had succoured him at Mirepoix. That, after all, was natural enough; for the minds of men in such reduced conditions as had been his upon that night are not prone to receive very clear impressions, and still less prone to retain such impressions as they do receive.

Before Marsac could answer me, Castelroux was at my side.

"A thousand apologies!" he laughed. "A fool might have guessed the errand that took you so quickly through that window, and none but a fool would have suspected you of seeking to escape. It was unworthy in me, Monsieur de Lesperon."

I turned to him while those others still stood gaping, and led him aside.

"Monsieur le Capitaine," said I, "you find it troublesome enough to reconcile your conscience with such arrests as you are charged to make, is it not so?"

"Mordieu!" he cried, by way of emphatically assenting.

"Now, if you should chance to overhear words betraying to you certain people whom otherwise you would never suspect of being rebels, your soldier's duty would, nevertheless, compel you to apprehend them, would it not?"

"Why, true. I am afraid it would," he answered, with a grimace.

"But, if forewarned that by being present in a certain place you should overhear such words, what course would you pursue?"

"Avoid it like a pestilence, monsieur," he answered promptly.

"Then, Monsieur le Capitaine, may I trespass upon your generosity to beseech you to let me take these litigants to our room upstairs, and to leave us alone there for a half-hour?"

Frankness was my best friend in dealing with Castelroux – frankness and his distaste for the business they had charged him with. As for Marsac and Lesperon, they were both eager enough to have the mystery explained, and when – Castelroux having consented – I invited them to my chamber, they came readily enough.

Since Monsieur de Lesperon did not recognize me, there was no reason why I should enlighten him touching my identity, and every reason why I should not. As soon as they were seated, I went to the heart of the matter at once and without preamble.

"A fortnight ago, gentlemen," said I, "I was driven by a pack of dragoons across the Garonne. I was wounded in the shoulder and very exhausted, and I knocked at the gates of Lavédan to crave shelter.

"That shelter, gentlemen, was afforded me, and when I had announced myself as Monsieur de Lesperon, it was all the more cordially because one Monsieur de Marsac, who was a friend of the Vicomte de Lavédan, and a partisan in the lost cause of Orléans, happened often to have spoken of a certain Monsieur de Lesperon as his very dear friend. I have no doubt, gentlemen, that you will think harshly of me because I did not enlighten the Vicomte. But there were reasons for which I trust you will not press me, since I shall find it difficult to answer you with truth."

"But is your name Lesperon?" cried Lesperon.

"That, monsieur, is a small matter. Whether my name is Lesperon or not, I confess to having practised a duplicity upon the Vicomte and his family, since I am certainly not the Lesperon whose identity I accepted. But if I accepted that identity, monsieur, I also accepted your liabilities, and so I think that you should find it in your heart to extend me some measure of forgiveness. As René de Lesperon, of Lesperon in Gascony, I was arrested last night at Lavédan, and, as you may observe, I am being taken to Toulouse to stand the charge of high treason. I have not demurred; I have not denied in the hour of trouble the identity that served me in my hour of need. I am taking the bitter with the sweet, and I assure you, gentlemen, that the bitter predominates in a very marked degree."

"But this must not be," cried Lesperon, rising. "I know not what use you may have made of my name, but I have no reason to think that you can have brought discredit upon it, and so – "

"I thank you, monsieur, but – "

"And so I cannot submit that you shall go to Toulouse in my stead. Where is this officer whose prisoner you are? Pray summon him, monsieur, and let us set the matter right."

"This is very generous," I answered calmly. "But I have crimes enough upon my head, and so, if the worst should befall me, I am simply atoning in one person for the errors of two."

"But that is no concern of mine!" he cried.

"It is so much your concern that if you commit so egregious a blunder as to denounce yourself, you will have ruined yourself, without materially benefiting me."

He still objected, but in this strain I argued for some time, and to such good purpose that in the end I made him realize that by betraying himself he would not save me, but only join me on the journey to the scaffold.

"Besides, gentlemen," I pursued, "my case is far from hopeless. I have every confidence that, as matters stand, by putting forth my hand at the right moment, by announcing my identity at the proper season, I can, if I am so inclined, save my neck from the headsman."

"If you are so inclined?" they both cried, their looks charged with inquiry.

"Let that be," I answered; "it does not at present concern us. What I desire you to understand, Monsieur de Lesperon, is that if I go to Toulouse alone, when the time comes to proclaim myself, and it is found that I am not René de Lesperon, of Lesperon in Gascony, they will assume that you are dead, and there will be no count against me.

"But if you come with me, and thereby afford proof that you are alive, my impersonation of you may cause me trouble. They may opine that I have been an abettor of treason, that I have attempted to circumvent the ends of justice, and that I may have impersonated you in order to render possible your escape. For that, you may rest assured, they will punish me.

"You will see, therefore, that my own safety rests on your passing quietly out of France and leaving the belief behind you that you are dead – a belief that will quickly spread once I shall have cast off your identity. You apprehend me?"

"Vaguely, monsieur; and perhaps you are right. What do you say, Stanislas?"

"Say?" cried the fiery Marsac. "I am weighed down with shame, my poor René, for having so misjudged you."

More he would have said in the same strain, but Lesperon cut him short and bade him attend to the issue now before him. They discussed it at some length, but always under the cloud in which my mysteriousness enveloped it, and, in the end, encouraged by my renewed assurances that I could best save myself if Lesperon were not taken with me, the Gascon consented to my proposals.

Marsac was on his way to Spain. His sister, he told us, awaited him at Carcassonne. Lesperon should set out with him at once, and in forty-eight hours they would be beyond the reach of the King's anger.

"I have a favour to ask of you, Monsieur de Marsac," said I, rising; for our business was at an end. "It is that if you should have an opportunity of communicating with Mademoiselle de Lavédan, you will let her know that I am not – not the Lesperon that is betrothed to your sister."

"I will inform her of it, monsieur," he answered readily; and then, of a sudden, a look of understanding and of infinite pity came into his eyes. "My God!" he cried.

"What is it, monsieur?" I asked, staggered by that sudden outcry.

"Do not ask me, monsieur, do not ask me. I had forgotten for the moment, in the excitement of all these revelations. But – " He stopped short.

"Well, monsieur?"

He seemed to ponder a moment, then looking at me again with that same compassionate glance, "You had better know," said he. "And yet – it is a difficult thing to tell you. I understand now much that I had not dreamt of. You – you have no suspicion of how you came to be arrested?"

"For my alleged participation in the late rebellion?"

"Yes, yes. But who gave the information of your whereabouts? Who told the Keeper of the Seals where you were to be found?"

"Oh, that?" I answered easily. "Why, I never doubted it. It was the coxcomb Saint-Eustache. I whipped him – "

I stopped short. There was something in Marsac's black face, something in his glance, that forced the unspoken truth upon my mind.

"Mother in Heaven!" I cried. "Do you mean that it was Mademoiselle de Lavédan?"

He bowed his head in silence. Did she hate me, then, so much as that? Would nothing less than my death appease her, and had I utterly crushed the love that for a little while she had borne me, that she could bring herself to hand me over to the headsman?

God! What a stab was that! It turned me sick with grief – aye, and with some rage not against her, oh, not against her; against the fates that had brought such things to pass.

I controlled myself while their eyes were yet upon me. I went to the door and held it open for them, and they, perceiving something of my disorder, were courteous enough to omit the protracted leave-takings that under other auspices there might have been.

Marsac paused a moment on the threshold as if he would have offered me some word of comfort. Then, perceiving, perhaps, how banal must be all comfort that was of words alone, and how it might but increase the anger of the wound it was meant to balm, he sighed a simple, "Adieu, monsieur!" and went his way.

When they were gone, I returned to the table, and, sitting down, I buried my head in my arms, and there I lay, a prey to the most poignant grief that in all my easy, fortunate life I had ever known.

That she should have done this thing! That the woman I loved, the pure, sweet, innocent girl that I had wooed so ardently in my unworthiness at Lavédan, should have stooped to such an act of betrayal! To what had I not reduced her, since such things could be!

Then, out of my despair grew comfort, slowly at first, and more vigorously anon. The sudden shock of the news had robbed me of some of my wit, and had warped my reasoning. Later, as the pain of the blow grew duller, I came to reflect that what she had done was but a proof – an overwhelming proof – of how deeply she had cared. Such hatred as this can be but born of a great love; reaction is ever to be measured by the action that occasions it, and a great revulsion can only come of a great affection. Had she been indifferent to me, or had she but entertained for me a passing liking, she would not have suffered so.

And so I came to realize how cruel must have been the pang that had driven her to this. But she had loved me; aye, and she loved me still, for all that she thought she hated, and for all that she had acted as if she hated. But even if I were wrong – even if she did hate me – what a fresh revulsion would not be hers when anon she learnt that – whatever my sins – I had not played lightly with her love; that I was not, as she had imagined, the betrothed of another woman!

The thought fired me like wine. I was no longer listless – no longer indifferent as to whether I lived or died. I must live. I must enlighten the Keeper of the Seals and the judges at Toulouse concerning my identity. Why, indeed, had I ever wavered? Bardelys the Magnificent must come to life again, and then – what then?

As suddenly as I had been exalted was I cast down. There was a rumour abroad that Bardelys was dead. In the wake of that rumour I shrewdly guessed that the report of the wager that had brought him into Languedoc would not be slow to follow. What then? Would she love me any the better? Would she hate me any the less? If now she was wounded by the belief that I had made sport of her love, would not that same belief be with her again when she came to know the truth?

Aye, the tangle was a grievous one. Yet I took heart. My old resolve returned to me, and I saw the need for urgency – in that alone could lie now my redemption in her eyes. My wager must be paid before I again repaired to her, for all that it should leave me poor indeed. In the meanwhile, I prayed God that she might not hear of it ere I returned to tell her.

# Chapter 11

## The King's Commissioner

For that most amiable of Gascon cadets, Monsieur de Castelroux, I have naught but the highest praise. In his every dealing with me he revealed himself so very gallant, generous, and high-minded a gentleman that it was little short of a pleasure to be his prisoner.

He made no inquiries touching the nature of my interview with those two gentlemen at the Hôtel de la Couronne, and when at the moment of leaving I requested him to deliver a packet to the taller of those same two he did so without comment or question. That packet contained the portrait of Mademoiselle de Marsac, but on the inner wrapper was a note requesting Lesperon not to open it until he should be in Spain.

Neither Marsac nor Lesperon did I see again before we resumed our journey to Toulouse.

At the moment of setting out a curious incident occurred.

Castelroux's company of dragoons had ridden into the courtyard as we were mounting. They lined up under their lieutenant's command, to allow us to pass; but as we reached the porte-cochère we were delayed for a moment by a travelling-carriage, entering for relays, and coming, apparently, from Toulouse. Castelroux and I backed our horses until we were in the midst of the dragoons, and so we stood while the vehicle passed in. As it went by, one of the leather curtains was drawn back, and my heart was quickened by the sight of a pale girl face, with eyes of blue, and brown curls lying upon the slender neck. Her glance lighted on me, swordless and in the midst of that company of troopers, and I bowed low upon the withers of my horse, doffing my hat in distant salutation.

The curtain dropped again, and eclipsed the face of the woman that had betrayed me. With my mind full of wild surmisings as to what emotions might have awakened in her upon beholding me, I rode away in silence at Monsieur de Castelroux's side. Had she experienced any remorse? Any shame? Whether or not such feelings had been aroused at sight of me, it certainly would not be long ere she experienced them, for at the Hôtel de la Couronne were those who would enlighten her.

The contemplation of the remorseful grief that might anon beset her when she came to ponder the truth of matters, and, with that truth, those things that at Lavédan I had uttered, filled me presently with regret and pity. I grew impatient to reach Toulouse and tell the judges of the mistake that there had been. My name could not be unknown to them, and the very mention of it, I thought, should suffice to give them pause and lead them to make inquiries before sending me to the scaffold. Yet I was not without uneasiness, for the summariness with which Castelroux had informed me they were in the habit of dealing with those accused of high treason occasioned me some apprehensive pangs.

This apprehension led me to converse with my captor touching those trials, seeking to gather from him who were the judges. I learnt then that besides the ordinary Tribunal, a Commissioner had been dispatched by His Majesty, and was hourly expected to arrive at Toulouse. It would be his mission to supervise and direct the inquiries that were taking place. It was said, he added, that the King himself was on his way thither, to be present at the trial of Monsieur le Duc de Montmorency. But he was travelling by easy stages, and was not yet expected for some days. My heart, which had leapt at the news, as suddenly sank again with the consideration that I should probably be disposed of before the King's arrival.

It would behove me, therefore, to look elsewhere for help and for someone to swear to my identity.

"Do you know the name of this King's Commissioner?" I asked.

"It is a certain Comte de Chatellerault, a gentleman said to stand very high in His Majesty's favour."

"Chatellerault!" I cried in wondering joy.

"You know him?"

"Most excellently!" I laughed. "We are very intimately acquainted."

"Why, then, monsieur, I augur you this gentleman's friendship, and that it may pilot you through your trouble. Although – " Being mercifully minded, he stopped short.

But I laughed easily. "Indeed, my dear Captain, I think it will," said I; "although friendship in this world is a thing of which the unfortunate know little."

But I rejoiced too soon, as you shall hear.

We rode diligently on, our way lying along the fertile banks of the Garonne, now yellow with the rustling corn. Towards evening we made our last halt at Fenouillet, whence a couple of hours' riding should bring us to Toulouse.

At the post-house we overtook a carriage that seemingly had halted for relays, but upon which I scarce bestowed a glance as I alighted.

Whilst Castelroux went to arrange for fresh horses, I strode into the common room, and there for some moments I stood discussing the viands with our host. When at last I had resolved that a cold pasty and a bottle of Armagnac would satisfy our wants, I looked about me to take survey of those in the room. One group in a remote corner suddenly riveted my attention to such a degree that I remained deaf to the voice of Castelroux, who had just entered, and who stood now beside me. In the centre of this group was the Comte de Chatellerault himself, a thick-set, sombre figure, dressed with that funereal magnificence he affected.

But it was not the sight of him that filled me with amazement. For that, Castelroux's information had prepared me, and I well understood in what capacity he was there. My surprise sprang rather from the fact that amongst the half-dozen gentlemen about him – and evidently in attendance – I beheld the Chevalier de Saint-Eustache. Now, knowing as I did the Chevalier's treasonable leanings, there was ample cause for my astonishment at finding him in such company.

Apparently, too, he was on very intimate terms with the Count, for in raising my glance I had caught him in the act of leaning over to whisper familiarly in Chatellerault's ear.

Their eyes – indeed, for that matter the eyes of the entire company – were turned in my direction.

Perhaps it was not a surprising thing that Chatellerault should gaze upon me in that curious fashion, for was it not probable that he had heard that I was dead? Besides, the fact that I was without a sword, and that at my side stood a King's officer, afforded evidence enough of my condition, and well might Chatellerault stare at beholding me so manifestly a prisoner.

Even as I watched him, he appeared to start at something that Saint-Eustache was saying, and a curious change spread over his face.

Its whilom expression had been rather one of dismay; for, having believed me dead, he no doubt accounted his wager won, whereas seeing me alive had destroyed that pleasant conviction. But now it took on a look of relief and of something that suggested malicious cunning.

"That," said Castelroux in my ear, "is the King's Commissioner."

Did I not know it? I never waited to answer him, but, striding across the room, I held out my hand over the table – to Chatellerault.

"My dear Comte," I cried, "you are most choicely met."

I would have added more, but there was something in his attitude that silenced me. He had turned half from me, and stood now, hand on hip, his great head thrown back and tilted towards his shoulder, his expression one of freezing and disdainful wonder.

Now, if his attitude filled me with astonishment and apprehension, consider how these feelings were heightened by his words.

"Monsieur de Lesperon, I can but express amazement at your effrontery. If we have been acquainted in the past, do you think that is a sufficient reason for me to take your hand now that you have placed yourself in a position which renders it impossible for His Majesty's loyal servants to know you?"

I fell back a pace, my mind scarce grasping yet the depths of this inexplicable attitude.

"This to me, Chatellerault?" I gasped.

"To you?" he blazed, stirred to a sudden passion. "What else did you expect, Monsieur de Lesperon?"

I had it in me to give him the lie, to denounce him then for a low, swindling trickster. I understood all at once the meaning of this wondrous make-believe. From Saint-Eustache he had gathered the mistake there was, and for his wager's sake he would let the error prevail, and hurry me to the scaffold. What else might I have expected from the man that had lured me into such a wager – a wager which the knowledge he possessed had made him certain of winning?

Would he who had cheated at the dealing of the cards neglect an opportunity to cheat again during the progress of the game?

As I have said, I had it in my mind to cry out that he lied – that I was not Lesperon; that he knew I was Bardelys. But the futility of such an outcry came to me simultaneously with the thought of it.

And, I fear me, I stood before him and his satellites – the mocking Saint-Eustache amongst them – a very foolish figure.

"There is no more to be said," I murmured at last.

"But there is!" he retorted. "There is much more to be said. You shall render yet an account of your treason, and I am afraid, my poor rebel, that your comely head will part company with your shapely body. You and I will meet at Toulouse. What more is to be said will be said in the Tribunal there."

A chill encompassed me. I was doomed, it seemed. This man, ruling the province pending the King's arrival, would see to it that none came forward to recognize me. He would expedite the comedy of my trial, and close it with the tragedy of my execution. My professions of a mistake of identity – if I wasted breath upon them would be treated with disdain and disregarded utterly. God! What a position had I got myself into, and what a vein of comedy ran through it – grim, tragic comedy, if you will, yet comedy to all faith. The very woman whom I had wagered to wed had betrayed me into the hands of the very man with whom I laid my wager.

But there was more in it than that. As I had told Mironsac that night in Paris, when the thing had been initiated, it was a duel that was being fought betwixt Chatellerault and me – a duel for supremacy in the King's good graces. We were rivals, and he desired my removal from the Court. To this end had he lured me into a bargain that should result in my financial ruin, thereby compelling me to withdraw from the costly life of the Luxembourg, and leaving him supreme, the sole and uncontested recipient of our master's favour. Now into his hand Fate had thrust a stouter weapon and a deadlier: a weapon which not only should make him master of the wealth that I had pledged, but one whereby he might remove me for all time, a thousandfold more effectively than the mere encompassing of my ruin would have done.

I was doomed. I realized it fully and very bitterly.

I was to go out of the ways of men unnoticed and unmourned; as a rebel, under the obscure name of another and bearing another's sins upon my shoulders, I was to pass almost unheeded to the gallows.

Bardelys the Magnificent – the Marquis Marcel de Saint-Pol de Bardelys, whose splendour had been a byword in France – was to go out like a guttering candle.

The thought filled me with the awful frenzy that so often goes with impotency, such a frenzy as the damned in hell may know. I forgot in that hour my precept that under no conditions should a gentleman give way to anger. In a blind access of fury I flung myself across the table and caught that villainous cheat by the throat, before any there could put out a hand to stop me.

He was a heavy man, if a short one, and the strength of his thick-set frame was a thing abnormal. Yet at that moment such nervous power did I gather from my rage, that I swung him from his feet as though he had been the puniest weakling. I dragged him down on to the table, and there I ground his face with a most excellent goodwill and relish.

"You liar, you cheat, you thief!" I snarled like any cross-grained mongrel. "The King shall hear of this, you knave! By God, he shall!"

They dragged me from him at last – those lapdogs that attended him – and with much rough handling they sent me sprawling among the sawdust on the floor. It is more than likely that but for Castelroux's intervention they had made short work of me there and then.

But with a bunch of Mordieus, Sangdieus, and Po' Cap de Dieus, the little Gascon flung himself before my prostrate figure, and bade them in the King's name, and at their peril, to stand back.

Chatellerault, sorely shaken, his face purple, and with blood streaming from his nostrils, had sunk into a chair. He rose now, and his first words were incoherent, raging gasps.

"What is your name, sir?" he bellowed at last, addressing the Captain.

"Amedée de Mironsac de Castelroux, of Château Rouge in Gascony," answered my captor, with a grand manner and a flourish, and added, "Your servant."

"What authority have you to allow your prisoners this degree of freedom?"

"I do not need authority, monsieur," replied the Gascon.

"Do you not?" blazed the Count. "We shall see. Wait until I am in Toulouse, my malapert friend."

Castelroux drew himself up, straight as a rapier, his face slightly flushed and his glance angry, yet he had the presence of mind to restrain himself, partly at least.

"I have my orders from the Keeper of the Seals, to effect the apprehension of Monsieur de Lesperon; and to deliver him up, alive or dead, at Toulouse. So that I do this, the manner of it is my own affair, and who presumes to criticize my methods censoriously impugns my honour and affronts me. And who affronts me, monsieur, be he whosoever he may be, renders me satisfaction. I beg that you will bear that circumstance in mind."

His moustaches bristled as he spoke, and altogether his air was very fierce and truculent. For a moment I trembled for him. But the Count evidently thought better of it than to provoke a quarrel, particularly one in which he would be manifestly in the wrong, King's Commissioner though he might be. There was an exchange of questionable compliments betwixt the officer and the Count, whereafter, to avoid further unpleasantness, Castelroux conducted me to a private room, where we took our meal in gloomy silence.

It was not until an hour later, when we were again in the saddle and upon the last stage of our journey, that I offered Castelroux an explanation of my seemingly mad attack upon Chatellerault.

"You have done a very rash and unwise thing, monsieur," he had commented regretfully, and it was in answer to this that I poured out the whole story. I had determined upon this course while we were supping, for Castelroux was now my only hope, and as we rode beneath the stars of that September night I made known to him my true identity.

I told him that Chatellerault knew me, and I informed him that a wager lay between us – withholding the particulars of its nature – which had brought me into Languedoc and into the position wherein he had found and arrested me. At first he hesitated to believe me, but when at last I had convinced him by the vehemence of my assurances as much as by the assurances themselves, he expressed such opinions of the Comte de Chatellerault as made my heart go out to him.

"You see, my dear Castelroux, that you are now my last hope," I said.

"A forlorn one, my poor gentleman!" he groaned.

"Nay, that need not be. My intendant Rodenard and some twenty of my servants should be somewhere betwixt this and Paris. Let them be sought for, monsieur, and let us pray God that they be still in Languedoc and may be found in time."

"It shall be done, monsieur, I promise you," he answered me solemnly. "But I implore you not to hope too much from it. Chatellerault has it in his power to act promptly, and you may depend that he will waste no time after what has passed."

"Still, we may have two or three days, and in those days you must do what you can, my friend."

"You may depend upon me," he promised.

"And meanwhile, Castelroux," said I, "you will say no word of this to anyone."

That assurance also he gave me, and presently the lights of our destination gleamed out to greet us.

That night I lay in a dank and gloomy cell of the prison of Toulouse, with never a hope to bear company during those dark, wakeful hours.

A dull rage was in my soul as I thought of my position, for it had not needed Castelroux's recommendation to restrain me from building false hopes upon his chances of finding Rodenard and my followers in time to save me. Some little ray of consolation I culled, perhaps, from my thoughts of Roxalanne. Out of the gloom of my cell my fancy fashioned her sweet girl face and stamped it with a look of gentle pity, of infinite sorrow for me and for the hand she had had in bringing me to this.

That she loved me I was assured, and I swore that if I lived I would win her yet, in spite of every obstacle that I myself had raised for my undoing.

# Chapter 12

# The Tribunal of Toulouse

I had hoped to lie some days in prison before being brought to trial, and that during those days Castelroux might have succeeded in discovering those who could witness to my identity. Conceive, therefore, something of my dismay when on the morrow I was summoned an hour before noon to go present myself to my judges.

From the prison to the Palace I was taken in chains like any thief – for the law demanded this indignity to be borne by one charged with the crimes they imputed to me. The distance was but short, yet I found it over-long, which is not wonderful considering that the people stopped to line up as I went by and to cast upon me a shower of opprobrious derision – for Toulouse was a very faithful and loyal city. It was within some two hundred yards of the Palace steps that I suddenly beheld a face in the crowd, at the sight of which I stood still in my amazement. This earned me a stab in the back from the butt-end of the pike of one of my guards.

"What ails you now?" quoth the man irritably. "Forward, monsieur le traite!"

I moved on, scarce remarking the fellow's roughness; my eyes were still upon that face – the white, piteous face of Roxalanne. I smiled reassurance and encouragement, but even as I smiled the horror in her countenance seemed to increase. Then, as I passed on, she vanished from my sight, and I was left to conjecture the motives that had occasioned her return to Toulouse. Had the message that Marsac would yesterday have conveyed to her caused her to retrace her steps that she might be near me in my extremity; or had some weightier reason influenced her return? Did she hope to undo some of the evil she had done? Alas, poor child! If such were her hopes, I sorely feared me they would prove very idle.

Of my trial I should say but little did not the exigencies of my story render it necessary to say much. Even now, across the gap of years, my gorge rises at the mockery which, in the King's name, those gentlemen made of justice. I can allow for the troubled conditions of the times, and I can realize how in cases of civil disturbances and rebellion it may be expedient to deal summarily with traitors, yet not all the allowances that I can think of would suffice to condone the methods of that Tribunal.

The trial was conducted in private by the Keeper of the Seals – a lean, wizened individual, with an air as musty and dry as that of the parchments among which he had spent his days. He was supported by six judges, and on his right sat the King's Commissioner, Monsieur de Chatellerault – the bruised condition of whose countenance still advertised the fact that we had met but yesterday.

Upon being asked my name and place of abode, I created some commotion by answering boldly, "I am the Sieur Marcel de Saint-Pol, Marquis of Bardelys, of Bardelys in Picardy."

The President – that is to say, the Keeper of the Seals – turned inquiringly to Chatellerault. The Count, however, did no more than smile and point to something written on a paper that lay spread upon the table. The President nodded.

"Monsieur René de Lesperon," said he, "the Court may perhaps not be able to discriminate whether this statement of yours is a deliberate attempt to misguide or frustrate the ends of justice, or whether, either in consequence of your wounds or as a visitation of God for your treason, you are the victim of a deplorable hallucination. But the Court wishes you to understand that it is satisfied of your identity. The papers found upon your person at the time of your arrest, besides other evidence in our power, remove all possibility of doubt in that connection. Therefore, in your own interests, we implore you to abandon these false statements, if so be that you are master of your wits. Your only hope of saving your head must lie in your truthfully answering our questions, and even then, Monsieur de Lesperon, the hope that we hold out to you is so slight as to be no hope at all."

There was a pause, during which the other judges nodded their heads in sage approval of their President's words. For myself, I kept silent, perceiving how little it could avail me to continue to protest, and awaited his next question.

"You were arrested, monsieur, at the Château de Lavédan two nights ago by a company of dragoons under the command of Captain de Castelroux. Is that so?"

"It is so, monsieur."

"And at the time of your arrest, upon being apprehended as René de Lesperon, you offered no repudiation of the identity; on the contrary, when Monsieur de Castelroux called for Monsieur de Lesperon, you stepped forward and acknowledged that you were he."

"Pardon, monsieur. What I acknowledged was that I was known by that name."

The President chuckled evilly, and his satellites smiled in polite reflection of his mood.

"This acute differentiating is peculiar, Monsieur de Lesperon, to persons of unsound mental condition," said he. "I am afraid that it will serve little purpose. A man is generally known by his name, is he not?" I did not answer him. "Shall we call Monsieur de Castelroux to confirm what I have said?"

"It is not necessary. Since you allow that I may have said I was known by the name, but refuse to recognize the distinction between that and a statement that 'Lesperon' is my name, it would serve no purpose to summon the Captain."

The President nodded, and with that the point was dismissed, and he proceeded as calmly as though there never had been any question of my identity.

"You are charged, Monsieur de Lesperon, with high treason in its most virulent and malignant form. You are accused of having borne arms against His Majesty. Have you anything to say?"

"I have to say that it is false, monsieur; that His Majesty has no more faithful or loving subject than am I."

The President shrugged his shoulders, and a shade of annoyance crossed his face.

"If you are come here for no other purpose than to deny the statements that I make, I am afraid that we are but wasting time," he cried testily. "If you desire it, I can summon Monsieur de Castelroux to swear that at the time of your arrest and upon being charged with the crime you made no repudiation of that charge."

"Naturally not, monsieur," I cried, somewhat heated by this seemingly studied ignoring of important facts, "because I realized that it was Monsieur de Castelroux's mission to arrest and not to judge me. Monsieur de Castelroux was an officer, not a Tribunal, and to have denied this or that to him would have been so much waste of breath."

"Ah! Very nimble; very nimble, in truth, Monsieur de Lesperon, but scarcely convincing. We will proceed. You are charged with having taken part in several of the skirmishes against the armies of Marshals de Schomberg and La Force, and finally, with having been in close attendance upon Monsieur de Montmorency at the battle of Castelnaudary. What have you to say?"

"That it is utterly untrue."

"Yet your name, monsieur, is on a list found among the papers in the captured baggage of Monsieur le Duc de Montmorency."

"No, monsieur," I denied stoutly, "it is not."

The President smote the table a blow that scattered a flight of papers.

"Par la mort Dieu!" he roared, with a most indecent exhibition of temper in one so placed. "I have had enough of your contradictions. You forget, monsieur, your position – "

"At least," I broke in harshly, "no less than you forget yours."

The Keeper of the Seals gasped for breath at that, and his fellow judges murmured angrily amongst themselves. Chatellerault maintained his sardonic smile, but permitted himself to utter no word.

"I would, gentlemen," I cried, addressing them all, "that His Majesty were here to see how you conduct your trials and defile his Courts. As for you, Monsieur le President, you violate the sanctity of your office in giving way to anger; it is a thing unpardonable in a judge. I have told you in plain terms, gentlemen, that I am not this René de Lesperon with whose crimes you charge me. Yet, in spite of my denials, ignoring them, or setting them down either to a futile attempt at defence or to an hallucination of which you suppose me the victim, you proceed to lay those crimes to my charge, and when I deny your charges you speak of proofs that can only apply to another.

"How shall the name of Lesperon having been found among the Duke of Montmorency's papers convict me of treason, since I tell you that I am not Lesperon? Had you the slightest, the remotest sense of your high duty, messieurs, you would ask me rather to explain how, if what I state be true, I come to be confounded with Lesperon and arrested in his place. Then, messieurs, you might seek to test the accuracy of what statements I may make; but to proceed as you are proceeding is not to judge but to murder. Justice is represented as a virtuous woman with bandaged eyes, holding impartial scales; in your hands, gentlemen, by my soul, she is become a very harlot clutching a veil."

Chatellerault's cynical smile grew broader as my speech proceeded and stirred up the rancour in the hearts of those august gentlemen.

The Keeper of the Seals went white and red by turns, and when I paused there was an impressive silence that lasted for some moments.

At last the President leant over to confer in a whisper with Chatellerault. Then, in a voice forcedly calm – like the calm of Nature when thunder is brewing – he asked me, "Who do you insist that you are, monsieur?"

"Once already have I told you, and I venture to think that mine is a name not easily forgotten. I am the Sieur Marcel de Saint-Pol, Marquis of Bardelys, of Bardelys in Picardy."

A cunning grin parted his thin lips.

"Have you any witnesses to identify you?"

"Hundreds, monsieur!" I answered eagerly, seeing salvation already within my grasp.

"Name some of them."

"I will name one – one whose word you will not dare to doubt."

"That is?"

"His Majesty the King. I am told that he is on his way to Toulouse, and I but ask, messieurs, that you await his arrival before going further with my trial."

"Is there no other witness of whom you can think, monsieur? Some witness that might be produced more readily. For if you can, indeed, establish the identity you claim, why should you languish in prison for some weeks?"

His voice was soft and oily. The anger had all departed out of it, which I – like a fool – imagined to be due to my mention of the King.

"My friends, Monsieur le Garde des Sceaux, are all either in Paris or in His Majesty's train, and so not likely to be here before him.

"There is my intendant, Rodenard, and there are my servants – some twenty of them – who may perhaps be still in Languedoc, and for whom I would entreat you to seek. Them you might succeed in finding within a few days if they have not yet determined to return to Paris in the belief that I am dead."

He stroked his chin meditatively, his eyes raised to the sunlit dome of glass overhead.

"Ah-h!" he gasped. It was a long-drawn sigh of regret, of conclusion, or of weary impatience. "There is no one in Toulouse who will swear to your identity, monsieur?" he asked.

"I am afraid there is not," I replied. "I know of no one."

As I uttered those words the President's countenance changed as abruptly as if he had flung off a mask. From soft and cat-like that he had been during the past few moments, he grew of a sudden savage as a tiger. He leapt to his feet, his face crimson, his eyes seeming to blaze, and the words he spoke came now in a hot, confused, and almost incoherent torrent.

"Miserable!" he roared, "out of your own mouth have you convicted yourself. And to think that you should have stood there and wasted the time of this Court – His Majesty's time – with your damnable falsehoods! What purpose did you think to serve by delaying your doom? Did you imagine that haply, whilst we sent to Paris for your witnesses, the King might grow weary of justice, and in some fit of clemency announce a general pardon? Such things have been known, and it may be that in your cunning you played for such a gain based upon such a hope. But justice, fool, is not to be cozened. Had you, indeed, been Bardelys, you had seen that here in this Court sits a gentleman who is very intimate with him. He is there, monsieur; that is Monsieur le Comte de Chatellerault, of whom perhaps you may have heard. Yet, when I ask you whether in Toulouse there is anyone who can bear witness to your identity, you answer me that you know of no one. I will waste no more time with you, I promise you."

He flung himself back into his chair like a man exhausted, and mopped his brow with a great kerchief which he had drawn from his robes. His fellow judges laid their heads together, and with smiles and nods, winks and leers, they discussed and admired the miraculous subtlety and acumen of this Solomon. Chatellerault sat, calmly smiling, in solemn mockery.

For a spell I was too thunderstruck to speak, aghast at this catastrophe. Like a fool, indeed, I had tumbled into the pit that had been dug for me by Chatellerault for I never doubted that it was of his contriving. At last, "My masters," said I, "these conclusions may appear to you most plausible, but, believe me, they are fallacious. I am perfectly acquainted with Monsieur de Chatellerault, and he with me, and if he were to speak the truth and play the man and the gentleman for once, he would tell you that I am, indeed, Bardelys. But Monsieur le Comte has ends of his own to serve in sending me to my doom. It is in a sense through his agency that I am at present in this position, and that I have been confounded with Lesperon. What, then, could it have availed me to have made appeal to him? And yet, Monsieur le President, he was born a gentleman, and he may still retain some notion of honour.

"Ask him, sir – ask him point-blank, whether I am or not Marcel de Bardelys."

The firmness of my tones created some impression upon those feeble minds. Indeed, the President went so far as to turn an interrogative glance upon the Count. But Chatellerault, supremely master of the situation, shrugged his shoulders, and smiled a pitying, long-suffering smile.

"Must I really answer such a question, Monsieur le President?" he inquired in a voice and with a manner that clearly implied how low would be his estimate of the President's intelligence if he were, indeed, constrained to do so.

"But no, Monsieur le Comte," replied the President with sudden haste, and in scornful rejection of the idea. "There is no necessity that you should answer."

"But the question, Monsieur le President!" I thundered, my hand outstretched towards Chatellerault. "Ask him – if you have any sense of your duty – ask him am I not Marcel de Bardelys."

"Silence!" blazed the President back at me. "You shall not fool us any longer, you nimble-witted liar!"

My head drooped. This coward had, indeed, shattered my last hope.

"Some day, monsieur," I said very quietly, "I promise you that your behaviour and these gratuitous insults shall cost you your position. Pray God they do not cost you also your head!"

My words they treated as one might treat the threats of a child.

That I should have had the temerity to utter them did but serve finally to decide my doom, if, indeed, anything had been wanting.

With many epithets of opprobrium, such as are applied to malefactors of the lowest degree, they passed sentence of death upon me, and with drooping spirits, giving myself up for lost and assured that I should be led to the block before many hours were sped, I permitted them to reconduct me through the streets of Toulouse to my prison.

I could entertain you at length upon my sensations as I walked between my guards, a man on the threshold of eternity, with hundreds of men and women gaping at me – men and women who would live for years to gape upon many another wretch in my position. The sun shone with a brilliance that to such eyes as mine was a very mockery.

Thus would it shine on through centuries, and light many another unfortunate to the scaffold. The very sky seemed pitiless in the intensity of its cobalt. Unfeeling I deemed the note that everywhere was struck by man and Nature, so discordant was it with my gloomy outlook. If you would have food for reflection upon the evanescent quality of life, upon the nothingness of man, upon the empty, heartless egoism implicit in human nature, get yourselves sentenced to death, and then look around you. With such a force was all this borne in upon me, and with such sufficiency, that after the first pang was spent I went near to rejoicing that things were as they were, and that I was to die, haply before sunset. It was become such a world as did not seem worth a man's while to live in: a world of vainness, of hollowness, of meanness, of nothing but illusions.

The knowledge that I was about to die, that I was about to quit all this, seemed to have torn some veil from my eyes, and to have permitted me to recognize the worthless quality of what I left.

Well may it be that such are but the thoughts of a man's dying moments, whispered into his soul by a merciful God to predispose him for the wrench and agony of his passing.

I had been a half-hour in my cell when the door was opened to admit Castelroux, whom I had not seen since the night before. He came to condole with me in my extremity, and yet to bid me not utterly lose hope.

"It is too late today to carry out the sentence," said he, "and as tomorrow will be Sunday, you will have until the day after. By then much may betide, monsieur. My agents are everywhere scouring the province for your servants, and let us pray Heaven that they may succeed in their search."

"It is a forlorn hope, Monsieur de Castelroux," I sighed, "and I will pin no faith to it lest I suffer a disappointment that will embitter my last moments, and perhaps rob me of some of the fortitude I shall have need of."

He answered me, nevertheless, with words of encouragement. No effort was being spared, and if Rodenard and my men were still in Languedoc there was every likelihood that they would be brought to Toulouse in time. Then he added that that, however, was not the sole object of his visit. A lady had obtained permission of the Keeper of the Seals to visit me, and she was waiting to be admitted.

"A lady?" I exclaimed, and the thought of Roxalanne flitted through my mind. "Mademoiselle de Lavédan?" I inquired.

He nodded. "Yes," said he; then added, "She seems in sore affliction, monsieur."

I besought him to admit her forthwith, and presently she came.

Castelroux closed the door as he withdrew, and we were left alone together. As she put aside her cloak, and disclosed to me the pallor of her face and the disfiguring red about her gentle eyes, telling of tears and sleeplessness, all my own trouble seemed to vanish in the contemplation of her affliction.

We stood a moment confronting each other with no word spoken. Then, dropping her glance, and advancing a step, in a faltering, hesitating manner, "Monsieur, monsieur," she murmured in a suffocating voice.

In a bound I was beside her, and I had gathered her in my arms, her little brown head against my shoulder.

"Roxalanne!" I whispered as soothingly as I might – "Roxalanne!"

But she struggled to be free of my embrace.

"Let me go, monsieur," she pleaded, a curious shrinking in her very voice. "Do not touch me, monsieur. You do not know – you do not know."

For answer, I enfolded her more tightly still.

"But I do know, little one," I whispered; "and I even understand."

At that, her struggles ceased upon the instant, and she seemed to lie limp and helpless in my arms.

"You know, monsieur," she questioned me – "you know that I betrayed you?"

"Yes," I answered simply.

"And you can forgive me? I am sending you to your death and you have no reproaches for me! Oh, monsieur, it will kill me!"

"Hush, child!" I whispered. "What reproaches can I have for you? I know the motives that impelled you."

"Not altogether, monsieur; you cannot know them. I loved you, monsieur. I do love you, monsieur. Oh! this is not a time to consider words. If I am bold and unmaidenly, I – I – "

"Neither bold nor unmaidenly, but – oh, the sweetest damsel in all France, my Roxalanne!" I broke in, coming to her aid. "Mine was a leprous, sinful soul, child, when I came into Languedoc. I had no faith in any human good, and I looked as little for an honest man or a virtuous woman as one looks for honey in a nettle. I was soured, and my life had hardly been such a life as it was meet to bring into contact with your own. Then, among the roses at Lavédan, in your dear company, Roxalanne, it seemed that some of the good, some of the sweetness, some of the purity about you were infused anew into my heart. I became young again, and I seemed oddly cleansed. In that hour of my rejuvenation I loved you, Roxalanne."

Her face had been raised to mine as I spoke. There came now a flutter of the eyelids, a curious smile about the lips. Then her head drooped again and was laid against my breast; a sigh escaped her, and she began to weep softly.

"Nay, Roxalanne, do not fret. Come, child, it is not your way to be weak."

"I have betrayed you!" she moaned. "I am sending you to your death!"

"I understand, I understand," I answered, smoothing her brown hair.

"Not quite, monsieur. I loved you so, monsieur, that you can have no thought of how I suffered that morning when Mademoiselle de Marsac came to Lavédan.

"At first it was but the pain of thinking that – that I was about to lose you; that you were to go out of my life, and that I should see you no more – you whom I had enshrined so in my heart.

"I called myself a little fool that morning for having dreamed that you had come to care for me; my vanity I thought had deluded me into imagining that your manner towards me had a tenderness that spoke of affection. I was bitter with myself, and I suffered, oh, so much! Then later, when I was in the rose garden, you came to me.

"You remember how you seized me, and how by your manner you showed me that it was not vanity alone had misled me. You had fooled me, I thought; even in that hour I imagined you were fooling me; you made light of me; and my sufferings were naught to you so that I might give you some amusement to pass the leisure and monotony of your sojourn with us."

"Roxalanne – my poor Roxalanne!" I whispered.

"Then my bitterness and sorrow all turned to anger against you. You had broken my heart, and I thought that you had done it wantonly. For that I burned to punish you. Ah! and not only that, perhaps. I think, too, that some jealousy drove me on. You had wooed and slighted me, yet you had made me love you, and if you were not for me I swore you should be for no other. And so, while my madness endured, I quitted Lavédan, and telling my father that I was going to Auch, to his sister's house, I came to Toulouse and betrayed you to the Keeper of the Seals.

"Scarce was the thing done than I beheld the horror of it, and I hated myself. In my despair, I abandoned all idea of pursuing the journey to Auch, but turned and made my way back in haste, hoping that I might still come to warn you. But at Grenade I met you already in charge of the soldiers. At Grenade, too, I learnt the truth – that you were not Lesperon. Can you not guess something of my anguish then? Already loathing my act, and beside myself for having betrayed you, think into what despair I was plunged by Monsieur de Marsac's intimation.

"Then I understood that for reasons of your own you had concealed your identity. You were not perhaps, betrothed; indeed, I remembered then how, solemnly, you had sworn that you were not; and so I bethought me that your vows to me may have been sincere and such as a maid might honourably listen to."

"They were, Roxalanne! they were!" I cried.

But she continued, "That you had Mademoiselle de Marsac's portrait was something that I could not explain; but then I hear that you had also Lesperon's papers upon you; so that you may have become possessed of the one with the others. And now, monsieur – "

She ceased, and there against my breast she lay weeping and weeping in her bitter passion of regret, until it seemed to me she would never regain her self-control.

"It has been all my fault, Roxalanne," said I, "and if I am to pay the price they are exacting, it will be none too high. I embarked upon a dastardly business, which brought me to Languedoc under false colours. I wish, indeed, that I had told you when first the impulse to tell you came upon me. Afterwards it grew impossible."

"Tell me now," she begged. "Tell me who you are."

Sorely was I tempted to respond. Almost was I on the point of doing so, when suddenly the thought of how she might shrink from me, of how, even then, she might come to think that I had but simulated love for her for infamous purposes of gain, restrained and silenced me. During the few hours of life that might be left me I would at least be lord and master of her heart. When I was dead – for I had little hope of Castelroux's efforts – it would matter less, and perhaps because I was dead she would be merciful.

"I cannot, Roxalanne. Not even now. It is too vile! If – if they carry out the sentence on Monday, I shall leave a letter for you, telling you everything."

She shuddered, and a sob escaped her. From my identity her mind fled back to the more important matter of my fate.

127

"They will not carry it out, monsieur! Oh, they will not! Say that you can defend yourself, that you are not the man they believe you to be!"

"We are in God's hands, child. It may be that I shall save myself yet. If I do, I shall come straight to you, and you shall know all that there is to know. But, remember, child" – and raising her face in my hands, I looked down into the blue of her tearful eyes – "remember, little one, that in one thing I have been true and honourable, and influenced by nothing but my heart – in my wooing of you. I love you, Roxalanne, with all my soul, and if I should die you are the only thing in all this world that I experience a regret at leaving."

"I do believe it; I do, indeed. Nothing can ever alter my belief again. Will you not, then, tell me who you are, and what is this thing, which you call dishonourable, that brought you into Languedoc?"

A moment again I pondered. Then I shook my head.

"Wait, child," said I; and she, obedient to my wishes, asked no more.

It was the second time that I neglected a favourable opportunity of making that confession, and as I had regretted having allowed the first occasion to pass unprofited, so was I, and still more poignantly, to regret this second silence.

A little while she stayed with me yet, and I sought to instil some measure of comfort into her soul. I spoke of the hopes that I based upon Castelroux's finding friends to recognize me – hopes that were passing slender. And she, poor child, sought also to cheer me and give me courage.

"If only the King were here!" she sighed. "I would go to him, and on my knees I would plead for your enlargement. But they say he is no nearer than Lyons; and I could not hope to get there and back by Monday. I will go to the Keeper of the Seals again, monsieur, and I will beg him to be merciful, and at least to delay the sentence."

I did not discourage her; I did not speak of the futility of such a step. But I begged her to remain in Toulouse until Monday, that she might visit me again before the end, if the end were to become inevitable.

Then Castelroux came to reconduct her, and we parted. But she left me a great consolation, a great strengthening comfort. If I were destined, indeed, to walk to the scaffold, it seemed that I could do it with a better grace and a gladder courage now.

# Chapter 13

## The Eleventh Hour

Castelroux visited me upon the following morning, but he brought no news that might be accounted encouraging. None of his messengers were yet returned, nor had any sent word that they were upon the trail of my followers. My heart sank a little, and such hope as I still fostered was fast perishing. Indeed, so imminent did my doom appear and so unavoidable, that later in the day I asked for pen and paper that I might make an attempt at setting my earthly affairs to rights. Yet when the writing materials were brought me, I wrote not. I sat instead with the feathered end of my quill between my teeth, and thus pondered the matter of the disposal of my Picardy estates.

Coldly I weighed the wording of the wager and the events that had transpired, and I came at length to the conclusion that Chatellerault could not be held to have the least claim upon my lands. That he had cheated at the very outset, as I have earlier shown, was of less account than that he had been instrumental in violently hindering me.

I took at last the resolve to indite a full memoir of the transaction, and to request Castelroux to see that it was delivered to the King himself. Thus not only would justice be done, but I should – though tardily – be even with the Count. No doubt he relied upon his power

130

to make a thorough search for such papers as I might leave, and to destroy everything that might afford indication of my true identity.

But he had not counted upon the good feeling that had sprung up betwixt the little Gascon captain and me, nor yet upon my having contrived to convince the latter that I was, indeed, Bardelys, and he little dreamt of such a step as I was about to take to ensure his punishment hereafter.

Resolved at last, I was commencing to write when my attention was arrested by an unusual sound. It was at first no more than a murmuring noise, as of a sea breaking upon its shore. Gradually it grew its volume and assumed the shape of human voices raised in lusty clamour. Then, above the din of the populace, a gun boomed out, then another, and another.

I sprang up at that, and, wondering what might be toward, I crossed to my barred window and stood there listening. I overlooked the courtyard of the jail, and I could see some commotion below, in sympathy, as it were, with the greater commotion without.

Presently, as the populace drew nearer, it seemed to me that the shouting was of acclamation. Next I caught a blare of trumpets, and, lastly, I was able to distinguish above the noise, which had now grown to monstrous proportions, the clattering hoofs of some cavalcade that was riding past the prison doors.

It was borne in upon me that some great personage was arriving in Toulouse, and my first thought was of the King. At the idea of such a possibility my brain whirled and I grew dizzy with hope. The next moment I recalled that but last night Roxalanne had told me that he was no nearer than Lyons, and so I put the thought from me, and the hope with it, for, travelling in that leisurely, indolent fashion that was characteristic of his every action, it would be a miracle if His Majesty should reach Toulouse before the week was out, and this but Sunday.

The populace passed on, then seemed to halt, and at last the shouts died down on the noontide air. I went back to my writing, and to wait until from my jailer, when next he should chance to appear, I might learn the meaning of that uproar.

131

An hour perhaps went by, and I had made some progress with my memoir, when my door was opened and the cheery voice of Castelroux greeted me from the threshold.

"Monsieur, I have brought a friend to see you."

I turned in my chair, and one glance at the gentle, comely face and the fair hair of the young man standing beside Castelroux was enough to bring me of a sudden to my feet.

"Mironsac!" I shouted, and sprang towards him with hands outstretched.

But though my joy was great and my surprise profound, greater still was the bewilderment that in Mironsac's face I saw depicted.

"Monsieur de Bardelys!" he exclaimed, and a hundred questions were contained in his astonished eyes.

"Po' Cap de Dieu!" growled his cousin, "I was well advised, it seems, to have brought you."

"But," Mironsac asked his cousin, as he took my hands in his own, "why did you not tell me, Amedée, that it was to Monsieur le Marquis de Bardelys that you were conducting me?"

"Would you have had me spoil so pleasant a surprise?" his cousin demanded.

"Armand," said I, "never was a man more welcome than are you. You are but come in time to save my life."

And then, in answer to his questions, I told him briefly of all that had befallen me since that night in Paris when the wager had been laid, and of how, through the cunning silence of Chatellerault, I was now upon the very threshold of the scaffold. His wrath burst forth at that, and what he said of the Count did me good to hear.

At last I stemmed his invective.

"Let that be for the present, Mironsac," I laughed. "You are here, and you can thwart all Chatellerault's designs by witnessing to my identity before the Keeper of the Seals."

And then of a sudden a doubt closed like a cold hand upon my brain.

I turned to Castelroux.

"Mon Dieu!" I cried. "What if they were to deny me a fresh trial?"

"Deny it you!" he laughed. "They will not be asked to grant you one."

"There will be no need," added Mironsac. "I have but to tell the King – "

"But, my friend," I exclaimed impatiently, "I am to die in the morning!"

"And the King shall be told today – now, at once. I will go to him."

I stared askance a moment; then the thought of the uproar that I had heard recurring to me, "Has the King arrived already?" I exclaimed.

"Naturally, monsieur. How else do I come to be here? I am in His Majesty's train."

At that I grew again impatient. I thought of Roxalanne and of how she must be suffering, and I bethought me that every moment Mironsac now remained in my cell was another moment of torture for that poor child. So I urged him to be gone at once and carry news of my confinement to His Majesty. He obeyed me, and I was left alone once more, to pace up and down in my narrow cell, a prey to an excitement such as I should have thought I had outlived.

At the end of a half-hour Castelroux returned alone.

"Well?" I cried the moment the door opened, and without giving him so much as time to enter. "What news?"

"Mironsac tells me that His Majesty is more overwrought than he has ever seen him. You are to come to the Palace at once. I have an order here from the King."

We went in a coach, and with all privacy, for he informed me that His Majesty desired the affair to be kept secret, having ends of his own to serve thereby.

I was left to wait some moments in an ante-chamber, whilst Castelroux announced me to the King; then I was ushered into a small apartment, furnished very sumptuously in crimson and gold, and evidently set apart for His Majesty's studies or devotions. As I entered, Louis' back was towards me. He was standing – a tall, spare figure in black – leaning against the frame of a window, his head supported on his raised left arm and his eyes intent upon the gardens below.

He remained so until Castelroux had withdrawn and the door had closed again; then, turning suddenly, he confronted me, his back to the light, so that his face was in a shadow that heightened its gloom and wonted weariness.

"Voilà, Monsieur de Bardelys!" was his greeting, and unfriendly. "See the pass to which your disobedience of my commands has brought you."

"I would submit, Sire," I answered, "that I have been brought to it by the incompetence of Your Majesty's judges and the ill-will of others whom Your Majesty honours with too great a confidence, rather than by this same disobedience of mine."

"The one and the other, perhaps," he said more softly. "Though, after all, they appear to have had a very keen nose for a traitor. Come, Bardelys, confess yourself that."

"I? A traitor?"

He shrugged his shoulders, and laughed without any conspicuous mirth.

"Is not a traitor one who runs counter to the wishes of his King? And are you not, therefore, a traitor, whether they call you Lesperon or Bardelys? But there," he ended more softly still, and flinging himself into a chair as he spoke, "I have been so wearied since you left me, Marcel. They have the best intentions in the world, these dullards, and some of them love me even; but they are tiresome all. Even Chatellerault, when he has a fancy for a jest – as in your case – perpetrates it with the grace of a bear, the sprightliness of an elephant."

"Jest?" said I.

"You find it no jest, Marcel? Pardieu, who shall blame you? He would be a man of unhealthy humour that could relish such a pleasantry as that of being sentenced to death. But tell me of it. The whole story, Marcel. I have not heard a story worth the listening to since – since you left us."

"Would it please you, Sire, to send for the Comte de Chatellerault ere I begin?" I asked.

"Chatellerault? No, no." He shook his head whimsically. "Chatellerault has had his laugh already, and, like the ill-mannered dog he is, he has kept it to himself. I think, Marcel, that it is our turn now. I have purposely sent Chatellerault away that he may gain no notion of the catastrophic jest we are preparing him in return."

The words set me in the very best of humours, and to that it may be due that presently, as I warmed to my narrative, I lent it a vigour that drew His Majesty out of his wonted apathy and listlessness. He leaned forward when I told him of my encounter with the dragoons at Mirepoix, and how first I had committed the false step of representing myself to be Lesperon.

Encouraged by his interest, I proceeded, and I told my story with as much piquancy as I was master of, repressing only those slight matters which might reflect upon Monsieur de Lavédan's loyalty, but otherwise dealing frankly with His Majesty, even down to the genuineness of the feelings I entertained for Roxalanne. Often he laughed, more often still he nodded approvingly, in understanding and sympathy, whilst now and then he purred his applause. But towards the end, when I came to the matter of the Tribunal of Toulouse, of how my trial was conducted, and of the part played in it by Chatellerault, his face grew set and hard.

"It is true – all this that you tell me?" he cried harshly.

"As true as the Gospels. If you deem an oath necessary, Sire, I swear by my honour that I have uttered nothing that is false, and that, in connection with Monsieur de Chatellerault, even as I have suppressed nothing, so also have I exaggerated nothing."

"The dastard!" he snapped. "But we will avenge you, Marcel. Never fear it."

Then the trend of his thoughts being changed, he smiled wearily.

"By my faith, you may thank God every night of your worthless life that I came so opportunely to Toulouse, and so may that fair child whose beauty you have limned with such a lover's ardour. Nay, never redden, Marcel. What? At your age, and with such a heavy score of affaires to your credit, has it been left for a simple Languedoc maiden to call a blush to your callous cheek? Ma foi, they say truly that love is a great regenerator, a great rejuvenator!"

I made him no answer other than a sigh, for his words set me thinking, and with thought came a tempering of the gay humour that had pervaded me. Remarking this, and misreading it, he laughed outright.

"There, Marcel, never fear. We will not be rigorous. You have won both the maid and the wager, and, by the Mass, you shall enjoy both."

"Hélas, Sire," I sighed again, "when the lady comes to know of the wager – "

"Waste no time in telling her, Marcel, and cast yourself upon her mercy. Nay, go not with so gloomy a face, my friend. When woman loves, she can be very merciful; leastways, they tell me so."

Then, his thoughts shifting ground once more, he grew stern again.

"But first we have Chatellerault to deal with. What shall we do with him?"

"It is for Your Majesty to decide."

"For me?" he cried, his voice resuming the harshness that was never far from it. "I have a fancy for having gentlemen about me. Think you I will set eyes again upon that dastard? I am already resolved concerning him, but it entered my mind that it might please you to be the instrument of the law for me."

"Me, Sire?"

"Aye, and why not? They say you can play a very deadly sword upon necessity. This is an occasion that demands an exception from our edict. You have my sanction to send the Comte de Chatellerault a challenge. And see that you kill him, Bardelys!" he continued viciously. "For, by the Mass, if you don't, I will! If he escapes your sword, or if he survives such hurt as you may do him, the headsman shall have him. Mordieu! is it for nothing that I am called Louis the Just?"

I stood in thought for a moment. Then –

"If I do this thing, Sire," I ventured, "the world will say of me that I did so to escape the payment I had incurred."

"Fool, you have not incurred it. When a man cheats, does he not forfeit all his rights?"

"That is very true. But the world – "

"Peste!" he snapped impatiently, "you are beginning to weary me, Marcel – and all the world does that so excellently that it needs not your collaboration. Go your ways, man, and do as you elect. But take my sanction to slay this fellow Chatellerault, and I shall be the better pleased if you avail yourself of it. He is lodged at the Auberge Royale, where probably you will find him at present. Now, go. I have more justice to dispense in this rebellious province."

I paused a moment.

"Shall I not resume my duties near Your Majesty?"

He pondered a moment, then he smiled in his weary way.

"It would please me to have you, for these creatures are so dismally dull, all of them. Je m'ennuie tellement, Marcel!" he sighed. "Ough! But, no, my friend, I do not doubt you would be as dull as any of them at present. A man in love is the weariest and most futile thing in all this weary, futile world. What shall I do with your body what time your soul is at Lavédan? I doubt me you are in haste to get you there. So go, Marcel. Get you wed, and live out your amorous intoxication; marriage is the best antidote. When that is done, return to me."

"That will be never, Sire," I answered slyly.

"Say you so, Master Cupid Bardelys?" And he combed his beard reflectively. "Be not too sure. There have been other passions – aye, as great as yours – yet have they staled. But you waste my time. Go, Marcel; you are excused your duties by me for as long as your own affairs shall hold you elsewhere – for as long as you please. We are here upon a gloomy business – as you know. There are my cousin

Montmorency and the others to be dealt with, and we are holding no levées, countenancing no revels. But come to me when you will, and I will see you. Adieu!"

I murmured my thanks, and very deep and sincere were they. Then, having kissed his hand, I left him.

Louis XIII is a man who lacks not maligners. Of how history may come to speak of him it is not mine to hazard. But this I can say, that I, at least, did never find him other than a just and kindly master, an upright gentleman, capricious at times and wilful, as must inevitably be the case with such spoilt children of fortune as are princes, but of lofty ideals and high principles. It was his worst fault that he was always tired, and through that everlasting weariness he came to entrust the determining of most affairs to His Eminence. Hence has it resulted that the censure for many questionable acts of his reign, which were the work of my Lord Cardinal, has recoiled upon my august master's head.

But to me, with all the faults that may be assigned him, he was ever Louis the Just, and wherever his name be mentioned in my hearing, I bare my head.

# Chapter 14

## Eavesdropping

I turned it over in my mind, after I had left the King's presence, whether or not I should visit with my own hands upon Chatellerault the punishment he had so fully earned. That I would have gone about the task rejoicing you may readily imagine; but there was that accursed wager, and – to restrain me – the thought of how such an action might be construed into an evasion of its consequences.

Better a thousand times that His Majesty should order his arrest and deal with him for his attempted perversion of justice to the service of his own vile ends. The charge of having abused his trust as King's Commissioner to the extent of seeking to do murder through the channels of the Tribunal was one that could not fail to have fatal results for him – as, indeed, the King had sworn.

That was the position of affairs as it concerned Chatellerault, the world, and me. But the position must also be considered as it concerned Roxalanne, and deeply, indeed, did I so consider it. Much pondering brought me again to the conclusion that until I had made the only atonement in my power, the only atonement that would leave me with clean hands, I must not again approach her.

Whether Chatellerault had cheated or not could not affect the question as it concerned Mademoiselle and me. If I paid the wager – whether in honour bound to do so or not – I might then go to her, impoverished, it is true, but at least with no suspicion attaching to my suit of any ulterior object other than that of winning Roxalanne herself.

I could then make confession, and surely the fact that I had paid where clearly there was no longer any need to pay must earn me forgiveness and afford proof of the sincerity of my passion.

Upon such a course, then, did I decide, and, with this end in view, I took my way towards the Auberge Royale, where His Majesty had told me that the Count was lodged. It was my purpose to show myself fully aware of the treacherous and unworthy part he had played at the very inception of the affair, and that if I chose to consider the wager lost it was that I might the more honestly win the lady.

Upon inquiring at the hostelry for Monsieur de Chatellerault I was informed by the servant I addressed that he was within, but that at the moment he had a visitor. I replied that I would wait, and demanded a private room, since I desired to avoid meeting any Court acquaintances who might chance into the auberge before I had seen the Count.

My apparel at the moment may not have been all that could have been desired, but when a gentleman's rearing has taken place amid an army of servitors to minister to his every wish, he is likely to have acquired an air that is wont to win him obedience. With all celerity was I ushered into a small chamber, opening on the one side upon the common room, and being divided on the other by the thinnest of wooden partitions from the adjoining apartment.

Here, the landlord having left me, I disposed myself to wait, and here I did a thing I would not have believed myself capable of doing, a thing I cannot think of without blushing to this very day. In short, I played the eavesdropper – I, Marcel de Saint-Pol de Bardelys.

Yet, if you who read and are nice-minded shudder at this confession, or, worse still, shrug your shoulders in contempt, with the reflection that such former conduct of mine as I have avowed had already partly disposed you against surprise at this, I do but ask that you measure my sin by my temptation, and think honestly whether in my position you might not yourselves have fallen. Aye – be you never so noble and high-principled – I make bold to say that you had done no less, for the voice that penetrated to my ears was that of Roxalanne de Lavédan.

"I sought an audience with the King," she was saying, "but I could not gain his presence. They told me that he was holding no levées, and that he refused to see anyone not introduced by one of those having the private entrée."

"And so," answered the voice of Chatellerault, in tones that were perfectly colourless, "you come to me that I may present you to his Majesty?"

"You have guessed it, Monsieur le Comte. You are the only gentleman of His Majesty's suite with whom I can claim acquaintance – however slight – and, moreover, it is well known how high you stand in his royal favour. I was told that they that have a boon to crave can find no better sponsor."

"Had you gone to the King, mademoiselle," said he, "had you gained audience, he would have directed you to make your appeal to me. I am his Commissioner in Languedoc, and the prisoners attainted with high treason are my property."

"Why then, monsieur," she cried in an eager voice, that set my pulses throbbing, "you'll not deny me the boon I crave? You'll not deny me his life?"

There was a short laugh from Chatellerault, and I could hear the deliberate fall of his feet as he paced the chamber.

"Mademoiselle, mademoiselle, you must not overrate my powers. You must not forget that I am the slave of Justice. You may be asking more than is in my power to grant. What can you advance to show that I should be justified in proceeding as you wish?"

"Hélas, monsieur, I can advance nothing but my prayers and the assurance that a hideous mistake is being made."

"What is your interest in this Monsieur de Lesperon?"

"He is not Monsieur de Lesperon," she cried.

"But, since you cannot tell me who he is, you must be content that we speak of him at least as Lesperon," said he, and I could imagine the evil grin with which he would accompany the words.

141

The better that you may appreciate that which followed, let me here impart to you the suspicions which were already sinking into my mind, to be changed later into absolute convictions touching the course the Count intended to pursue concerning me. The sudden arrival of the King had thrown him into some measure of panic, and no longer daring to carry out his plans concerning me, it was his object, I made no doubt, to set me at liberty that very evening. Ere he did so, however, and presuming upon my ignorance of His Majesty's presence in Toulouse, Chatellerault would of a certainty have bound me down by solemn promise – making that promise the price of my liberty and my life – to breathe no word of my captivity and trial. No doubt, his cunning brain would have advanced me plausible and convincing reasons so to engage myself.

He had not calculated upon Castelroux, nor that the King should already have heard of my detention. Now that Roxalanne came to entreat him to do that which already he saw himself forced to do, he turned his attention to the profit that he might derive from her interestedness on my behalf. I could guess also something of the jealous rage that must fill him at this signal proof of my success with her, and already I anticipated, I think, the bargain that he would drive.

"Tell me, then," he was repeating, "what is your interest in this gentleman?"

There was a silence. I could imagine her gentle face clouded with the trouble that sprang from devising an answer to that question; I could picture her innocent eyes cast down, her delicate cheeks pinked by some measure of shame, as at last, in a low, stifled voice, the four words broke from her, "I love him, monsieur."

Ah, Dieu! To hear her confess it so! If yesternight it had stirred me to the very depths of my poor, sinful soul to have her say so much to me, how infinitely more did it not affect me to overhear this frank avowal of it to another! And to think that she was undergoing all this to the end that she might save me!

From Chatellerault there came an impatient snort in answer, and his feet again smote the floor as he resumed the pacing that for a moment he had suspended. Then followed a pause, a long silence, broken only by the Count's restless walking to and fro. At last, "Why are you silent, monsieur?" she asked in a trembling voice.

"Hélas, mademoiselle, I can do nothing. I had feared that it might be thus with you; and, if I put the question, it was in the hope that I was wrong."

"But he, monsieur?" she exclaimed in anguish. "What of him?"

"Believe me, mademoiselle, if it lay in my power I would save him were he never so guilty, if only that I might spare you sorrow."

He spoke with tender regret, foul hypocrite that he was!

"Oh, no, no!" she cried, and her voice was of horror and despair. "You do not mean that – " She stopped short; and then, after a pause, it was the Count who finished the sentence for her.

"I mean, mademoiselle, that this Lesperon must die!"

You will marvel that I let her suffer so, that I did not break down the partition with my hands and strike that supple gentleman dead at her feet in atonement for the anguish he was causing her. But I had a mind to see how far he would drive this game he was engaged upon.

Again there was a spell of silence, and at last, when Mademoiselle spoke, I was amazed at the calm voice in which she addressed him, marvelling at the strength and courage of one so frail and childlike to behold.

"Is your determination, indeed, irrevocable, monsieur? If you have any pity, will you not at least let me bear my prayers and my tears to the King?"

"It would avail you nothing. As I have said, the Languedoc rebels are in my hands." He paused as if to let those words sink well into her understanding; then, "If I were to set him at liberty, mademoiselle, if I were to spirit him out of prison in the night, bribing his jailers to keep silent and binding him by oath to quit France at once and never to betray me, I should be, myself, guilty of high treason. Thus alone could the thing be done, and you will see, mademoiselle, that by doing it I should be endangering my neck."

There was an ineffable undercurrent of meaning in his words – an intangible suggestion that he might be bribed to do all this to which he so vaguely alluded.

"I understand, monsieur," she answered, choking – "I understand that it would be too much to ask of you."

"It would be much, mademoiselle," he returned quickly, and his voice was now subdued and invested with an odd quiver. "But nothing that your lips might ask of me and that it might lie in the power of mortal man to do, would be too much!"

"You mean?" she cried, a catch in her breath. Had she guessed – as I, without sight of her face, had guessed – what was to follow? My gorge was rising fast. I clenched my hands, and by an effort I restrained myself to learn that I had guessed aright.

"Some two months ago," he said, "I journeyed to Lavédan, as you may remember. I saw you, mademoiselle – for a brief while only, it is true – and ever since I have seen nothing else but you." His voice went a shade lower, and passion throbbed in his words.

She, too, perceived it, for the grating of a chair informed me that she had risen.

"Not now, monsieur – not now!" she exclaimed. "This is not the season. I beg of you think of my desolation."

"I do, mademoiselle, and I respect your grief, and, with all my heart, believe me, I share it. Yet this is the season, and if you have this man's interests at heart, you will hear me to the end."

Through all the imperiousness of his tone an odd note of respect – real or assumed – was sounding.

"If you suffer, mademoiselle, believe me that I suffer also, and if I make you suffer more by what I say, I beg that you will think how what you have said, how the very motive of your presence here, has made me suffer. Do you know, mademoiselle, what it is to be torn by jealousy? Can you imagine it? If you can, you can imagine also something of the torture I endured when you confessed to me that you loved this Lesperon, when you interceded for his life. Mademoiselle, I love you – with all my heart and soul I love you. I have loved you, I think, since the first moment of our meeting at Lavédan, and to win you there is no risk that I would not take, no danger that I would not brave."

"Monsieur, I implore you – "

"Hear me out, mademoiselle!" he cried. Then in quieter voice he proceeded: "At present you love this Monsieur de Lesperon – "

"I shall always love him! Always, monsieur!"

"Wait, wait, wait!" he exclaimed, annoyed by her interruption. "If he were to live, and you were to wed him and be daily in his company, I make no doubt your love might endure. But if he were to die, or if he were to pass into banishment and you were to see him no more, you would mourn him for a little while, and then – Hélas! it is the way of men and women – time would heal first your sorrow, then your heart."

"Never, monsieur – oh, never!"

"I am older, child, than you are. I know. At present you are anxious to save his life; anxious because you love him, and also because you betrayed him, and you would not have his death upon your conscience." He paused a moment; then raising his voice, "Mademoiselle," said he, "I offer you your lover's life."

"Monsieur, monsieur!" cried the poor child, "I knew you were good! I knew – "

"A moment! Do not misapprehend me. I do not say that I give it – I offer it."

"But the difference?"

"That if you would have it, mademoiselle, you must buy it. I have said that for you I would brave all dangers. To save your lover, I brave the scaffold. If I am betrayed, or if the story transpire, my head will assuredly fall in the place of Lesperon's. This I will risk, mademoiselle – I will do it gladly – if you will promise to become my wife when it is done."

There was a moan from Roxalanne, then silence; then – "Oh, monsieur, you are pitiless! What bargain is this that you offer me?"

"A fair one, surely," said that son of hell, "a very fair one. The risk of my life against your hand in marriage."

"If you – if you truly loved me as you say, monsieur," she reasoned, "you would serve me without asking guerdon."

"In any other thing I would. But is it fair to ask a man who is racked by love of you to place another in your arms, and that at the risk of his own life? Ah, mademoiselle, I am but a man, and I am subject to human weaknesses. If you will consent, this Lesperon shall go free, but you must see him no more; and I will carry my consideration so far as to give you six months in which to overcome your sorrow, ere I present myself to you again to urge my suit."

"And if I refuse, monsieur?"

He sighed.

"To the value which I set upon my life you must add my very human jealousy. From such a combination what can you hope for?"

"You mean, in short, that he must die?"

"Tomorrow," was that infernal cheat's laconic answer.

They were silent a little while, then she fell a-sobbing.

"Be pitiful, monsieur! Have mercy if you, indeed, love me. Oh, he must not die! I cannot, I dare not, let him die! Save him, monsieur, and I will pray for you every night of my life; I will pray for you to our Holy Mother as I am now praying to you for him."

Lived there the man to resist that innocent, devout appeal? Lived there one who in answer to such gentle words of love and grief could obtrude his own coarse passions? It seems there did, for all he answered was, "You know the price, child."

"And God pity me! I must pay it. I must, for if he dies I shall have his blood upon my conscience!" Then she checked her grief, and her voice grew almost stern in the restraint she set upon herself.

"If I give you my promise to wed you hereafter – say in six months' time – what proof will you afford me that he who is detained under the name of Lesperon shall go free?"

I caught the sound of something very like a gasp from the Count.

"Remain in Toulouse until tomorrow, and tonight ere he departs he shall come to take his leave of you. Are you content?"

"Be it so, monsieur," she answered.

Then at last I leapt to my feet. I could endure no more. You may marvel that I had had the heart to endure so much, and to have so let her suffer that I might satisfy myself how far this scoundrel Chatellerault would drive his trickster's bargain.

A more impetuous man would have beaten down the partition, or shouted to her through it the consolation that Chatellerault's bargain was no bargain at all, since I was already at large. And that is where a more impetuous man would have acted upon instinct more wisely than did I upon reason. Instead, I opened the door, and, crossing the common room, I flung myself down a passage that I thought must lead to the chamber in which they were closeted. But in this I was at fault, and ere I had come upon a waiter and been redirected some precious moments were lost. He led me back through the common room to a door opening upon another corridor. He pushed it wide, and I came suddenly face to face with Chatellerault, still flushed from his recent contest.

"You here!" he gasped, his jaw falling, and his cheeks turning pale, as well they might; for all that he could not dream I had overheard his bargaining.

"We will go back, if you please, Monsieur le Comte," said I.

"Back where?" he asked stupidly.

"Back to Mademoiselle. Back to the room you have just quitted."

And none too gently I pushed him into the corridor again, and so, in the gloom, I missed the expression of his face.

"She is not there," said he.

I laughed shortly.

"Nevertheless, we will go back," I insisted.

And so I had my way, and we gained the room where his infamous traffic had been held. Yet for once he spoke the truth. She was no longer there.

"Where is she?" I demanded angrily.

147

"Gone," he answered; and when I protested that I had not met her, "You would not have a lady go by way of the public room, would you?" he demanded insolently. "She left by the side door into the courtyard."

"That being so, Monsieur le Comte," said I quietly, "I will have a little talk with you before going after her." And I carefully closed the door.

# Chapter 15

# M. de Chatellerault is Angry

Within the room Chatellerault and I faced each other in silence. And how vastly changed were the circumstances since our last meeting!

The disorder that had stamped itself upon his countenance when first he had beheld me still prevailed. There was a lowering, sullen look in his eyes and a certain displacement of their symmetry which was peculiar to them when troubled.

Although a cunning plotter and a scheming intriguer in his own interests, Chatellerault, as I have said before, was not by nature a quick man. His wits worked slowly, and he needed leisure to consider a situation and his actions therein ere he was in a position to engage with it.

"Monsieur le Comte," quoth I ironically, "I make you my compliments upon your astuteness and the depth of your schemes, and my condolences upon the little accident owing to which I am here, and in consequence of which your pretty plans are likely to miscarry."

He threw back his great head like a horse that feels the curb, and his smouldering eyes looked up at me balefully. Then his sensuous lips parted in scorn.

"How much do you know?" he demanded with sullen contempt.

"I have been in that room for the half of an hour," I answered, rapping the partition with my knuckles.

"The dividing wall, as you will observe, is thin, and I heard everything that passed between you and Mademoiselle de Lavédan."

"So that Bardelys, known as the Magnificent; Bardelys the mirror of chivalry; Bardelys the arbiter elegantiarum of the Court of France, is no better, it seems, than a vulgar spy."

If he sought by that word to anger me, he failed.

"Lord Count," I answered him very quietly, "you are of an age to know that the truth alone has power to wound. I was in that room by accident, and when the first words of your conversation reached me I had not been human had I not remained and strained my ears to catch every syllable you uttered. For the rest, let me ask you, my dear Chatellerault, since when have you become so nice that you dare cast it at a man that he has been eavesdropping?"

"You are obscure, monsieur. What is it that you suggest?"

"I am signifying that when a man stands unmasked for a cheat, a liar, and a thief, his own character should give him concern enough to restrain him from strictures upon that of another."

A red flush showed through the tan of his skin, then faded and left him livid – a very evil sight, as God lives. He flung his heavily-feathered hat upon the table, and carried his hand to his hilt.

"God's blood!" he cried. "You shall answer me for this."

I shook my head and smiled; but I made no sign of drawing.

"Monsieur, we must talk a while. I think that you had better."

He raised his sullen eyes to mine. Perhaps the earnest impressiveness of my tones prevailed. Be that as it may, his half-drawn sword was thrust back with a click, and, "What have you to say?" he asked.

"Be seated." I motioned him to a chair by the table and when he had taken it I sat down opposite to him. Taking up a quill, I dipped it in the ink-horn that stood by, and drew towards me a sheet of paper.

"When you lured me into the wager touching Mademoiselle de Lavédan," said I calmly, "you did so, counting upon certain circumstances, of which you alone had knowledge, that should render impossible the urging of my suit. That, Monsieur le Comte, was undeniably the action of a cheat. Was it not?"

"Damnation!" he roared, and would have risen, but, my hand upon his arm, I restrained him and pressed him back into his chair.

"By a sequence of fortuitous circumstances," I pursued, "it became possible for me to circumvent the obstacle upon which you had based your calculations. Those same circumstances led later to my being arrested in error and in place of another man. You discovered how I had contravened the influence upon which you counted; you trembled to see how the unexpected had befriended me, and you began to fear for your wager.

"What did you do? Seeing me arraigned before you in your quality as King's Commissioner, you pretended to no knowledge of me; you became blind to my being any but Lesperon the rebel, and you sentenced me to death in his place, so that being thus definitely removed I should be unable to carry out my undertaking, and my lands should consequently pass into your possession. That, monsieur, was at once the act of a thief and a murderer. Wait, monsieur; restrain yourself until I shall have done. Today again fortune comes to my rescue. Again you see me slipping from your grasp, and you are in despair. Then, in the eleventh hour, Mademoiselle de Lavédan comes to you to plead for my life. By that act she gives you the most ample proof that your wager is lost. What would a gentleman, a man of honour, have done under these circumstances?

"What did you do? You seized that last chance; you turned it to the best account; you made this poor girl buy something from you; you made her sell herself to you for nothing – pretending that your nothing was a something of great value. What term shall we apply to that? To say that you cheated again seems hardly adequate."

"By God, Bardelys!"

"Wait!" I thundered, looking him straight between the eyes, so that again he sank back, cowed. Then resuming the calm with which hitherto I had addressed him, "Your cupidity," said I, "your greed for the estates of Bardelys, and your jealousy and thirst to see me impoverished and so ousted from my position at Court, to leave you supreme in His Majesty's favour, have put you to strange shifts for a gentleman, Chatellerault. Yet, wait."

And, dipping my pen in the ink-horn, I began to write. I was conscious of his eyes upon me, and I could imagine his surmisings and bewildered speculations as my pen scratched rapidly across the paper. In a few moments it was done, and I tossed the pen aside.

I took up the sandbox.

"When a man cheats, Monsieur le Comte, and is detected, he is invariably adjudged the loser of his stakes. On that count alone everything that you have is now mine by rights." Again I had to quell an interruption. "But if we waive that point, and proceed upon the supposition that you have dealt fairly and honourably with me, why, then, monsieur, you have still sufficient evidence – the word of Mademoiselle, herself, in fact – that I have won my wager.

"And so, if we take this, the most lenient view of the case" – I paused to sprinkle the sand over my writing – "your estates are still lost to you, and pass to be my property."

"Do they, by God?" he roared, unable longer to restrain himself, and leaping to his feet. "You have done, have you not? You have said all that you can call to mind? You have flung insults and epithets at me enough to earn the cutting of a dozen throats. You have dubbed me cheat and thief" – he choked in his passion – "until you have had your fill – is it not so? Now, listen to me, Master Bardelys, master spy, master buffoon, master masquerader! What manner of proceeding was yours to go to Lavédan under a false name? How call you that? Was that, perhaps, not cheating?"

"No, monsieur, it was not," I answered quietly. "It was in the terms of your challenge that I was free to go to Lavédan in what guise I listed, employing what wiles I pleased. But let that be," I ended, and, creasing the paper, I poured the sand back into the box, and dusted the document. "The point is hardly worth discussing at this time of day. If not one way, why, then, in another, your wager is lost."

"Is it?" He set his arms akimbo and eyed me derisively, his thick-set frame planted squarely before me. "You are satisfied that it is so? Quite satisfied, eh?" He leered in my face. "Why, then, Monsieur le

Marquis, we will see whether a few inches of steel will win it back for me." And once more his hand flew to his hilt.

Rising, I flung the document I had accomplished upon the table.

"Glance first at that," said I.

He stopped to look at me in inquiry, my manner sowing so great a curiosity in him that his passion was all scattered before it. Then he stepped up to the table and lifted the paper. As he read, his hand shook, amazement dilated his eyes and furrowed his brow.

"What – what does it signify?" he gasped.

"It signifies that, although fully conscious of having won, I prefer to acknowledge that I have lost. I make over to you thus my estates of Bardelys, because, monsieur, I have come to realize that that wager was an infamous one – one in which a gentleman should have had no part – and the only atonement I can make to myself, my honour, and the lady whom we insulted – is that."

"I do not understand," he complained.

"I apprehend your difficulty, Comte. The point is a nice one. But understand at least that my Picardy estates are yours. Only, monsieur, you will be well advised to make your will forthwith, for you are not destined, yourself, to enjoy them."

He looked at me, his glance charged with inquiry.

"His Majesty," I continued, in answer to his glance, "is ordering your arrest for betraying the trust he had reposed in you and for perverting the ends of justice to do your own private murdering."

"Mon Dieu!" he cried, falling of a sudden unto a most pitiful affright. "The King knows?"

"Knows?" I laughed. "In the excitement of these other matters you have forgotten to ask how I come to be at liberty. I have been to the King, monsieur, and I have told him what has taken place here at Toulouse, and how I was to have gone to the block tomorrow!"

"Scélérat!" he cried. "You have ruined me!" Rage and grief were blent in his accents. He stood before me, livid of face and with hands clenching and unclenching at his sides.

"Did you expect me to keep such a matter silent? Even had I been so inclined it had not been easy, for His Majesty had questions to ask me. From what the King said, monsieur, you may count upon mounting the scaffold in my stead. So be advised, and make your will without delay, if you would have your heirs enjoy my Picardy chateau."

I have seen terror and anger distort men's countenances, but never have I seen aught to compare with the disorder of Chatellerault at that moment. He stamped and raved and fumed. He poured forth a thousand ordures of speech in his frenzy; he heaped insults upon me and imprecations upon the King, whose lapdog he pronounced me. His short, stout frame was quivering with passion and fear, his broad face distorted by his hideous grimaces of rage. And then, while yet his ravings were in full flow, the door opened, and in stepped the airy Chevalier de Saint-Eustache.

He stood still, amazed, beneath the lintel – marvelling to see all this anger, and abashed at beholding me. His sudden appearance reminded me that I had last seen him at Grenade in the Count's company, on the day of my arrest. The surprise it had occasioned me now returned upon seeing him so obviously and intimately seeking Chatellerault.

The Count turned on him in his anger.

"Well, popinjay?" he roared. "What do you want with me?"

"Monsieur le Comte!" cried the other, in blent indignation and reproach.

"You will perceive that you are come inopportunely," I put in. "Monsieur de Chatellerault is not quite himself."

But my speech again drew his attention to my presence; and the wonder grew in his eyes at finding me there, for to him I was still Lesperon the rebel, and he marvelled naturally that I should be at large.

Then in the corridor there was a sound of steps and voices, and as I turned I beheld in the doorway, behind Saint-Eustache, the faces of Castelroux, Mironsac, and my old acquaintance, the babbling, irresponsible buffoon, La Fosse. From Mironsac he had heard of my presence in Toulouse, and, piloted by Castelroux, they were both come to seek me out. I'll swear it was not thus they had looked to find me.

They pushed their way into the room, impelling Saint-Eustache forward, and there were greetings exchanged and felicitations, whilst Chatellerault, curbing his disorder, drew the Chevalier into a corner of the room, and stood there listening to him.

At length I heard the Count exclaim –

"Do as you please, Chevalier. If you have interests of your own to serve, serve them. As for myself – I am past being interested."

"But why, monsieur?" the Chevalier inquired.

"Why?" echoed Chatellerault, his ferocity welling up again. Then, swinging round, he came straight at me, as a bull makes a charge.

"Monsieur de Bardelys!" he blazed.

"Bardelys!" gasped Saint-Eustache in the background.

"What now?" I inquired coldly, turning from my friends.

"All that you said may be true, and I may be doomed, but I swear before God that you shall not go unpunished."

"I think, monsieur, that you run a grave risk of perjuring yourself!" I laughed.

"You shall render me satisfaction ere we part!" he cried.

"If you do not deem that paper satisfaction enough, then, monsieur, forgive me, but your greed transcends all possibility of being ever satisfied."

"The devil take your paper and your estates! What shall they profit me when I am dead?"

"They may profit your heirs," I suggested.

"How shall that profit me?"

"That is a riddle that I cannot pretend to elucidate."

"You laugh, you knave!" he snorted. Then, with an abrupt change of manner, "You do not lack for friends," said he. "Beg one of these gentlemen to act for you, and if you are a man of honour let us step out into the yard and settle the matter."

I shook my head.

"I am so much a man of honour as to be careful with whom I cross steel. I prefer to leave you to His Majesty's vengeance; his headsman may be less particular than am I. No, monsieur, on the whole, I do not think that I can fight you."

His face grew a shade paler. It became grey; the jaw was set, and the eyes were more out of symmetry than I had ever seen them. Their glance approached what is known in Italy as the *mal'occhio*, and to protect themselves against the baneful influences of which men carry charms. A moment he stood so, eyeing me. Then, coming a step nearer –

"You do not think that you can fight me, eh? You do not think it? Pardieu! How shall I make you change your mind? To the insult of words you appear impervious. You imagine your courage above dispute because by a lucky accident you killed La Vertoile some years ago and the fame of it has attached to you." In the intensity of his anger he was breathing heavily, like a man overburdened. "You have been living ever since by the reputation which that accident gave you. Let us see if you can die by it, Monsieur de Bardelys." And, leaning forward, he struck me on the breast, so suddenly and so powerfully – for he was a man of abnormal strength – that I must have fallen but that La Fosse caught me in his arms.

"Kill him!" lisped the classic-minded fool. "Play Theseus to this bull of Marathon."

Chatellerault stood back, his hands on his hips, his head inclined towards his right shoulder, and an insolent leer of expectancy upon his face.

"Will that resolve you?" he sneered.

"I will meet you," I answered, when I had recovered breath. "But I swear that I shall not help you to escape the headsman."

He laughed harshly.

"Do I not know it?" he mocked. "How shall killing you help me to escape? Come, messieurs, sortons. At once!"

"Sor," I answered shortly; and thereupon we crowded from the room, and went pêle-mêle down the passage to the courtyard at the back.

# Chapter 16

## Swords

La Fosse led the way with me, his arm through mine, swearing that he would be my second. He had such a stomach for a fight, had this irresponsible, irrepressible rhymester, that it mounted to the heights of passion with him, and when I mentioned, in answer to a hint dropped in connection with the edict, that I had the King's sanction for this combat, he was nearly mad with joy.

"Blood of La Fosse!" was his oath. "The honour to stand by you shall be mine, my Bardelys! You owe it me, for am I not in part to blame for all this ado? Nay, you'll not deny me. That gentleman yonder, with the wild-cat moustaches and a name like a Gascon oath – that cousin of Mironsac's, I mean – has the flair of a fight in his nostrils, and a craving to be in it. But you'll grant me the honour, will you not? Pardieu! It will earn me a place in history."

"Or the graveyard," quoth I, by way of cooling his ardour.

"Peste! What an augury!" Then, with a laugh: "But," he added, indicating Saint-Eustache, "that long, lean saint – I forget of what he is patron – hardly wears a murderous air."

To win peace from him, I promised that he should stand by me. But the favour lost much of its value in his eyes when presently I added that I did not wish the seconds to engage, since the matter was of so very personal a character.

157

Mironsac and Castelroux, assisted by Saint-Eustache, closed the heavy porte-cochère, and so shut us in from the observation of passers-by. The clanging of those gates brought the landlord and a couple of his knaves, and we were subjected to the prayers and intercessions, to the stormings and ravings that are ever the prelude of a stable-yard fight, but which invariably end, as these ended, in the landlord's withdrawal to run for help to the nearest corps-de-garde.

"Now, my myrmillones," cried La Fosse in bloodthirsty jubilation, "to work before the host returns."

"Po' Cap de Dieu!" growled Castelroux, "is this a time for jests, master joker?"

"Jests?" I heard him retorting, as he assisted me to doff my doublet.

"Do I jest? Diable! you Gascons are a slow-witted folk! I have a taste for allegory, my friend, but that never yet was accounted so low a thing as jesting."

At last we were ready, and I shifted the whole of my attention to the short, powerful figure of Chatellerault as he advanced upon me, stripped to the waist, his face set and his eyes full of stern resolve. Despite his low stature, and the breadth of frame which argue sluggish motion, there was something very formidable about the Count. His bared arms were great masses of muscular flesh, and if his wrist were but half as supple as it looked powerful, that alone should render him a dangerous antagonist.

Yet I had no qualm of fear, no doubt, even, touching the issue. Not that I was an habitual ferrailleur. As I have indicated, I had fought but one man in all my life. Nor yet am I of those who are said to know no fear under any circumstances. Such men are not truly brave; they are stupid and unimaginative, in proof of which I will advance the fact that you may incite a timid man to deeds of reckless valour by drugging him with wine. But this is by the way.

It may be that the very regular fencing practice that in Paris I was wont to take may so have ordered my mind that the fact of meeting unbaited steel had little power to move me.

Be that as it may, I engaged the Count without a tremor either of the flesh or of the spirit. I was resolved to wait and let him open the play, that I might have an opportunity of measuring his power and seeing how best I might dispose of him. I was determined to do him no hurt, and to leave him, as I had sworn, to the headsman; and so, either by pressure or by seizure, it was my aim to disarm him.

But on his side also he entered upon the duel with all caution and wariness. From his rage I had hoped for a wild, angry rush that should afford me an easy opportunity of gaining my ends with him.

Not so, however. Now that he came with steel to defend his life and to seek mine, he appeared to have realized the importance of having keen wits to guide his hand; and so he put his anger from him, and emerged calm and determined from his whilom disorder.

Some preliminary passes we made from the first engagement in the lines of tierce, each playing warily for an opening, yet neither of us giving ground or betraying haste or excitement. Now his blade slithered on mine with a ceaseless tremor; his eyes watched mine from under lowering brows, and with knees bent he crouched like a cat making ready for a spring. Then it came. Sudden as lightning was his disengage; he darted under my guard, then over it, then back and under it again, and stretching out in the lunge – his double-feint completed – he straightened his arm to drive home the botte.

But with a flying point I cleared his blade out of the line of my body. There had been two sharp tinkles of our meeting swords, and now Chatellerault stood at his fullest stretch, the half of his steel past and behind me, for just a fraction of time completely at my mercy. Yet I was content to stand, and never move my blade from his until he had recovered and we were back in our first position once again.

I heard the deep bass of Castelroux's "Mordieu!" the sharp gasp of fear from Saint-Eustache, who already in imagination beheld his friend stretched lifeless on the ground, and the cry of mortification from La Fosse as the Count recovered. But I heeded these things little. As I have said, to kill the Count was not my object. It had been wise, perhaps, in Chatellerault to have appreciated that fact; but he did not. From the manner in which he now proceeded to press me, I was assured that he set his having recovered guard to slowness on my part, never thinking of the speed that had been necessary to win myself such an opening as I had obtained.

My failure to run him through in that moment of jeopardy inspired him with a contempt of my swordplay. This he now made plain by the recklessness with which he fenced, in his haste to have done ere we might chance to be interrupted. Of this recklessness I suddenly availed myself to make an attempt at disarming him. I turned aside a vicious thrust by a close – a dangerously close – parry, and whilst in the act of encircling his blade I sought by pressure to carry it out of his hand. I was within an ace of succeeding, yet he avoided me, and doubled back.

He realized then, perhaps, that I was not quite so contemptible an antagonist as he had been imagining, and he went back to his earlier and more cautious tactics. Then I changed my plans. I simulated an attack, and drove him hard for some moments. Strong he was, but there were advantages of reach and suppleness with me, and even these advantages apart, had I aimed at his life, I could have made short work of him. But the game I played was fraught with perils to myself, and once I was in deadly danger, and as near death from the sword as a man may go and live. My attack had lured him, as I desired that it should, into making a riposte. He did so, and as his blade twisted round mine and came slithering at me, I again carried it off by encircling it, and again I exerted pressure to deprive him of it. But this time I was farther from success than before. He laughed at the attempt, as with a suddenness that I had been far from expecting he disengaged again, and his point darted like a snake upwards at my throat.

I parried that thrust, but I only parried it when it was within some three inches of my neck, and even as I turned it aside it missed me as narrowly as it might without tearing my skin. The imminence of the peril had been such that, as we mutually recovered, I found a cold sweat bathing me.

After that, I resolved to abandon the attempt to disarm him by pressure, and I turned my attention to drawing him into a position that might lend itself to seizure. But even as I was making up my mind to this – we were engaged in sixte at the time – I saw a sudden chance. His point was held low while he watched me; so low that his arm was uncovered and my point was in line with it. To see the opening, to estimate it, and to take my resolve was all the work of a fraction of a second. The next instant I had straightened my elbow, my blade shot out in a lightning stroke and transfixed his sword-arm.

There was a yell of pain, followed by a deep growl of fury, as, wounded but not vanquished, the enraged Count caught his falling sword in his left hand, and whilst my own blade was held tight in the bone of his right arm, he sought to run me through. I leapt quickly aside, and then, before he could renew the attempt, my friends had fallen upon him and wrenched his sword from his hand and mine from his arm.

It would ill have become me to taunt a man in his sorry condition, else might I now have explained to him what I had meant when I had promised to leave him for the headsman even though I did consent to fight him.

Mironsac, Castelroux, and La Fosse stood babbling around me, but I paid no heed either to Castelroux's patois or to La Fosse's misquotations of classic authors. The combat had been protracted, and the methods I had pursued had been of a very exhausting nature.

I leaned now against the porte-cochère, and mopped myself vigorously.

Then Saint-Eustache, who was engaged in binding up his principal's arm, called to La Fosse.

I followed my second with my eyes as he went across to Chatellerault.

The Count stood white, his lips compressed, no doubt from the pain his arm was causing him. Then his voice floated across to me as he addressed La Fosse.

"You will do me the favour, monsieur, to inform your friend that this was no first blood combat, but one à outrance. I fence as well with my left arm as with my right, and if Monsieur de Bardelys will do me the honour to engage again, I shall esteem it."

La Fosse bowed and came over with the message that already we had heard.

"I fought," said I in answer, "in a spirit very different from that by which Monsieur de Chatellerault appears to have been actuated. He made it incumbent upon me to afford proof of my courage. That proof I have afforded; I decline to do more. Moreover, as Monsieur de Chatellerault himself must perceive, the light is failing us, and in a few minutes it will be too dark for sword-play."

"In a few minutes there will be need for none, monsieur," shouted Chatellerault, to save time. He was boastful to the end.

"Here, monsieur, in any case, come those who will resolve the question," I answered, pointing to the door of the inn.

As I spoke, the landlord stepped into the yard, followed by an officer and a half-dozen soldiers. These were no ordinary keepers of the peace, but musketeers of the guard, and at sight of them I knew that their business was not to interrupt a duel, but to arrest my erstwhile opponent upon a much graver charge.

The officer advanced straight to Chatellerault.

"In the King's name, Monsieur le Comte," said he. "I demand your sword."

It may be that at bottom I was still a man of soft heart, unfeeling cynic though they accounted me; for upon remarking the misery and gloom that spread upon Chatellerault's face I was sorry for him, notwithstanding the much that he had schemed against me. Of what his fate would be he could have no shadow of doubt. He knew – none better – how truly the King loved me, and how he would punish such an attempt as had been made upon my life, to say nothing of the prostitution of justice of which he had been guilty, and for which alone he had earned the penalty of death.

He stood a moment with bent head, the pain of his arm possibly forgotten in the agony of his spirit. Then, straightening himself suddenly, with a proud, half scornful air, he looked the officer straight between the eyes.

"You desire my sword, monsieur?" he inquired.

The musketeer bowed respectfully.

"Saint-Eustache, will you do me the favour to give it to me?"

And while the Chevalier picked up the rapier from the ground where it had been flung, that man waited with an outward calm for which at the moment I admired him, as we must ever admire a tranquil bearing in one smitten by a great adversity. And than this I can conceive few greater. He had played for much, and he had lost everything. Ignominy, degradation, and the block were all that impended for him in this world, and they were very imminent.

He took the sword from the Chevalier. He held it for a second by the hilt, like one in thought, like one who is resolving upon something, whilst the musketeer awaited his good pleasure with that deference which all gentle minds must accord to the unfortunate.

Still holding his rapier, he raised his eyes for a second and let them rest on me with a grim malevolence. Then he uttered a short laugh, and, shrugging his shoulders, he transferred his grip to the blade, as if about to offer the hilt to the officer. Holding it so, halfway betwixt point and quillons, he stepped suddenly back, and before any there could put forth a hand to stay him, he had set the pummel on the ground and the point at his breast, and so dropped upon it and impaled himself.

A cry went up from every throat, and we sprang towards him. He rolled over on his side, and with a grin of exquisite pain, yet in words of unconquerable derision, "You may have my sword now, Monsieur l'Officier," he said, and sank back, swooning.

With an oath, the musketeer stepped forward. He obeyed Chatellerault to the letter, by kneeling beside him and carefully withdrawing the sword. Then he ordered a couple of his men to take up the body.

"Is he dead?" asked someone; and someone else replied, "Not yet, but he soon will be."

Two of the musketeers bore him into the inn and laid him on the floor of the very room in which, an hour or so ago, he had driven a bargain with Roxalanne. A cloak rolled into a pillow was thrust under his head, and there we left him in charge of his captors, the landlord, Saint-Eustache, and La Fosse, the latter inspired, I doubt not, by that morbidity which is so often a feature of the poetic mind, and which impelled him now to witness the death-agony of my Lord of Chatellerault.

Myself, having resumed my garments, I disposed myself to repair at once to the Hotel de l'Épée, there to seek Roxalanne, that I might set her fears and sorrows at rest, and that I might at last make my confession.

As we stepped out into the street, where the dusk was now thickening, I turned to Castelroux to inquire how Saint-Eustache came into Chatellerault's company.

"He is of the family of the Iscariot, I should opine," answered the Gascon. "As soon as he had news that Chatellerault was come to Languedoc as the King's Commissioner, he repaired to him to offer his services in the work of bringing rebels to justice. He urged that his thorough acquaintance with the province should render him of value to the King, as also that he had had particular opportunities of becoming acquainted with many treasonable dealings on the part of men whom the State was far from suspecting."

"Mort Dieu!" I cried, "I had suspected something of such a nature. You do well to call him of the family of the Iscariot. He is more so than you imagine: I have knowledge of this – ample knowledge. He was until lately a rebel himself, and himself a follower of Gaston d'Orléans – though of a lukewarm quality. What reasons have driven him to such work, do you know?"

"The same reason that impelled his forefather, Judas of old. The desire to enrich himself. For every hitherto unsuspected rebel that shall be brought to justice and whose treason shall be proven by his agency, he claims the half of that rebel's confiscated estates."

"Diable!" I exclaimed. "And does the Keeper of the Seals sanction this?"

"Sanction it? Saint-Eustache holds a commission, has a free hand and a company of horse to follow him in his rebel-hunting."

"Has he done much so far?" was my next question.

"He has reduced half a dozen noblemen and their families. The wealth he must thereby have amassed should be very considerable, indeed."

"Tomorrow, Castelroux, I will see the King in connection with this pretty gentleman, and not only shall we find him a dungeon deep and dank, but we shall see that he disgorges his blood-money."

"If you can prove his treason you will be doing blessed work," returned Castelroux. "Until tomorrow, then, for here is the Hotel de l'Épée."

From the broad doorway of an imposing building a warm glow of light issued out and spread itself fanwise across the ill-paved street.

In this – like bats about a lamp – flitted the black figures of gaping urchins and other stragglers, and into this I now passed, having taken leave of my companions.

I mounted the steps and I was about to cross the threshold, when suddenly, above a burst of laughter that greeted my ears, I caught the sound of a singularly familiar voice. This seemed raised at present to address such company as might be within. One moment of doubt had I – for it was a month since last I had heard those soft, unctuous accents. Then I was assured that the voice I heard was, indeed, the voice of my steward Ganymède. Castelroux's messenger had found him at last, it seemed, and had brought him to Toulouse.

I was moved to spring into the room and greet that old retainer for whom, despite the gross and sensuous ways that with advancing years were claiming him more and more, I had a deep attachment. But even as I was on the point of entering, not only his voice, but the very words that he was uttering floated out to my ears, and they were of a quality that held me there to play the hidden listener for the second time in my life in one and the same day.

# Chapter 17

## The Babbling of Ganymède

Never until that hour, as I stood in the porch of the Hôtel de l'Épée, hearkening to my henchman's narrative and to the bursts of laughter which ever and anon it provoked from his numerous listeners, had I dreamed of the raconteur talents which Rodenard might boast. Yet was I very far from being appreciative now that I discovered them, for the story that he told was of how one Marcel de Saint-Pol, Marquis de Bardelys, had laid a wager with the Comte de Chatellerault that he would woo and win Mademoiselle de Lavédan to wife within three months. Nor did he stop there. Rodenard, it would seem, was well informed; he had drawn all knowledge of the state of things from Castelroux's messenger, and later – I know not from whom – at Toulouse, since his arrival.

He regaled the company, therefore, with a recital of our finding the dying Lesperon, and of how I had gone off alone, and evidently assumed the name and role of that proscribed rebel, and thus conducted my wooing under sympathy inspiring circumstances at Lavédan. Then came, he announced, the very cream of the jest, when I was arrested as Lesperon and brought to Toulouse and to trial in Lesperon's stead; he told them how I had been sentenced to death in the other man's place, and he assured them that I would certainly have been beheaded upon the morrow but that news had been borne to him – Rodenard – of my plight, and he was come to deliver me.

My first impulse upon hearing him tell of the wager had been to stride into the room and silence him by my coming. That I did not obey that impulse was something that presently I was very bitterly to regret. How it came that I did not I scarcely know. I was tempted, perhaps, to see how far this henchman whom for years I had trusted was unworthy of that trust. And so, there in the porch, I stayed until he had ended by telling the company that he was on his way to inform the King – who by great good chance was that day arrived in Toulouse – of the mistake that had been made, and thus obtain my immediate enlargement and earn my undying gratitude.

Again I was on the point of entering to administer a very stern reproof to that talkative rogue, when of a sudden there was a commotion within. I caught a scraping of chairs, a dropping of voices, and then suddenly I found myself confronted by Roxalanne de Lavédan herself, issuing with a page and a woman in attendance.

For just a second her eyes rested on me, and the light coming through the doorway at her back boldly revealed my countenance. And a very startled countenance it must have been, for in that fraction of time I knew that she had heard all that Rodenard had been relating. Under that instant's glance of her eyes I felt myself turn pale; a shiver ran through me, and the sweat started cold upon my brow. Then her gaze passed from me, and looked beyond into the street, as though she had not known me; whether in her turn she paled or reddened I cannot say, for the light was too uncertain. Next followed what seemed to me an interminable pause, although, indeed, it can have been no more than a matter of seconds – aye, and of but few. Then, her gown drawn well aside, she passed me in that same irrecognizing way, whilst I, abashed, shrank back into the shadows of the porch, burning with shame and rage and humiliation.

From under her brows her woman glanced at me inquisitively; her liveried page, his nose in the air, eyed me so pertly that I was hard put to it not to hasten with my foot his descent of the steps.

At last they were gone, and from the outside the shrill voice of her page was wafted to me. He was calling to the ostler for her carriage. Standing, in my deep mortification, where she had passed me, I conjectured from that demand that she was journeying to Lavédan.

She knew now how she had been cheated on every hand, first by me and later, that very afternoon, by Chatellerault, and her resolve to quit Toulouse could but signify that she was done with me for good.

That it had surprised her to find me at large already, I fancied I had seen in her momentary glance, but her pride had been quick to conquer and stifle all signs of that surprise.

I remained where she had passed me until her coach had rumbled away into the night, and during the moments that elapsed I had stood arguing with myself and resolving upon my course of action. But despair was fastening upon me.

I had come to the Hôtel de l'Épée, exulting, joyous, and confident of victory. I had come to confess everything to her, and by virtue of what I had done that confession was rendered easy. I could have said to her: "The woman whom I wagered to win was not you, Roxalanne, but a certain Mademoiselle de Lavédan. Your love I have won, but that you may foster no doubts of my intentions, I have paid my wager and acknowledge defeat. I have made over to Chatellerault and to his heirs for all time my estates of Bardelys."

Oh, I had rehearsed it in my mind, and I was confident – I knew – that I should win her. And now – the disclosure of that shameful traffic coming from other lips than mine had ruined everything by forestalling my avowal.

Rodenard should pay for it – by God, he should! Once again did I become a prey to the passion of anger which I have ever held to be unworthy in a gentleman, but to which it would seem that I was growing accustomed to give way. The ostler was mounting the steps at the moment. He carried in his hand a stout horsewhip with a long knotted thong. Hastily muttering a "By your leave," I snatched it from him and sprang into the room.

My intendant was still talking of me. The room was crowded, for Rodenard alone had brought with him my twenty followers. One of these looked up as I brushed past him, and uttered a cry of surprise upon recognizing me. But Rodenard talked on, engrossed in his theme to the exclusion of all else.

"Monsieur le Marquis," he was saying, "is a gentleman whom it is, indeed, an honour to serve – "

A scream burst from him with the last word, for the lash of my whip had burnt a wheal upon his well-fed sides.

"It is an honour that shall be yours no more, you dog!" I cried.

He leapt high into the air as my whip cut him again. He swung round, his face twisted with pain, his flabby cheeks white with fear, and his eyes wild with anger, for as yet the full force of the situation had not been borne in upon him. Then, seeing me there, and catching something of the awful passion that must have been stamped upon my face, he dropped on his knees and cried out something that I did not understand for I was past understanding much just then.

The lash whistled through the air again and caught him about the shoulders. He writhed and roared in his anguish of both flesh and spirit. But I was pitiless. He had ruined my life for me with his talking, and, as God lived, he should pay the only price that it lay in his power to pay – the price of physical suffering. Again and again my whip hissed about his head and cut into his soft white flesh, whilst roaring for mercy he moved and rocked on his knees before me. Instinctively he approached me to hamper my movements, whilst I moved back to give my lash the better play. He held out his arms and joined his fat hands in supplication, but the lash caught them in its sinuous tormenting embrace, and started a red wheal across their whiteness. He tucked them into his armpits with a scream, and fell prone upon the ground.

Then I remember that some of my men essayed to restrain me, which to my passion was as the wind to a blaze. I cracked my whip about their heads, commanding them to keep their distance lest they were minded to share his castigation. And so fearful an air must I have worn, that, daunted, they hung back and watched their leader's punishment in silence.

When I think of it now, I take no little shame at the memory of how I beat him. It is, indeed, with deep reluctance and yet deeper shame that I have brought myself to write of it. If I offend you with this account of that horsewhipping, let necessity be my apology; for the horsewhipping itself I have, unfortunately, no apology, save the blind fury that obsessed me – which is no apology at all.

Upon the morrow I repented me already with much bitterness. But in that hour I knew no reason. I was mad, and of my madness was born this harsh brutality.

"You would talk of me and my affairs in a tavern, you hound!" I cried, out of breath both by virtue of my passion and my exertions. "Let the memory of this act as a curb upon your poisonous tongue in future."

"Monseigneur!" he screamed. "Misericorde, monseigneur!"

"Aye, you shall have mercy – just so much mercy as you deserve. Have I trusted you all these years, and did my father trust you before me, for this? Have you grown sleek and fat and smug in my service that you should requite me thus? Sangdieu, Rodenard! My father had hanged you for the half of the talking that you have done this night. You dog! You miserable knave!"

"Monseigneur," he shrieked again, "forgive! For your sainted mother's sake, forgive! Monseigneur, I did not know – "

"But you are learning, cur; you are learning by the pain of your fat carcase; is it not so, carrion?"

He sank down, his strength exhausted, a limp, moaning, bleeding mass of flesh, into which my whip still cut relentlessly.

I have a picture in my mind of that ill-lighted room, of the startled faces on which the flickering glimmer of the candles shed odd shadows; of the humming and cracking of my whip; of my own voice raised in oaths and epithets of contempt; of Rodenard's screams; of the cries raised here and there in remonstrance or in entreaty, and of some more bold that called shame upon me. Then others took up that cry of "Shame!" so that at last I paused and stood there drawn up to my full height, as if in challenge. Towering above the heads of any in that room, I held my whip menacingly. I was unused to criticism, and their expressions of condemnation roused me.

"Who questions my right?" I demanded arrogantly, whereupon they one and all fell silent. "If any here be bold enough to step out, he shall have my answer." Then, as none responded, I signified my contempt for them by a laugh.

"Monseigneur!" wailed Rodenard at my feet, his voice growing feeble.

By way of answer, I gave him a final cut, then I flung the whip – which had grown ragged in the fray – back to the ostler from whom I had borrowed it.

"Let that suffice you, Rodenard," I said, touching him with my foot. "See that I never set eyes upon you again, if you cherish your miserable life!"

"Not that, monseigneur," groaned the wretch. "Oh, not that! You have punished me; you have whipped me until I cannot stand; forgive me, monseigneur, forgive me now!"

"I have forgiven you, but I never wish to see you again, lest I should forget that I have forgiven you. Take him away, some of you," I bade my men, and in swift, silent obedience two of them stepped forward and bore the groaning, sobbing fellow from the room. When that was done, "Host," I commanded, "prepare me a room. Attend me, a couple of you."

I gave orders thereafter for the disposal of my baggage, some of which my lacqueys brought up to the chamber that the landlord had in haste made ready for me. In that chamber I sat until very late; a prey to the utmost misery and despair. My rage being spent, I might have taken some thought for poor Ganymède and his condition, but my own affairs crowded over-heavily upon my mind, and sat the undisputed rulers of my thoughts that night.

At one moment I considered journeying to Lavédan, only to dismiss the idea the next. What could it avail me now? Would Roxalanne believe the tale I had to tell? Would she not think, naturally enough, that I was but making the best of the situation, and that my avowal of the truth of a story which it was not in my power to deny was not spontaneous, but forced from me by circumstances? No, there was nothing more to be done. A score of amours had claimed my attention in the past and received it; yet there was not one of those affairs whose miscarriage would have afforded me the slightest concern or mortification. It seemed like an irony, like a Dies Irae, that it should have been left to this first true passion of my life to have gone awry.

I slept ill when at last I sought my bed, and through the night I nursed my bitter grief, huddling to me the corpse of the love she had borne me as a mother may the corpse of her first-born.

On the morrow I resolved to leave Toulouse – to quit this province wherein so much had befallen me and repair to Beaugency, there to grow old in misanthropical seclusion. I had done with Courts, I had done with love and with women; I had done, it seemed to me, with life itself. Prodigal had it been in gifts that I had not sought of it. It had spread my table with the richest offerings, but they had been little to my palate, and I had nauseated quickly. And now, when here in this remote corner of France it had shown me the one prize I coveted, it had been swift to place it beyond my reach, thereby sowing everlasting discontent and misery in my hitherto pampered heart.

I saw Castelroux that day, but I said no word to him of my affliction. He brought me news of Chatellerault. The Count was lying in a dangerous condition at the Auberge Royale, and might not be moved. The physician attending him all but despaired of his life.

"He is asking to see you," said Castelroux.

But I was not minded to respond. For all that he had deeply wronged me, for all that I despised him very cordially, the sight of him in his present condition might arouse my pity, and I was in no mood to waste upon such a one as Chatellerault – even on his deathbed – a quality of which I had so dire a need just then for my own case.

"I will not go," said I, after deliberation. "Tell him from me that I forgive him freely if it be that he seeks my forgiveness; tell him that I bear him no rancour, and – that he had better make his will, to save me trouble hereafter, if he should chance to die."

I said this because I had no mind, if he should perish intestate, to go in quest of his next heirs and advise them that my late Picardy estates were now their property.

Castelroux sought yet to persuade me to visit the Count, but I held firmly to my resolve.

"I am leaving Toulouse today," I announced.

"Whither do you go?"

"To hell, or to Beaugency – I scarce know which, nor does it matter."

He looked at me in surprise, but, being a man of breeding, asked no questions upon matters that he accounted secret.

"But the King?" he ventured presently.

"His Majesty has already dispensed me from my duties by him."

Nevertheless, I did not go that day. I maintained the intention until sunset; then, seeing that it was too late, I postponed my departure until the morrow. I can assign no reason for my dallying mood. Perhaps it sprang from the inertness that pervaded me, perhaps some mysterious hand detained me. Be that as it may, that I remained another night at the Hôtel de l'Épée was one of those contingencies which, though slight and seemingly inconsequential in themselves, lead to great issues. Had I departed that day for Beaugency, it is likely that you had never heard of me – leastways, not from my own pen – for in what so far I have told you, without that which is to follow, there is haply little that was worth the labour of setting down.

In the morning, then, I set out; but having started late, we got no farther than Grenade, where we lay the night once more at the Hôtel de la Couronne. And so, through having delayed my departure by a single day, did it come to pass that a message reached me before it might have been too late.

It was high noon of the morrow. Our horses stood saddled; indeed, some of my men were already mounted – for I was not minded to disband them until Beaugency was reached – and my two coaches were both ready for the journey. The habits of a lifetime are not so easy to abandon even when Necessity raises her compelling voice.

I was in the act of settling my score with the landlord when of a sudden there were quick steps in the passage, the clank of a rapier against the wall, and a voice – the voice of Castelroux – calling excitedly, "Bardelys! Monsieur de Bardelys!"

"What brings you here?" I cried in greeting, as he stepped into the room.

"Are you still for Beaugency?" he asked sharply, throwing back his head.

"Why, yes," I answered, wondering at this excitement.

"Then you have seen nothing of Saint-Eustache and his men?"

"Nothing."

"Yet they must have passed this way not many hours ago." Then tossing his hat on the table and speaking with sudden vehemence: "If you have any interest in the family of Lavédan, you will return upon the instant to Toulouse."

The mention of Lavédan was enough to quicken my pulses. Yet in the past two days I had mastered resignation, and in doing that we school ourselves to much restraint. I turned slowly, and surveyed the little Captain attentively. His black eyes sparkled, and his moustaches bristled with excitement. Clearly he had news of import.

I turned to the landlord.

"Leave us, Monsieur l'Hôte," said I shortly; and when he had departed, "What of the Lavédan family, Castelroux?" I inquired as calmly as I might.

"The Chevalier de Saint-Eustache left Toulouse at six o'clock this morning for Lavédan."

Swift the suspicion of his errand broke upon my mind.

"He has betrayed the Vicomte?" I half inquired, half asserted.

Castelroux nodded. "He has obtained a warrant for his apprehension from the Keeper of the Seals, and is gone to execute it. In the course of a few days Lavédan will be in danger of being no more than a name. This Saint-Eustache is driving a brisk trade, by God, and some fine prizes have already fallen to his lot. But if you add them all together, they are not likely to yield as much as this his latest expedition. Unless you intervene, Bardelys, the Vicomte de Lavédan is doomed and his family houseless."

"I will intervene," I cried. "By God, I will! And as for Saint-Eustache – he was born under a propitious star, indeed, if he escapes the gallows. He little dreams that I am still to be reckoned with. There, Castelroux, I will start for Lavédan at once."

Already I was striding to the door, when the Gascon called me back.

"What good will that do?" he asked. "Were it not better first to return to Toulouse and obtain a counter-warrant from the King?"

There was wisdom in his words – much wisdom. But my blood was afire, and I was in too hot a haste to reason.

"Return to Toulouse?" I echoed scornfully. "A waste of time, Captain. No, I will go straight to Lavédan. I need no counter-warrant. I know too much of this Chevalier's affairs, and my very presence should be enough to stay his hand. He is as foul a traitor as you'll find in France; but for the moment God bless him for a very opportune knave.

"Gilles!" I called, throwing wide the door. "Gilles!"

"Monseigneur," he answered, hastening to me.

"Put back the carriages and saddle me a horse," I commanded. "And bid your fellows mount at once and await me in the courtyard. We are not going to Beaugency, Gilles. We ride north – to Lavédan."

# Chapter 18

## The Obstinacy of Saint-Eustache

On the occasion of my first visit to Lavédan I had disregarded – or, rather, Fate had contrived that I should disregard – Chatellerault's suggestion that I should go with all the panoply of power – with my followers, my liveries, and my equipages to compose the magnificence all France had come to associate with my name, and thus dazzle by my brilliant lustre the lady I was come to win. As you may remember, I had crept into the chateau like a thief in the night, – wounded, bedraggled, and of miserable aspect, seeking to provoke compassion rather than admiration.

Not so now that I made my second visit. I availed myself of all the splendour to which I owed my title of "Magnificent", and rode into the courtyard of the Château de Lavédan preceded by twenty well-mounted knaves wearing the gorgeous Saint-Pol liveries of scarlet and gold, with the Bardelys escutcheon broidered on the breasts of their doublets – on a field or a bar azure surcharged by three lilies of the field. They were armed with swords and musketoons, and had more the air of a royal bodyguard than of a company of attendant servants.

Our coming was in a way well timed. I doubt if we could have stayed the execution of Saint-Eustache's warrant even had we arrived earlier. But for effect – to produce a striking coup de théâtre – we could not have come more opportunely.

A coach stood in the quadrangle, at the foot of the chateau steps: down these the Vicomte was descending, with the Vicomtesse – grim and blasphemant as ever, on one side, and his daughter, white of face and with tightly compressed lips, on the other. Between these two women – his wife and his child – as different in body as they were different in soul, came Lavédan with a firm step, a good colour, and a look of well-bred, lofty indifference to his fate.

He disposed himself to enter the carriage which was to bear him to prison with much the same air he would have assumed had his destination been a royal levée.

Around the coach were grouped a score of men of Saint-Eustache's company – half soldiers, half ploughboys – ill-garbed and indifferently accoutred in dull breastplates and steel caps, many of which were rusted. By the carriage door stood the long, lank figure of the Chevalier himself, dressed with his wonted care, and perfumed, curled, and beribboned beyond belief. His weak, boyish face sought by scowls and by the adoption of a grim smile to assume an air of martial ferocity.

Such was the grouping in the quadrangle when my men, with Gilles at their head, thundered across the drawbridge, giving pause to those within, and drawing upon themselves the eyes of all, as they rode, two by two, under the old-world arch of the keep into the courtyard.

And Gilles, who knew our errand, and who was as ready-witted a rogue as ever rode with me, took in the situation at a glance. Knowing how much I desired to make a goodly show, he whispered an order.

This resulted in the couples dividing at the gateway, one going to the left and one to the right, so that as they came they spread themselves in a crescent, and drawing rein, they faced forward, confronting and half surrounding the Chevalier's company.

As each couple appeared, the curiosity – the uneasiness, probably – of Saint-Eustache and his men, had increased, and their expectancy was on tiptoe to see what lord it was went abroad with such regal pomp, when I appeared in the gateway and advanced at the trot into

177

the middle of the quadrangle. There I drew rein and doffed my hat
to them as they stood, open-mouthed and gaping one and all. If it
was a theatrical display, a parade worthy of a tilt-ground, it was yet
a noble and imposing advent, and their gaping told me that it was
not without effect. The men looked uneasily at the Chevalier; the
Chevalier looked uneasily at his men; Mademoiselle, very pale,
lowered her eyes and pressed her lips yet more tightly; the Vicomtesse
uttered an oath of astonishment; whilst Lavédan, too dignified to
manifest surprise, greeted me with a sober bow.

Behind them on the steps I caught sight of a group of domestics,
old Anatole standing slightly in advance of his fellows, and
wondering, no doubt, whether this were, indeed, the bedraggled
Lesperon of a little while ago – for if I had thought of pomp in the
display of my lacqueys, no less had I considered it in the decking of
my own person. Without any of the ribbons and fopperies that mark
the coxcomb, yet was I clad, plumed, and armed with a magnificence
such as I'll swear had not been seen within the grey walls of that old
castle in the lifetime of any of those that were now present.

Gilles leapt from his horse as I drew rein, and hastened to hold
my stirrup, with a murmured, "Monsieur," which title drew a fresh
astonishment into the eyes of the beholders.

I advanced leisurely towards Saint-Eustache, and addressed him
with such condescension as I might a groom; to impress and quell a
man of this type your best weapon is the arrogance that a nobler
spirit would resent.

"A world of odd meetings this, Saint-Eustache," I smiled
disdainfully. "A world of strange comings and goings, and of strange
transformations. The last time we were here we stood mutually as
guests of Monsieur le Vicomte; at present you appear to be officiating
as a – a tipstaff."

"Monsieur!" He coloured, and he uttered the word in accents of
awakening resentment. I looked into his eyes, coldly, impassively, as
if waiting to hear what he might have to add, and so I stayed until
his glance fell and his spirit was frozen in him. He knew me, and he
knew how much I was to be feared. A word from me to the King

might send him to the wheel. It was upon this I played. Presently, as his eye fell, "Is your business with me, Monsieur de Bardelys?" he asked, and at that utterance of my name there was a commotion on the steps, whilst the Vicomte started, and his eyes frowned upon me, and the Vicomtesse looked up suddenly to scan me with a fresh interest.

She beheld at last in the flesh the gentleman who had played so notorious a part, ten years ago, in that scandal connected with the Duchesse de Bourgogne, of which she never tired of reciting the details. And think that she had sat at table with him day by day and been unconscious of that momentous fact! Such, I make no doubt, was what passed through her mind at the moment, and, to judge from her expression, I should say that the excitement of beholding the Magnificent Bardelys had for the nonce eclipsed beholding even her husband's condition and the imminent sequestration of Lavédan.

"My business is with you, Chevalier," said I. "It relates to your mission here."

His jaw fell. "You wish – ?"

"To desire you to withdraw your men and quit Lavédan at once, abandoning the execution of your warrant."

He flashed me a look of impotent hate. "You know of the existence of my warrant, Monsieur de Bardelys, and you must therefore realize that a royal mandate alone can exempt me from delivering Monsieur de Lavédan to the Keeper of the Seals."

"My only warrant," I answered, somewhat baffled, but far from abandoning hope, "is my word. You shall say to the Garde des Sceaux that you have done this upon the authority of the Marquis de Bardelys, and you have my promise that His Majesty shall confirm my action."

In saying that I said too much, as I was quickly to realize.

"His Majesty will confirm it, monsieur?" he said interrogatively, and he shook his head. "That is a risk I dare not run. My warrant sets me under imperative obligations which I must discharge – you will see the justice of what I state."

His tone was all humility, all subservience, nevertheless it was firm to the point of being hard. But my last card, the card upon which I was depending, was yet to be played.

"Will you do me the honour to step aside with me, Chevalier?" I commanded rather than besought.

"At your service, sir," said he; and I drew him out of earshot of those others.

"Now, Saint-Eustache, we can talk," said I, with an abrupt change of manner from the coldly arrogant to the coldly menacing. "I marvel greatly at your temerity in pursuing this Iscariot business after learning who I am, at Toulouse two nights ago."

He clenched his hands, and his weak face hardened.

"I would beg you to consider your expressions, monsieur, and to control them," said he in a thick voice.

I vouchsafed him a stare of freezing amazement. "You will no doubt remember in what capacity I find you employed. Nay, keep your hands still, Saint-Eustache. I don't fight catchpolls, and if you give me trouble my men are yonder." And I jerked my thumb over my shoulder.

"And now to business. I am not minded to talk all day. I was saying that I marvel at your temerity, and more particularly at your having laid information against Monsieur de Lavédan, and having come here to arrest him, knowing, as you must know, that I am interested in the Vicomte."

"I have heard of that interest, monsieur," said he, with a sneer for which I could have struck him.

"This act of yours," I pursued, ignoring his interpolation, "savours very much of flying in the face of Destiny. It almost seems to me as if you were defying me."

His lip trembled, and his eyes shunned my glance.

"Indeed – indeed, monsieur– " he was protesting, when I cut him short.

"You cannot be so great a fool but that you must realize that if I tell the King what I know of you, you will be stripped of your ill-gotten gains, and broken on the wheel for a double traitor – a betrayer of your fellow-rebels."

"But you will not do that, monsieur?" he cried. "It would be unworthy in you."

At that I laughed in his face. "Heart of God! Are you to be what you please, and do you still expect that men shall be nice in dealing with you? I would do this thing, and, by my faith, Monsieur de Saint-Eustache, I will do it, if you compel me!"

He reddened and moved his foot uneasily. Perhaps I did not take the best way with him, after all. I might have confined myself to sowing fear in his heart; that alone might have had the effect I desired; by visiting upon him at the same time the insults I could not repress, I may have aroused his resistance, and excited his desire above all else to thwart me.

"What do you want of me?" he demanded, with a sudden arrogance which almost cast mine into the shade.

"I want you," said I, deeming the time ripe to make a plain tale of it, "to withdraw your men, and to ride back to Toulouse without Monsieur de Lavédan, there to confess to the Keeper of the Seals that your suspicions were unfounded, and that you have culled evidence that the Vicomte has had no relations with Monsieur the King's brother."

He looked at me in amazement – amusedly, almost.

"A likely story that to bear to the astute gentlemen in Toulouse," said he.

"Aye, ma foi, a most likely story," said I. "When they come to consider the profit that you are losing by not apprehending the Vicomte, and can think of none that you are making, they will have little difficulty in believing you."

"But what of this evidence you refer to?"

"You have, I take it, discovered no incriminating evidence – no documents that will tell against the Vicomte?"

"No, monsieur, it is true that I have not – "

He stopped and bit his lip, my smile making him aware of his indiscretion.

"Very well, then, you must invent some evidence to prove that he was in no way associated with the rebellion."

"Monsieur de Bardelys," said he very insolently, "we waste time in idle words. If you think that I will imperil my neck for the sake of serving you or the Vicomte, you are most prodigiously at fault."

"I have never thought so. But I have thought that you might be induced to imperil your neck – as you have it – for its own sake, and to the end that you might save it."

He moved away. "Monsieur, you talk in vain. You have no royal warrant to supersede mine. Do what you will when you come to Toulouse," and he smiled darkly. "Meanwhile, the Vicomte goes with me."

"You have no evidence against him!" I cried, scarce believing that he would dare to defy me and that I had failed.

"I have the evidence of my word. I am ready to swear to what I know – that, whilst I was here at Lavédan, some weeks ago, I discovered his connection with the rebels."

"And what think you, miserable fool, shall your word weigh against mine?" I cried. "Never fear, Monsieur le Chevalier, I shall be in Toulouse to give you the lie by showing that your word is a word to which no man may attach faith, and by exposing to the King your past conduct. If you think that, after I have spoken, King Louis whom they name the Just will suffer the trial of the Vicomte to go further on your instigation, or if you think that you will be able to slip your own neck from the noose I shall have set about it, you are an infinitely greater fool than I deem you."

He stood and looked at me over his shoulder, his face crimson, and his brows black as a thundercloud.

"All this may betide when you come to Toulouse, Monsieur de Bardelys," said he darkly, "but from here to Toulouse it is a matter of some twenty leagues."

With that, he turned on his heel and left me, baffled and angry, to puzzle out the inner meaning of his parting words.

He gave his men the order to mount, and bade Monsieur de Lavédan enter the coach, whereupon Gilles shot me a glance of inquiry. For a second, as I stepped slowly after the Chevalier, I was minded to try armed resistance, and to convert that grey courtyard into a shambles. Then I saw betimes the futility of such a step, and I shrugged my shoulders in answer to my servant's glance.

I would have spoken to the Vicomte ere he departed, but I was too deeply chagrined and humiliated by my defeat. So much so that I had no room in my thoughts even for the very natural conjecture of what Lavédan must be thinking of me. I repented me then of my rashness in coming to Lavédan without having seen the King – as Castelroux had counselled me. I had come indulging vain dreams of a splendid overthrow of Saint-Eustache. I had thought to shine heroically in Mademoiselle's eyes, and thus I had hoped that both gratitude for having saved her father and admiration at the manner in which I had achieved it would predispose her to grant me a hearing in which I might plead my rehabilitation. Once that were accorded me, I did not doubt I should prevail.

Now my dream was all dispelled, and my pride had suffered just such a humiliating fall as the moralists tell us pride must ever suffer.

There seemed little left me but to go hence with lambent tail, like a dog that has been whipped – my dazzling escort become a mockery but that it served the more loudly to advertise my true impotency.

As I approached the carriage, the Vicomtesse swept suddenly down the steps and came towards me with a friendly smile. "Monsieur de Bardelys," said she, "we are grateful for your intervention in the cause of that rebel my husband."

"Madame," I besought her, under my breath, "if you would not totally destroy him, I beseech you to be cautious. By your leave, I will have my men refreshed, and thereafter I shall take the road to Toulouse again. I can only hope that my intervention with the King may bear better fruit."

Although I spoke in a subdued key, Saint-Eustache, who stood near us, overheard me, as his face very clearly testified.

"Remain here, sir," she replied, with some effusion, "and follow us when you are rested."

"Follow you?" I inquired. "Do you then go with Monsieur de Lavédan?"

"No, Anne," said the Vicomte politely from the carriage. "It will be tiring you unnecessarily. You were better advised to remain here until my return."

I doubt not that the poor Vicomte was more concerned with how she would tire him than with how the journey might tire her. But the Vicomtesse was not to be gainsaid. The Chevalier had sneered when the Vicomte spoke of returning. Madame had caught that sneer, and she swung round upon him now with the vehement fury of a virago.

"He'll not return, you think, you Judas!" she snarled at him, her lean, swarthy face growing very evil to see. "But he shall – by God, he shall! And look to your skin when he does, monsieur the catchpoll, for, on my honour, you shall have a foretaste of hell for your trouble in this matter."

The Chevalier smiled with much restraint. "A woman's tongue," said he, "does no injury."

"Will a woman's arm, think you?" demanded that warlike matron. "You musk-stinking tipstaff, I'll – "

"Anne, my love," implored the Vicomte soothingly, "I beg that you will control yourself."

"Shall I submit to the insolence of this misbegotten vassal? Shall I – "

"Remember rather that it does not become the dignity of your station to address the fellow. We avoid venomous reptiles, but we do not pause to reproach them with their venom. God made them so."

Saint-Eustache coloured to the roots of his hair, then, turning hastily to the driver, he bade him start. He would have closed the door with that, but that Madame thrust herself forward.

That was the Chevalier's chance to be avenged. "You cannot go," said he.

"Cannot?" Her cheeks reddened. "Why not, Monsieur de Saint-Eustache?"

"I have no reasons to afford you," he answered brutally. "You cannot go."

"Your pardon, Chevalier," I interposed. "You go beyond your rights in seeking to prevent her. Monsieur le Vicomte is not yet convicted. Do not, I beseech you, transcend the already odious character of your work."

And without more ado I shouldered him aside, and held the door that she might enter. She rewarded me with a smile – half vicious, half whimsical, and mounted the step. Saint-Eustache would have interfered. He came at me as if resenting that shoulder-thrust of mine, and for a second I almost thought he would have committed the madness of striking me.

"Take care, Saint-Eustache," I said very quietly, my eyes fixed on his. And much as dead Caesar's ghost may have threatened Brutus with Philippi, "We meet at Toulouse, Chevalier," said I, and closing the carriage door I stepped back.

There was a flutter of skirts behind me. It was Mademoiselle. So brave and outwardly so calm until now, the moment of actual separation – and added thereunto, perhaps, her mother's going and the loneliness that for herself she foresaw – proved more than she could endure. I stepped aside, and she swept past me and caught at the leather curtain of the coach.

"Father!" she sobbed.

There are some things that a man of breeding may not witness – some things to look upon which is near akin to eavesdropping or reading the letters of another. Such a scene did I now account the present one, and, turning, I moved away. But Saint-Eustache cut it short, for scarce had I taken three paces when his voice rang out the command to move. The driver hesitated, for the girl was still hanging at the window. But a second command, accompanied by a vigorous oath, overcame his hesitation. He gathered up his reins, cracked his whip, and the lumbering wheels began to move.

"Have a care, child!" I heard the Vicomte cry, "have a care! Adieu, mon enfant!"

She sprang back, sobbing, and assuredly she would have fallen, thrown out of balance by the movement of the coach, but that I put forth my hands and caught her.

I do not think she knew whose were the arms that held her for that brief space, so desolated was she by the grief so long repressed.

At last she realized that it was this worthless Bardelys against whom she rested; this man who had wagered that he would win and wed her; this impostor who had come to her under an assumed name; this knave who had lied to her as no gentleman could have lied, swearing to love her, whilst, in reality, he did no more than seek to win a wager. When all this she realized, she shuddered a second, then moved abruptly from my grasp, and, without so much as a glance at me, she left me, and, ascending the steps of the chateau, she passed from my sight.

I gave the order to dismount as the last of Saint-Eustache's followers vanished under the portcullis.

# Chapter 19

## The Flint and the Steel

"Mademoiselle will see you, monsieur," said Anatole at last.

Twice already had he carried unavailingly my request that Roxalanne should accord me an interview ere I departed. On this the third occasion I had bidden him say that I would not stir from Lavédan until she had done me the honour of hearing me. Seemingly that threat had prevailed where entreaties had been scorned.

I followed Anatole from the half-light of the hall in which I had been pacing into the salon overlooking the terraces and the river, where Roxalanne awaited me. She was standing at the farther end of the room by one of the long windows, which was open, for, although we were already in the first week of October, the air of Languedoc was as warm and balmy as that of Paris or Picardy is in summer.

I advanced to the centre of the chamber, and there I paused and waited until it should please her to acknowledge my presence and turn to face me. I was no fledgling. I had seen much, I had learnt much and been in many places, and my bearing was wont to convey it.

Never in my life had I been gauche, for which I thank my parents, and if years ago – long years ago – a certain timidity had marked my first introductions to the Louvre and the Luxembourg, that timidity was something from which I had long since parted company. And yet it seemed to me, as I stood in that pretty, sunlit room awaiting the

187

pleasure of that child, scarce out of her teens, that some of the awkwardness I had escaped in earlier years, some of the timidity of long ago, came to me then. I shifted the weight of my body from one leg to the other; I fingered the table by which I stood; I pulled at the hat I held; my colour came and went; I looked at her furtively from under bent brows, and I thanked God that her back being towards me she might not see the clown I must have seemed.

At length, unable longer to brook that discomposing silence –

"Mademoiselle!" I called softly. The sound of my own voice seemed to invigorate me, to strip me of my awkwardness and self-consciousness. It broke the spell that for a moment had been over me, and brought me back to myself – to the vain, self-confident, flamboyant Bardelys that perhaps you have pictured from my writings.

"I hope, monsieur," she answered, without turning, "that what you may have to say may justify in some measure your very importunate insistence."

On my life, this was not encouraging. But now that I was master of myself, I was not again so easily to be disconcerted. My eyes rested upon her as she stood almost framed in the opening of that long window. How straight and supple she was, yet how dainty and slight withal! She was far from being a tall woman, but her clean length of limb, her very slightness, and the high-bred poise of her shapely head, conveyed an illusion of height unless you stood beside her. The illusion did not sway me then. I saw only a child; but a child with a great spirit, with a great soul that seemed to accentuate her physical helplessness. That helplessness, which I felt rather than saw, wove into the warp of my love. She was in grief just then – in grief at the arrest of her father, and at the dark fate that threatened him; in grief at the unworthiness of a lover. Of the two which might be the more bitter it was not mine to judge, but I burned to gather her to me, to comfort and cherish her, to make her one with me, and thus, whilst giving her something of my man's height and strength, cull from her something of that pure, noble spirit, and thus sanctify my own.

I had a moment's weakness when she spoke. I was within an ace of advancing and casting myself upon my knees like any Lenten penitent, to sue forgiveness. But I set the inclination down betimes. Such expedients would not avail me here.

"What I have to say, mademoiselle," I answered after a pause, "would justify a saint descending into hell; or, rather, to make my metaphor more apt, would warrant a sinner's intrusion into heaven."

I spoke solemnly, yet not too solemnly; the least slur of a sardonic humour was in my tones.

She moved her head upon the white column of her neck, and with the gesture one of her brown curls became disordered. I could fancy the upward tilt of her delicate nose, the scornful curve of her lip as she answered shortly, "Then say it quickly, monsieur."

And, being thus bidden, I said quickly, "I love you, Roxalanne."

Her heel beat the shimmering parquet of the floor; she half turned towards me, her cheek flushed, her lip tremulous with anger.

"Will you say what you have to say, monsieur?" she demanded in a concentrated voice, "and having said it, will you go?"

"Mademoiselle, I have already said it," I answered, with a wistful smile.

"Oh!" she gasped. Then suddenly facing round upon me, a world of anger in her blue eyes – eyes that I had known dreamy, but which were now very wide awake. "Was it to offer me this last insult you forced your presence upon me? Was it to mock me with those words, me – a woman, with no man about me to punish you? Shame, sir! Yet it is no more than I might look for in you."

"Mademoiselle, you do me grievous wrong – " I began.

"I do you no wrong," she answered hotly, then stopped, unwilling haply to be drawn into contention with me. "Enfin, since you have said what you came to say will you go?" And she pointed to the door.

"Mademoiselle, mademoiselle – " I began in a voice of earnest intercession.

189

"Go!" she interrupted angrily, and for a second the violence of her voice and gesture almost reminded me of the Vicomtesse. "I will hear no more from you."

"Mademoiselle, you shall," I answered no whit less firmly.

"I will not listen to you. Talk if you will. You shall have the walls for audience." And she moved towards the door, but I barred her passage. I was courteous to the last degree; I bowed low before her as I put myself in her way.

"It is all that was wanting – that you should offer me violence!" she exclaimed.

"God forbid!" said I.

"Then let me pass."

"Aye, when you have heard me."

"I do not wish to hear you. Nothing that you may say can matter to me. Oh, monsieur, if you have any instincts of gentility, if you have any pretension to be accounted anything but a mauvais sujet, I beg of you to respect my grief. You witnessed, yourself, the arrest of my father. This is no season for such a scene as you are creating."

"Pardon! It is in such a season as this that you need the comfort and support that the man you love alone can give you."

"The man I love?" she echoed, and from flushed that they had been, her cheeks went very pale. Her eyes fell for an instant, then – they were raised again, and their blue depths were offered me. "I think, sir," she said, through her teeth, "that your insolence transcends all belief."

"Can you deny it?" I cried. "Can you deny that you love me? If you can – why, then, you lied to me three nights ago at Toulouse!"

That smote her hard – so hard that she forgot her assurance that she would not listen to me – her promise to herself that she would stoop to no contention with me.

"If, in a momentary weakness, in my nescience of you as you truly are, I did make some such admission, I did entertain such feelings for you, things have come to my knowledge since then, monsieur, that have revealed you to me as another man; I have learnt something that has utterly withered such love as I then confessed. Now, monsieur, are you satisfied, and will you let me pass?" She said the last words with a return of her imperiousness, already angry at having been drawn so far.

"I am satisfied, mademoiselle," I answered brutally, "that you did not speak the truth three nights ago. You never loved me. It was pity that deluded you, shame that urged you – shame at the Delilah part you had played and at your betrayal of me. Now, mademoiselle, you may pass," said I.

And I stood aside, assured that as she was a woman she would not pass me now. Nor did she. She recoiled a step instead. Her lip quivered. Then she recovered quickly. Her mother might have told her that she was a fool for engaging herself in such a duel with me – me, the veteran of a hundred amorous combats. Yet though I doubt not it was her first assault-at-arms of this description, she was more than a match for me, as her next words proved.

"Monsieur, I thank you for enlightening me. I cannot, indeed, have spoken the truth three nights ago. You are right, I do not doubt it now, and you lift from me a load of shame."

Dieu! It was like a thrust in the high lines, and its hurtful violence staggered me. I was finished, it seemed. The victory was hers, and she but a child with no practice of Cupid's art of fence!

"Now, monsieur," she added, "now that you are satisfied that you did wrong to say I loved you, now that we have disposed of that question – adieu!"

"A moment yet!" I cried. "We have disposed of that, but there was another point, an earlier one, which for the moment we have disregarded. We have – you have disproved the love I was so presumptuous as to believe you fostered for me. We have yet to reckon with the love I bear you, mademoiselle, and of that we shall not be able to dispose so readily."

With a gesture of weariness or of impatience, she turned aside.

"What is it you want? What do you seek to gain by thus provoking me? To win your wager?" Her voice was cold. Who to have looked upon that childlike face, upon those meek, pondering eyes, could have believed her capable of so much cruelty?

"There can no longer be any question of my wager; I have lost and paid it," said I.

She looked up suddenly. Her brows met in a frown of bewilderment.

Clearly this interested her. Again was she drawn.

"How?" she asked. "You have lost and paid it?"

"Even so. That odious, cursed, infamous wager, was the something which I hinted at so often as standing between you and me. The confession that so often I was on the point of making – that so often you urged me to make – concerned that wager. Would to God, Roxalanne, that I had told you!" I cried, and it seemed to me that the sincerity ringing in my voice drove some of the harshness from her countenance, some of the coldness from her glance.

"Unfortunately," I pursued, "it always seemed to me either not yet time, or already too late. Yet so soon as I regained my liberty, my first thought was of that. While the wager existed I might not ask you to become my wife, lest I should seem to be carrying out the original intention which embarked me upon the business of wooing you, and brought me here to Languedoc. And so my first step was to seek out Chatellerault and deliver him my note of hand for my Picardy possessions, the bulk – by far the greater bulk – of all my fortune. My second step was to repair to you at the Hôtel de l'Épée.

"At last I could approach you with clean hands; I could confess what I had done; and since it seemed to me that I had made the utmost atonement, I was confident of success. Alas! I came too late. In the porch of the auberge I met you as you came forth. From my talkative intendant you had learnt already the story of that bargain into which Bardelys had entered. You had learnt who I was, and you thought that you had learnt why I wooed you. Accordingly you could but despise me."

She had sunk into a chair. Her hands were folded in a listless manner in her lap, and her eyes were lowered, her cheeks pale. But the swift heave of her bosom told me that my words were not without effect. "Do you know nothing of the bargain that I made with Chatellerault?" she asked in a voice that held, I thought, some trace of misery.

"Chatellerault was a cheat!" I cried. "No man of honour in France would have accounted himself under obligation to pay that wager. I paid it, not because I thought the payment due, but that by its payment I might offer you a culminating proof of my sincerity."

"Be that as it may," said she, "I passed him my word to – to marry him, if he set you at liberty."

"The promise does not hold, for when you made it I was at liberty already. Besides, Chatellerault is dead by now – or very near it."

"Dead?" she echoed, looking up.

"Yes, dead. We fought–" The ghost of a smile, of sudden, of scornful understanding, passed like a ray of light across her face.

"Pardieu!" I cried, "you do me a wrong there. It was not by my hands that he fell. It was not by me that the duel was instigated."

And with that I gave her the whole details of the affair, including the information that Chatellerault had been no party to my release, and that for his attempted judicial murder of me the King would have dealt very hardly with him had he not saved the King the trouble by throwing himself upon his sword.

There was a silence when I had done. Roxalanne sat on, and seemed to ponder. To let all that I had said sink in and advocate my cause, as to me was very clear it must, I turned aside and moved to one of the windows.

"Why did you not tell me before?" she asked suddenly. "Why – oh, why – did you not confess to me the whole infamous affair as soon as you came to love me, as you say you did?"

"As I say I did?" I repeated after her. "Do you doubt it? Can you doubt it in the face of what I have done?"

"Oh, I don't know what to believe!" she cried, a sob in her voice. "You have deceived me so far, so often. Why did you not tell me that night on the river? Or later, when I pressed you in this very house? Or again, the other night in the prison of Toulouse?"

"You ask me why. Can you not answer the question for yourself? Can you not conceive the fear that was in me that you should shrink away from me in loathing? The fear that if you cared a little, I might for all time stifle such affection as you bore me? The fear that I must ruin your trust in me? Oh, mademoiselle, can you not see how my only hope lay in first owning defeat to Chatellerault, in first paying the wager?"

"How could you have lent yourself to such a bargain?" was her next question.

"How, indeed?" I asked in my turn. "From your mother you have heard something of the reputation that attaches to Bardelys. I was a man of careless ways, satiated with all the splendours life could give me, nauseated by all its luxuries. Was it wonderful that I allowed myself to be lured into this affair? It promised some excitement, a certain novelty, difficulties in a path that I had – alas! – ever found all too smooth – for Chatellerault had made your reputed coldness the chief bolster of his opinion that I should not win.

"Again, I was not given to over-nice scruples. I make no secret of my infirmities, but do not blame me too much. If you could see the fine demoiselles we have in Paris, if you could listen to their tenets and take a deep look into their lives, you would not marvel at me. I had never known any but these. On the night of my coming to Lavédan, your sweetness, your pure innocence, your almost childish virtue, dazed me by their novelty. From that first moment I became your slave. Then I was in your garden day by day. And here, in this old Languedoc garden with you and your roses, during the languorous days of my convalescence, is it wonderful that some of the purity, some of the sweetness that was of you and of your roses, should have crept into my heart and cleansed it a little? Ah, mademoiselle!" I cried – and, coming close to her, I would have bent my knee in intercession but that she restrained me.

"Monsieur," she interrupted, "we harass ourselves in vain. This can have but one ending."

Her tones were cold, but the coldness I knew was forced – else had she not said "we harass ourselves." Instead of quelling my ardour, it gave it fuel.

"True, mademoiselle," I cried, almost exultantly. "It can end but one way!"

She caught my meaning, and her frown deepened. I went too fast, it seemed.

"It had better end now, monsieur. There is too much between us. You wagered to win me to wife." She shuddered. "I could never forget it."

"Mademoiselle," I denied stoutly, "I did not."

"How?" She caught her breath. "You did not?"

"No," I pursued boldly. "I did not wager to win you. I wagered to win a certain Mademoiselle de Lavédan, who was unknown to me – but not you, not you."

She smiled, with never so slight a touch of scorn.

"Your distinctions are very fine – too fine for me, monsieur."

"I implore you to be reasonable. Think reasonably."

"Am I not reasonable? Do I not think? But there is so much to think of!" she sighed. "You carried your deception so far. You came here, for instance, as Monsieur de Lesperon. Why that duplicity?"

"Again, mademoiselle, I did not," said I.

She glanced at me with pathetic disdain.

"Indeed, indeed, monsieur, you deny things very bravely."

"Did I tell you that my name was Lesperon? Did I present myself to monsieur your father as Lesperon?"

"Surely – yes."

"Surely no; a thousand times no. I was the victim of circumstances in that, and if I turned them to my own account after they had been forced upon me, shall I be blamed and accounted a cheat? Whilst I was unconscious, your father, seeking for a clue to my identity, made an inspection of my clothes.

"In the pocket of my doublet they found some papers addressed to René de Lesperon – some love letters, a communication from the Duc d'Orléans, and a woman's portrait. From all of this it was assumed that I was that Lesperon. Upon my return to consciousness your father greeted me effusively, whereat I wondered; he passed on to discuss – nay, to tell me of – the state of the province and of his own connection with the rebels, until I lay gasping at his egregious temerity. Then, when he greeted me as Monsieur de Lesperon, I had the explanation of it, but too late. Could I deny the identity then?

"Could I tell him that I was Bardelys, the favourite of the King himself? What would have occurred? I ask you, mademoiselle. Would I not have been accounted a spy, and would they not have made short work of me here at your chateau?"

"No, no; they would have done no murder."

"Perhaps not, but I could not be sure just then. Most men situated as your father was would have despatched me. Ah, mademoiselle, have you not proofs enough? Do you not believe me now?"

"Yes, monsieur," she answered simply, "I believe you."

"Will you not believe, then, in the sincerity of my love?"

She made no rely. Her face was averted, but from her silence I took heart. I drew close to her. I set my hand upon the tall back of her chair, and, leaning towards her, I spoke with passionate heat as must have melted, I thought, any woman who had not a loathing for me.

"Mademoiselle; I am a poor man now," I ended. "I am no longer that magnificent gentleman whose wealth and splendour were a byword. Yet am I no needy adventurer. I have a little property at Beaugency – a very spot for happiness, mademoiselle. Paris shall know me no more. At Beaugency I shall live at peace, in seclusion, and, so that you come with me, in such joy as in all my life I have done nothing to deserve. I have no longer an army of retainers. A couple of men and a maid or two shall constitute our household. Yet I shall account my wealth well lost if for love's sake you'll share with me the peace of my obscurity. I am poor, mademoiselle, yet no poorer even now than that Gascon gentleman, René de Lesperon, for whom you held me, and on whom you bestowed the priceless treasure of your heart."

"Oh, might it have pleased God that you had remained that poor Gascon gentleman!" she cried.

"In what am I different, Roxalanne?"

"In that he had laid no wager," she answered, rising suddenly.

My hopes were withering. She was not angry. She was pale, and her gentle face was troubled – dear God! how sorely troubled! To me it almost seemed that I had lost.

She flashed me a glance of her blue eyes, and I thought that tears impended.

"Roxalanne!" I supplicated.

But she recovered the control that for a moment she had appeared upon the verge of losing. She put forth her hand.

"Adieu, monsieur!" said she.

I glanced from her hand to her face. Her attitude began to anger me, for I saw that she was not only resisting me, but resisting herself.

In her heart the insidious canker of doubt persisted. She knew – or should have known – that it no longer should have any place there, yet obstinately she refrained from plucking it out. There was that wager. But for that same obstinacy she must have realized the reason of my arguments, the irrefutable logic of my payment. She denied me, and in denying me she denied herself, for that she had loved me she had herself told me, and that she could love me again I was assured, if she would but see the thing in the light of reason and of justice.

"Roxalanne, I did not come to Lavédan to say 'Goodbye' to you. I seek from you a welcome, not a dismissal."

"Yet my dismissal is all that I can give. Will you not take my hand? May we not part in friendly spirit?"

"No, we may not; for we do not part at all."

It was as the steel of my determination striking upon the flint of hers. She looked up to my face for an instant; she raised her eyebrows in deprecation; she sighed, shrugged one shoulder, and, turning on her heel, moved towards the door.

"Anatole shall bring you refreshment ere you go," she said in a very polite and formal voice.

Then I played my last card. Was it for nothing that I had flung away my wealth? If she would not give herself, by God, I would compel her to sell herself. And I took no shame in doing it, for by doing it I was saving her and saving myself from a life of unhappiness.

"Roxalanne!" I cried. The imperiousness of my voice arrested and compelled her perhaps against her very will.

"Monsieur?" said she, as demurely as you please.

"Do you know what you are doing?"

"But yes – perfectly."

"Pardieu, you do not. I will tell you. You are sending your father to the scaffold."

She turned livid, her step faltered, and she leant against the frame of the doorway for support. Then she stared at me, wide-eyed in horror.

"That is not true," she pleaded, yet without conviction. "He is not in danger of his life. They can prove nothing against him. Monsieur de Saint-Eustache could find no evidence here – nothing."

"Yet there is Monsieur de Saint-Eustache's word; there is the fact – the significant fact – that your father did not take up arms for the King, to afford the Chevalier's accusation some measure of corroboration. At Toulouse in these times they are not particular. Remember how it had fared with me but for the King's timely arrival."

That smote home. The last shred of her strength fell from her. A great sob shook her, then covering her face with her hands, "Mother in Heaven, have pity on me!" she cried. "Oh, it cannot be, it cannot be!"

Her distress touched me sorely. I would have consoled her, I would have bidden her have no fear, assuring her that I would save her father. But for my own ends, I curbed the mood. I would use this as a cudgel to shatter her obstinacy, and I prayed that God might forgive me if I did aught that a gentleman should account unworthy.

My need was urgent, my love all-engrossing; winning her meant winning life and happiness, and already I had sacrificed so much.

Her cry rang still in my ears, "It cannot be, it cannot be!"

I trampled my nascent tenderness underfoot, and in its room I set a harshness that I did not feel – a harshness of defiance and menace.

"It can be, it will be, and, as God lives, it shall be, if you persist in your unreasonable attitude."

"Monsieur, have mercy!"

"Yes, when you shall be pleased to show me the way to it by having mercy upon me. If I have sinned, I have atoned. But that is a closed question now; to reopen it were futile. Take heed of this, Roxalanne: there is one thing – one only in all France can save your father."

"That is, monsieur?" she inquired breathlessly.

"My word against that of Saint-Eustache. My indication to His Majesty that your father's treason is not to be accepted on the accusation of Saint-Eustache. My information to the King of what I know touching this gentleman."

"You will go, monsieur?" she implored me. "Oh, you will save him! Mon Dieu, to think of the time that we have wasted here, you and I, whilst he is being carried to the scaffold! Oh, I did not dream it was so perilous with him! I was desolated by his arrest; I thought of some months' imprisonment, perhaps. But that he should die – ! Monsieur de Bardelys, you will save him! Say that you will do this for me!"

She was on her knees to me now, her arms clasping my boots, her eyes raised in entreaty – God, what entreaty! – to my own.

"Rise, mademoiselle, I beseech you," I said, with a quiet I was far from feeling. "There is no need for this. Let us be calm. The danger to your father is not so imminent. We may have some days yet – three or four, perhaps."

I lifted her gently and led her to a chair. I was hard put to it not to hold her supported in my arms. But I might not cull that advantage from her distress. A singular niceness, you will say, perhaps, as in your scorn you laugh at me. Perhaps you are right to laugh – yet are you not altogether right.

"You will go to Toulouse, monsieur?" she begged.

I took a turn in the room, then halting before her, "Yes," I answered, "I will go."

The gratitude that leapt to her eyes smote me hard, for my sentence was unfinished.

"I will go," I continued quickly, "when you shall have promised to become my wife."

The joy passed from her face. She glanced at me a moment as if without understanding.

"I came to Lavédan to win you, Roxalanne, and from Lavédan I shall not stir until I have accomplished my design," I said very quietly. "You will therefore see that it rests with you how soon I may set out."

She fell to weeping softly, but answered nothing. At last I turned from her and moved towards the door.

"Where are you going?" she cried.

"To take the air, mademoiselle. If upon deliberation you can bring yourself to marry me, send me word by Anatole or one of the others, and I shall set out at once for Toulouse."

"Stop!" she cried. Obediently I stopped, my hand already upon the doorknob. "You are cruel, monsieur!" she complained.

"I love you," said I, by way of explaining it. "To be cruel seems to be the way of love. You have been cruel to me."

"Would you – would you take what is not freely given?"

"I have the hope that when you see that you must give, you will give freely."

"If – if I make you this promise – "

"Yes?" I was growing white with eagerness.

"You will fulfil your part of the bargain?"

"It is a habit of mine, mademoiselle – as witnesses the case of Chatellerault." She shivered at the mention of his name. It reminded her of precisely such another bargain that three nights ago she had made. Precisely, did I say? Well, not quite precisely.

"I – I promise to marry you, then," said she in a choking voice, "whenever you choose, after my father shall have been set at liberty."

I bowed. "I shall start at once," said I.

And perhaps out of shame, perhaps out of – who shall say what sentiments? – I turned without another word and left her.

# Chapter 20

## At Blagnac

I was glad to be in the open once more – glad of the movement, as I rode at the head of my brave company along the bank of the Garonne and in the shade of the golden, autumn-tinted trees.

I was in a measure angry with myself that I had driven such a bargain with Roxalanne, in a measure angry with her that she had forced me to it by her obstinacy. A fine gentleman I, on my soul, to have dubbed Chatellerault a cheat for having done no worse than I had now brought myself to do! Yet, was it so? No, I assured myself, it was not. A thousand times no! What I had done I had done as much to win Roxalanne to me as to win her from her own unreasonableness. In the days to come she should thank me for my harshness, for that which now she perhaps accounted my unfairness.

Then, again, would I ask myself, was I very sure of this? And so the two questions were flung the one against the other; my conscience divided itself into two parties, and they waged a war that filled me with a depressing uncertainty.

In the end shame was overthrown, and I flung back my head with a snort of assurance. I was doing no wrong. On the contrary, I was doing right – both by myself and by Roxalanne. What matter that I was really cheating her? What matter that I had said I would not leave Lavédan until I had her promise, whilst in reality I had hurled my threat at Saint-Eustache that I would meet him at Toulouse, and passed my word to the Vicomtesse that I would succour her husband?

I gave no thought to the hidden threat with which Saint-Eustache had retorted that from Lavédan to Toulouse was a distance of some twenty leagues. Had he been a man of sterner purposes I might have been uneasy and on my guard. But Saint-Eustache – pshaw!

It is ill to underestimate an enemy, be he never so contemptible, and for my disdain of the Chevalier I might have paid dearly had not Fortune – which of late had been practising singular jests upon me after seemingly abandoning me, returned to my aid at the last moment.

It was Saint-Eustache's purpose that I should never reach Toulouse alive, for in all the world I was the one man he feared, the one man who would encompass his undoing and destruction by a word. And so he had resolved and disposed that I should be removed, and to accomplish this he had left a line of bravos along the road I was to pass.

He had counted upon my lying the night in one of the intervening towns, for the journey was over-long to be accomplished at a stretch, and wherever I might chance to lie, there I should have to reckon with his assassins. The nearer Toulouse – although I knew not this – the thicker grew my danger. Into the very thick of it I rode; in the very thick of it I lay, and all that came of it was that I obtained possession of one more and overwhelming piece of evidence against my murderous Chevalier. But I outrun my story.

It had been my purpose to change horses at Grenade, and so push on and reach Toulouse that very night or in the early hours of the following morning. At Grenade, however, there were no horses to be obtained, at least not more than three, and so, leaving the greater portion of my company behind, I set out, escorted only by Gilles and Antoine. Night had fallen long before we reached Lespinasse, and with it came foul weather. The wind rose from the west, grew to the violence of a hurricane, and brought with it such a deluge of cold, cutting rain as never had it been my ill-chance to ride through.

From Lespinasse to Fenouillet the road dips frequently, and wherever this occurred it seemed to us that we were riding in a torrent, our horses fetlock-deep in mud.

Antoine complained in groans; Gilles growled openly, and went the length of begging me, as we rode through the ill-paved, flooded streets of Fenouillet, to go no farther. But I was adamant in my resolve. Soaked to the skin, my clothes hanging sodden about me, and chilled to the marrow though I was, I set my chattering teeth, and swore that we should not sleep until we reached Toulouse.

"My God," he groaned, "and we but halfway!"

"Forward!" was all I answered; and so as midnight chimed we left Fenouillet behind us, and dashed on into the open country and the full fury of the tempest.

My servants came after me upon their stumbling horses, whining and cursing by turns, and forgetting in their misery the respect that they were accustomed to pay me. I think now that it was a providence that guided me. Had I halted at Fenouillet, as they would have had me do, it is odds that this chronicle would never have been penned, for likely enough I had had my throat cut as I slept. A providence was it also that brought my horse down within a half-mile of Blagnac, and so badly did it founder that it might not be ridden farther.

The beasts my men bestrode were in little better condition, and so, with infinite chagrin, I was forced to acknowledge defeat and to determine that at Blagnac we should lie for the remainder of the night. After all, it mattered little. A couple of hours' riding in the morning would bring us to Toulouse, and we would start betimes.

I bade Gilles dismount – he had been the louder in his complainings – and follow us afoot, bringing my horse to the Auberge de l'Étoile at Blagnac, where we would await him. Then I mounted his jaded beast, and, accompanied by Antoine – the last of my retainers – I rode into Blagnac, and pulled up at the sign of the "Star".

With my whip I smote the door, and I had need to smite hard if I would be heard above the wind that shrieked and howled under the eaves of that narrow street. Yet it almost seemed as if some one were expected, for scarce had my knocking ceased when the door was opened, and the landlord stood there, shading a taper with his hand. For a moment I saw the glow of its light on his rosy, white-bearded face, then a gust of wind extinguished it.

"Diable!" he swore, "an ugly night for travelling;" adding as an afterthought, "You ride late, monsieur."

"You are a man of supreme discernment, Monsieur l'Hôte," said I testily, as I pushed him aside and stepped into the passage. "Will you keep me in the rain till daylight whilst you perpend how late I ride? Is your ostler abed? See to those beasts yourself, then. Afterwards get me food – for me and for my man and beds for both of us."

"I have but one room, monsieur," he answered respectfully. "You shall have that, and your servant shall sleep in the hayloft."

"My servant sleeps in my room, if you have but one. Set a mattress on the floor for him. Is this a night to leave a dog to sleep in a hayloft? I have another servant following. He will be here in a few minutes. You must find room for him also – in the passage outside my door, if no other accommodation be possible."

"But, monsieur – " he began in a tone of protest, which I set down to the way a landlord has of making difficulties that he shall be the better paid for such lodging as he finds us.

"See to it," I ordered peremptorily. "You shall be well paid. Now go tend those horses."

On the wall of the passage fell a warm, reddish glow from the common room, which argued a fire, and this was too alluring to admit of my remaining longer in discussion with him. I strode forward, therefore.

The Auberge de l'Étoile was not an imposing hostelry, nor one at which from choice I had made a halt. This common room stank most vilely of oil, of burning tallow – from the smoky tapers – and of I know not what other noisome unsavourinesses.

As I entered, I was greeted by a resonant snore from a man seated in a corner by the fire. His head had fallen back, displaying the brown, sinewy neck, and he slept – or seemed to sleep – with mouth wide open. Full length on the hearth and in the red glare of the burning logs lay what at first glance I took to be a heap of rags, but which closer scrutiny showed me to be another man, seemingly asleep also.

I flung my sodden castor on the table; I dropped my drenched cloak on the ground, and stepped with heavy tread and a noisy rattle of spurs across the floor. Yet my ragged gentleman slept on. I touched him lightly with my whip.

"Holà! mon bonhomme," I cried to him. Still he did not move, whereat I lost patience and caught him a kick full in the side, so choicely aimed that first it doubled him up, then brought him into a sitting posture, with the snarl of a cross-grained dog that has been rudely aroused.

From out of an evil, dirty countenance a pair of gloomy, bloodshot eyes scowled threateningly upon me. The man on the chair awoke at the same instant, and sat forward.

"Eh bien?" said I to my friend on the hearth: "Will you stir yourself?"

"For whom?" he growled. "Is not the Étoile as much for me as for you, whoever you may be?"

"We have paid our lodging, pardieu!" swore he of the chair.

"My masters," said I grimly, "if you have not eyes to see my sodden condition, and if you therefore have not the grace to move that I may approach the fire; I'll see to it that you spend the night not only à l'Étoile, but à la belle étoile." With which pleasantry, and a touch of the foot, I moved my friend aside. My tone was not nice, nor do I generally have the air of promising more than I can fulfil.

They were growling together in a corner when Antoine came to draw off my doublet and my boots. They were still growling when Gilles joined us presently, although at his coming they paused to take his measure with their eyes. For Gilles was something of a giant, and men were wont to turn their heads – aye, and women too – to admire his fine proportions. We supped – so vilely that I have not the heart to tell you what we ate – and, having supped, I bade my host light me to my chamber. As for my men, I had determined that they should spend the night in the common room, where there was a fire, and where – notwithstanding the company of those two ruffians, into whose presence I had not troubled to inquire – they would doubtless be better than elsewhere in that poor hostelry.

In gathering up my cloak and doublet and other effects to bear them off to the kitchen, the host would have possessed himself also of my sword. But with a laugh I took it from him, remarking that it required no drying.

As we mounted the stairs, I heard something above me that sounded like the creaking of a door. The host heard it also, for he stood suddenly still, his glance very questioning.

"What was that?" said he.

"The wind, I should say," I answered idly; and my answer seemed to reassure him, for with a "Ah, yes – the wind," he went on.

Now, for all that I am far from being a man of tremors or unwarranted fears, to tell the truth the hostelry of the "Star" was beginning to fret my nerves. I could scarce have told you why had you asked me, as I sat upon the bed after mine host had left me, and turned my thoughts to it. It was none of the trivial incidents that had marked my coming; but it was, I think, the combination of them all. First there was the host's desire to separate me from my men by suggesting that they should sleep in the hayloft. Clearly unnecessary, when he was not averse to turning his common room into a dormitory. There was his very evident relief when, after announcing that I would have them sleep one in my room and one in the passage by my door, I consented to their spending the night below; there was the presence of those two very ill-looking cut-throats; there was the attempt to carry off my sword; and, lastly, there was that creaking door and the host's note of alarm.

What was that?

I stood up suddenly. Had my fancy, dwelling upon that very incident, tricked me into believing that a door had creaked again? I listened, but a silence followed, broken only by a drone of voices ascending from the common room. As I had assured the host upon the stairs, so I now assured myself that it was the wind, the signboard of the inn, perhaps, swaying in the storm.

And then, when I had almost dismissed my doubts, and was about to divest myself of my remaining clothes, I saw something at which I thanked Heaven that I had not allowed the landlord to carry off my rapier. My eyes were on the door, and, as I gazed, I beheld the slow raising of the latch. It was no delusion; my wits were keen and my eyes sharp; there was no fear to make me see things that were not. Softly I stepped to the bed-rail where I had hung my sword by the baldrick, and as softly I unsheathed it. The door was pushed open, and I caught the advance of a stealthy step. A naked foot shot past the edge of the door into my room, and for a second I thought of pinning it to the ground with my rapier; then came a leg, then a half-dressed body surmounted by a face – the face of Rodenard!

At sight of it, amazement and a hundred suspicions crossed my mind.

How, in God's name, came he here, and for what purpose did he steal so into my chamber?

But my suspicions perished even as they were begotten. There was so momentous, so alarmingly warning a look on his face as he whispered the one word "Monseigneur!" that clearly if danger there was to me it was not from him.

"What the devil – " I began.

But at the sound of my voice the alarm grew in his eyes.

"Sh!" he whispered, his finger on his lips. "Be silent, monseigneur, for Heaven's sake!"

Very softly he closed the door; softly, yet painfully, he hobbled forward to my side.

"There is a plot to murder you, monseigneur," he whispered.

"What! Here at Blagnac?"

He nodded fearfully.

"Bah!" I laughed. "You rave, man. Who was to know that I was to come this way? And who is there to plot against my life?"

"Monsieur de Saint-Eustache," he answered. "And for the rest, as to expecting you here, they did not, but they were prepared against the remote chance of your coming. From what I have gathered, there is not a hostelry betwixt this and Lavédan at which the Chevalier has not left his cut-throats with the promise of enormous reward to the men who shall kill you."

I caught my breath at that. My doubts vanished.

"Tell me what you know," said I. "Be brief."

Thereupon this faithful dog, whom I had so sorely beaten but four nights ago, told me how, upon finding himself able to walk once more, he had gone to seek me out, that he might implore me to forgive him and not cast him off altogether, after a lifetime spent in the service of my father and of myself.

He had discovered from Monsieur de Castelroux that I was gone to Lavédan, and he determined to follow me thither. He had no horse and little money, and so he had set out afoot that very day, and dragged himself as far as Blagnac, where, however, his strength had given out, and he was forced to halt. A providence it seemed that this had so befallen. For here at the Étoile he had that evening overheard Saint-Eustache in conversation with those two bravos below stairs. It would seem from what he had said that at every hostelry from Grenade to Toulouse – at which it was conceivable that I might spend the night – the Chevalier had made a similar provision.

At Blagnac, if I got so far without halting, I must arrive very late, and therefore the Chevalier had bidden his men await me until daylight. He did not believe, however, that I should travel so far, for he had seen to it that I should find no horses at the posthouses.

But it was just possible that I might, nevertheless, push on, and Saint-Eustache would let no possibility be overlooked. Here at Blagnac the landlord, Rodenard informed me, was also in Saint-Eustache's pay. Their intention was to stab me as I slept.

"Monseigneur," he ended, "knowing what danger awaited you along the road, I have sat up all night, praying God and His saints that you might come this far, and that thus I might warn you. Had I been less bruised and sore, I had got myself a horse and ridden out to meet you; as it was, I could but hope and pray that you would reach Blagnac, and that – "

I gathered him into my arms at that, but my embrace drew a groan from him, for the poor, faithful knave was very sore.

"My poor Ganymède!" I murmured, and I was more truly moved to sympathy, I think, than ever I had been in all my selfish life.

Hearing his sobriquet, a look of hope gleamed suddenly in his eye.

"You will take me back, monseigneur?" he pleaded. "You will take me back, will you not? I swear that I will never let my tongue – "

"Sh, my good Ganymède. Not only will I take you back, but I shall strive to make amends for my brutality. Come, my friend, you shall have twenty golden louis to buy unguents for your poor shoulders."

"Monseigneur is very good," he murmured, whereupon I would have embraced him again but that he shivered and drew back.

"No, no, monseigneur," he whispered fearfully. "It is a great honour, but it – it pains me to be touched."

"Then take the will for the deed. And now for these gentlemen below stairs." I rose and moved to the door.

"Order Gilles to beat their brains out," was Ganymède's merciful suggestion.

I shook my head. "We might be detained for doing murder. We have no proof yet of their intentions – I think – " An idea flashed suddenly across my mind. "Go back to your room, Ganymède," I bade him. "Lock yourself in, and do not stir until I call you. I do not wish their suspicions aroused."

I opened the door, and as Ganymède obediently slipped past me and vanished down the passage "Monsieur l'Hôte," I called. "Ho, there, Gilles!"

"Monsieur," answered the landlord.

"Monseigneur," replied Gilles; and there came a stir below.

"Is aught amiss?" the landlord questioned, a note of concern in his voice.

"Amiss?" I echoed peevishly, mincing my words as I uttered them. "Pardieu! Must I be put to it to undress myself, whilst those two lazy dogs of mine are snoring beneath me? Come up this instant, Gilles. And," I added as an afterthought, "you had best sleep here in my room."

209

"At once, monseigneur," answered he, but I caught the faintest tinge of surprise in his accents, for never yet had it fallen to the lot of sturdy, clumsy Gilles to assist me at my toilet.

The landlord muttered something, and I heard Gilles whispering his reply. Then the stairs creaked under his heavy tread.

In my room I told him in half a dozen words what was afoot. For answer, he swore a great oath that the landlord had mulled a stoup of wine for him, which he never doubted now was drugged. I bade him go below and fetch the wine, telling the landlord that I, too, had a fancy for it.

"But what of Antoine?" he asked. "They will drug him."

"Let them. We can manage this affair, you and I, without his help. If they did not drug him, they might haply stab him. So that in being drugged lies his safety."

As I bade him so he did, and presently he returned with a great steaming measure. This I emptied into a ewer, then returned it to him that he might take it back to the host with my thanks and our appreciation. Thus should we give them confidence that the way was clear and smooth for them.

Thereafter there befell precisely that which already you will be expecting, and nothing that you cannot guess. It was perhaps at the end of an hour's silent waiting that one of them came. We had left the door unbarred so that his entrance was unhampered. But scarce was he within when out of the dark, on either side of him, rose Gilles and I. Before he had realized it, he was lifted off his feet and deposited upon the bed without a cry; the only sound being the tinkle of the knife that dropped from his suddenly unnerved hand.

On the bed, with Gilles' great knee in his stomach, and Gilles' hands at his throat, he was assured in unequivocal terms that at his slightest outcry we would make an end of him. I kindled a light. We trussed him hand and foot with the bedclothes, and then, whilst he lay impotent and silent in his terror, I proceeded to discuss the situation with him.

I pointed out that we knew that what he had done he had done at Saint-Eustache's instigation, therefore the true guilt was Saint-Eustache's and upon him alone the punishment should fall.

But ere this could come to pass, he himself must add his testimony to ours – mine and Rodenard's. If he would come to Toulouse and do that – make a full confession of how he had been set to do this murdering – the Chevalier de Saint-Eustache, who was the real culprit, should be the only one to suffer the penalty of the law.

If he would not do that, why, then, he must stand the consequences himself – and the consequences would be the hangman. But in either case he was coming to Toulouse in the morning.

It goes without saying that he was reasonable. I never for a moment held his judgment in doubt; there is no loyalty about a cut-throat, and it is not the way of his calling to take unnecessary risk.

We had just settled the matter in a mutually agreeable manner when the door opened again, and his confederate – rendered uneasy, no doubt, by his long absence – came to see what could be occasioning this unconscionable delay in the slitting of the throats of a pair of sleeping men.

Beholding us there in friendly conclave, and no doubt considering that under the circumstances his intrusion was nothing short of an impertinence, that polite gentleman uttered a cry – which I should like to think was an apology for having disturbed us and turned to go with most indecorous precipitancy.

But Gilles took him by the nape of his dirty neck and haled him back into the room. In less time than it takes me to tell of it, he lay beside his colleague, and was being asked whether he did not think that he might also come to take the same view of the situation.

Overjoyed that we intended no worse by him, he swore by every saint in the calendar that he would do our will, that he had reluctantly undertaken the Chevalier's business, that he was no cut-throat, but a poor man with a wife and children to provide for.

And that, in short, was how it came to pass that the Chevalier de Saint-Eustache himself, by disposing for my destruction, disposed only for his own. With these two witnesses, and Rodenard to swear how Saint-Eustache had bribed them to cut my throat, with myself and Gilles to swear how the attempt had been made and frustrated, I could now go to His Majesty with a very full confidence, not only of having the Chevalier's accusations, against whomsoever they might be, discredited, but also of sending the Chevalier himself to the gallows he had so richly earned.

# Chapter 21

## Louis the Just

"For me," said the King, "these depositions were not necessary. Your word, my dear Marcel, would have sufficed. For the Courts, however, perhaps it is well that you have had them taken; moreover, they form a valuable corroboration of the treason which you lay to the charge of Monsieur de Saint-Eustache."

We were standing – at least, La Fosse and I were standing, Louis XIII sat – in a room, of the Palace of Toulouse, where I had had the honour of being brought before His Majesty. La Fosse was there, because it would seem that the King had grown fond of him, and could not be without him since his coming to Toulouse.

His Majesty was, as usual, so dull and weary – not even roused by the approaching trial of Montmorency, which was the main business that had brought him south – that even the company of this vapid, shallow, but irrepressibly good-humoured La Fosse, with his everlasting mythology, proved a thing desirable.

"I will see," said Louis, "that your friend the Chevalier is placed under arrest at once, and as much for his attempt upon your life as for the unstable quality of his political opinions, the law shall deal with him – conclusively." He sighed. "It always pains me to proceed to extremes against a man of his stamp. To deprive a fool of his head seems a work of supererogation."

I inclined my head, and smiled at his pleasantry. Louis the Just rarely permitted himself to jest, and when he did his humour was as like unto humour as water is like unto wine. Still, when a monarch jests, if you are wise, if you have a favour to sue, or a position at Court to seek or to maintain, you smile, for all that the ineptitude of his witless wit be rather provocative of sorrow.

"Nature needs meddling with at times," hazarded La Fosse, from behind His Majesty's chair. "This Saint-Eustache is a sort of Pandora's box, which it is well to close ere – "

"Go to the devil," said the King shortly. "We are not jesting. We have to do justice."

"Ah! Justice," murmured La Fosse; "I have seen pictures of the lady. She covers her eyes with a bandage, but is less discreet where the other beauties of her figure are in question."

His Majesty blushed. He was above all things a chaste-minded man, modest as a nun. To the immodesty rampant about him he was in the habit of closing his eyes and his ears, until the flagrancy or the noise of it grew to proportions to which he might remain neither blind nor deaf.

"Monsieur de la Fosse," said he in an austere voice, "you weary me, and when people weary me I send them away – which is one of the reasons why I am usually so much alone. I beg that you will glance at that hunting-book, so that when I have done with Monsieur de Bardelys you may give me your impressions of it."

La Fosse fell back, obedient but unabashed, and, moving to a table by the window, he opened the book Louis had pointed out.

"Now, Marcel, while that buffoon prepares to inform me that the book has been inspired by Diana herself, tell me what else you have to tell."

"Naught else, Sire."

"How naught? What of this Vicomte de Lavédan."

"Surely Your Majesty is satisfied that there is no charge – no heedful charge against him?"

"Aye, but there is a charge – a very heedful one. And so far you have afforded me no proofs of his innocence to warrant my sanctioning his enlargement."

"I had thought, Sire, that it would be unnecessary to advance proofs of his innocence until there were proofs of his guilt to be refuted. It is unusual, Your Majesty, to apprehend a gentleman so that he may show cause why he did not deserve such apprehension. The more usual course is to arrest him because there are proofs of his guilt to be preferred against him."

Louis combed his beard pensively, and his melancholy eyes grew thoughtful.

"A nice point, Marcel," said he, and he yawned. "A nice point. You should have been a lawyer." Then, with an abrupt change of manner, "Do you give me your word of honour that he is innocent?" he asked sharply.

"If Your Majesty's judges offer proof of his guilt, I give you my word that I will tear that proof to pieces."

"That is not an answer. Do you swear his innocence?"

"Do I know what he carries in his conscience?" quoth I still fencing with the question. "How can I give my word in such a matter? Ah, Sire, it is not for nothing that they call you Louis the Just," I pursued, adopting cajolery and presenting him with his own favourite phrase. "You will never allow a man against whom there is no shred of evidence to be confined in prison."

"Is there not?" he questioned. Yet his tone grew gentler. History, he had promised himself, should know him as Louis the Just, and he would do naught that might jeopardize his claim to that proud title. "There is the evidence of this Saint-Eustache!"

"Would Your Majesty hang a dog upon the word of that double traitor?"

"Hum! You are a great advocate, Marcel. You avoid answering questions; you turn questions aside by counter-questions." He seemed to be talking more to himself than to me. "You are a much better advocate than the Vicomte's wife, for instance. She answers questions and has a temper – Ciel! what a temper!"

215

"You have seen the Vicomtesse?" I exclaimed, and I grew cold with apprehension, knowing as I did the licence of that woman's tongue.

"Seen her?" he echoed whimsically. "I have seen her, heard her, well-nigh felt her. The air of this room is still disturbed as a consequence of her presence. She was here an hour ago."

"And it seemed," lisped La Fosse, turning from his hunting-book, "as if the three daughters of Acheron had quitted the domain of Pluto to take embodiment in a single woman."

"I would not have seen her," the King resumed, as though La Fosse had not spoken, "but she would not be denied. I heard her voice blaspheming in the antechamber when I refused to receive her; there was a commotion at my door; it was dashed open, and the Swiss who held it was hurled into my room here as though he had been a mannikin. Dieu! Since I have reigned in France I have not been the centre of so much commotion. She is a strong woman, Marcel. The saints defend you hereafter, when she shall come to be your mother-in-law. In all France, I'll swear, her tongue is the only stouter thing than her arm. But she's a fool."

"What did she say, Sire?" I asked in my anxiety.

"Say? She swore – Ciel! how she did swear! Not a saint in the calendar would she let rest in peace; she dragged them all by turns from their chapter-rolls to bear witness to the truth of what she said."

"That was – "

"That her husband was the foulest traitor out of hell. But that he was a fool with no wit of his own to make him accountable for what he did, and that out of folly he had gone astray. Upon those grounds she besought me to forgive him and let him go. When I told her that he must stand his trial, and that I could offer her but little hope of his acquittal, she told me things about myself, which in my conceit, and thanks to you flatterers who have surrounded me, I had never dreamed.

"She told me I was ugly, sour-faced, and malformed; that I was priest-ridden and a fool; unlike my brother, who, she assured me, is a mirror of chivalry and manly perfections. She promised me that Heaven should never receive my soul, though I told my beads from now till Doomsday, and she prophesied for me a welcome among the damned when my time comes. What more she might have foretold I cannot say. She wearied me at last, for all her novelty, and I dismissed her – that is to say," he amended, "I ordered four musketeers to carry her out. God pity you, Marcel, when you become her daughter's husband!"

But I had no heart to enter into his jocularity. This woman with her ungovernable passion and her rash tongue had destroyed everything.

"I see no likelihood of being her daughter's husband," I answered mournfully.

The King looked up, and laughed. "Down on your knees, then," said he, "and render thanks to Heaven."

But I shook my head very soberly. "To Your Majesty it is a pleasing comedy," said I, "but to me, hélas! it is nearer far to tragedy."

"Come, Marcel," said he, "may I not laugh a little? One grows so sad with being King of France! Tell me what vexes you."

"Mademoiselle de Lavédan has promised that she will marry me only when I have saved her father from the scaffold. I came to do it, very full of hope, Sire. But his wife has forestalled me and, seemingly, doomed him irrevocably."

His glance fell; his countenance resumed its habitual gloom. Then he looked up again, and in the melancholy depths of his eyes I saw a gleam of something that was very like affection.

"You know that I love you, Marcel," he said gently. "Were you my own son I could not love you more. You are a profligate, dissolute knave, and your scandals have rung in my ears more than once; yet you are different from these other fools, and at least you have never wearied me. To have done that is to have done something.

"I would not lose you, Marcel; as lose you I shall if you marry this rose of Languedoc, for I take it that she is too sweet a flower to let wither in the stale atmosphere of Courts. This man, this Vicomte de

217

Lavédan, has earned his death. Why should I not let him die, since if he dies you will not wed?"

"Do you ask me why, Sire?" said I. "Because they call you Louis the Just, and because no king was ever more deserving of the title."

He winced; he pursed his lips, and shot a glance at La Fosse, who was deep in the mysteries of his volume. Then he drew towards him a sheet of paper, and, taking a quill, he sat toying with it.

"Because they call me the Just, I must let justice take its course," he answered presently.

"But," I objected, with a sudden hope, "the course of justice cannot lead to the headsman in the case of the Vicomte de Lavédan."

"Why not?" And his solemn eyes met mine across the table.

"Because he took no active part in the revolt. If he was a traitor, he was no more than a traitor at heart, and until a man commits a crime in deed he is not amenable to the law's rigour. His wife has made his defection clear; but it were unfair to punish him in the same measure as you punish those who bore arms against you, Sire."

"Ah!" he pondered. "Well? What more?"

"Is that not enough, Sire?" I cried. My heart beat quickly, and my pulses throbbed with the suspense of that portentous moment.

He bent his head, dipped his pen and began to write.

"What punishment would you have me mete out to him?" he asked as he wrote. "Come, Marcel, deal fairly with me, and deal fairly with him – for as you deal with him, so shall I deal with you through him."

I felt myself paling in my excitement. "There is banishment, Sire – it is usual in cases of treason that are not sufficiently flagrant to be punished by death."

"Yes!" He wrote busily. "Banishment for how long, Marcel? For his lifetime?"

"Nay, Sire. That were too long."

"For my lifetime, then?"

"Again that were too long."

He raised his eyes and smiled. "Ah! You turn prophet? Well, for how long, then? Come, man."

"I should think five years – "

"Five years be it. Say no more."

He wrote on for a few moments; then he raised the sandbox and sprinkled the document.

"Tiens!" he cried, as he dusted it and held it out to me. "There is my warrant for the disposal of Monsieur le Vicomte Léon de Lavédan. He is to go into banishment for five years, but his estates shall suffer no sequestration, and at the end of that period he may return and enjoy them – we hope with better loyalty than in the past. Get them to execute that warrant at once, and see that the Vicomte starts today under escort for Spain. It will also be your warrant to Mademoiselle de Lavédan, and will afford proof to her that your mission has been successful."

"Sire!" I cried. And in my gratitude I could say no more, but I sank on my knee before him and raised his hand to my lips.

"There," said he in a fatherly voice. "Go now, and be happy."

As I rose, he suddenly put up his hand.

"Ma foi, I had all but forgotten, so much has Monsieur de Lavédan's fate preoccupied us." He picked up another paper from his table, and tossed it to me. It was my note of hand to Chatellerault for my Picardy estates.

"Chatellerault died this morning," the King pursued. "He had been asking to see you, but when he was told that you had left Toulouse, he dictated a long confession of his misdeeds, which he sent to me together with this note of yours. He could not, he wrote, permit his heirs to enjoy your estates; he had not won them; he had really forfeited his own stakes, since he had broken the rules of play. He has left me to deliver judgment in the matter of his own lands passing into your possession. What do you say to it, Marcel?"

It was almost with reluctance that I took up that scrap of paper. It had been so fine and heroic a thing to have cast my wealth to the winds of Heaven for love's sake, that on my soul I was loath to see myself master of more than Beaugency. Then a compromise suggested itself.

"The wager, Sire," said I, "is one that I take shame in having entered upon; that shame made me eager to pay it, although fully conscious that I had not lost. But even now, I cannot, in any case, accept the forfeit Chatellerault was willing to suffer. Shall we – shall we forget that the wager was ever laid?"

"The decision does you honour. It was what I had hoped from you. Go now, Marcel. I doubt me you are eager. When your love-sickness wanes a little we shall hope to see you at Court again."

I sighed. "Hélas, Sire, that would be never."

"So you said once before, monsieur. It is a foolish spirit upon which to enter into matrimony; yet – like many follies – a fine one. Adieu, Marcel!"

"Adieu, Sire!"

I had kissed his hands; I had poured forth my thanks; I had reached the door already, and he was in the act of turning to La Fosse, when it came into my head to glance at the warrant he had given me.

He noticed this and my sudden halt.

"Is aught amiss?" he asked.

"You – you have omitted something, Sire," I ventured, and I returned to the table. "I am already so grateful that I hesitate to ask an additional favour. Yet it is but troubling you to add a few strokes of the pen, and it will not materially affect the sentence itself."

He glanced at me, and his brows drew together as he sought to guess my meaning.

"Well, man, what is it?" he demanded impatiently.

"It has occurred to me that this poor Vicomte, in a strange land, alone, among strange faces, missing the loved ones that for so many years he has seen daily by his side, will be pitiably lonely."

The King's glance was lifted suddenly to my face. "Must I then banish his family as well?"

"All of it will not be necessary, Your Majesty."

For once his eyes lost their melancholy, and as hearty a burst of laughter as ever I heard from that poor, weary gentleman he vented then.

"Ciel! what a jester you are! Ah, but I shall miss you!" he cried, as, seizing the pen, he added the word I craved of him.

"Are you content at last?" he asked, returning the paper to me.

I glanced at it. The warrant now stipulated that Madame la Vicomtesse de Lavédan should bear her husband company in his exile.

"Sire, you are too good!" I murmured.

"Tell the officer to whom you entrust the execution of this warrant that he will find the lady in the guardroom below, where she is being detained, pending my pleasure. Did she but know that it was your pleasure she has been waiting upon, I should tremble for your future when the five years expire."

# Chapter 22

## We Unsaddle

Mademoiselle held the royal warrant of her father's banishment in her hand. She was pale, and her greeting of me had been timid. I stood before her, and by the door stood Rodenard, whom I had bidden attend me.

As I had approached Lavédan that day, I had been taken with a great, an overwhelming shame at the bargain I had driven. I had pondered, and it had come to me that she had been right to suggest that in matters of love what is not freely given it is not worth while to take. And out of my shame and that conclusion had sprung a new resolve. So that nothing might weaken it, and lest, after all, the sight of Roxalanne should bring me so to desire her that I might be tempted to override my purpose, I had deemed it well to have the restraint of a witness at our last interview. To this end had I bidden Ganymède follow me into the very salon.

She read the document to the very end, then her glance was raised timidly again to mine, and from me it shifted to Ganymède, stiff at his post by the door.

"This was the best that you could do, monsieur?" she asked at last.

"The very best, mademoiselle," I answered calmly. "I do not wish to magnify my service, but it was that or the scaffold. Madame your mother had, unfortunately, seen the King before me, and she had prejudiced your father's case by admitting him to be a traitor. There was a moment when in view of that I was almost led to despair.

"I am glad, however, mademoiselle, that I was so fortunate as to persuade the King to just so much clemency."

"And for five years, then, I shall not see my parents." She sighed, and her distress was very touching.

"That need not be. Though they may not come to France, it still remains possible for you to visit them in Spain."

"True," she mused; "that will be something – will it not?"

"Assuredly something; under the circumstances, much."

She sighed again, and for a moment there was silence.

"Will you not sit, monsieur?" said she at last. She was very quiet today, this little maid – very quiet and very wondrously subdued.

"There is scarce the need," I answered softly; whereupon her eyes were raised to ask a hundred questions. "You are satisfied with my efforts, mademoiselle?" I inquired.

"Yes, I am satisfied, monsieur."

That was the end, I told myself, and involuntarily I also sighed.

Still, I made no shift to go.

"You are satisfied that I – that I have fulfilled what I promised?"

Her eyes were again cast down, and she took a step in the direction of the window.

"But yes. Your promise was to save my father from the scaffold. You have done so, and I make no doubt you have done as much to reduce the term of his banishment as lay within your power. Yes, monsieur, I am satisfied that your promise has been well fulfilled."

Heigh-ho! The resolve that I had formed in coming whispered it in my ear that nothing remained but to withdraw and go my way. Yet not for all that resolve – not for a hundred such resolves – could I have gone thus. One kindly word, one kindly glance at least would I take to comfort me. I would tell her in plain words of my purpose, and she should see that there was still some good, some sense of honour in me, and thus should esteem me after I was gone.

"Ganymède," said I.

"Monseigneur?"

"Bid the men mount."

At that she turned, wonder opening her eyes very wide, and her glance travelled from me to Rodenard with its unspoken question.

But even as she looked at him he bowed and, turning to do my bidding, left the room. We heard his steps pass with a jingle of spurs across the hall and out into the courtyard. We heard his raucous voice utter a word of command, and there was a stamping of hoofs, a cramping of harness, and all the bustle of preparation.

"Why have you ordered your men to mount?" she asked at last.

"Because my business here is ended, and we are going."

"Going?" said she. Her eyes were lowered now, but a frown suggested their expression to me. "Going whither?"

"Hence," I answered. "That for the moment is all that signifies."

I paused to swallow something that hindered a clear utterance.

Then, "Adieu!" said I, and I abruptly put forth my hand.

Her glance met mine fearlessly, if puzzled.

"Do you mean, monsieur, that you are leaving Lavédan – thus?"

"So that I leave, what signifies the manner of my going?"

"But" – the trouble grew in her eyes; her cheeks seemed to wax paler than they had been – "but I thought that – that we made a bargain."

"Sh! mademoiselle, I implore you," I cried. "I take shame at the memory of it. Almost as much shame as I take at the memory of that other bargain which first brought me to Lavédan. The shame of the former one I have wiped out – although, perchance, you think it not. I am wiping out the shame of the latter one. It was unworthy in me, mademoiselle, but I loved you so dearly that it seemed to me that no matter how I came by you, I should rest content if I but won you. I have since seen the error if it, the injustice of it. I will not take what is not freely given. And so, farewell."

"I see, I see," she murmured, and ignored the hand that I held out. "I am very glad of it, monsieur."

I withdrew my hand sharply. I took up my hat from the chair on which I had cast it. She might have spared me that, I thought.

She need not have professed joy. At least she might have taken my hand and parted in kindness.

"Adieu, mademoiselle!" I said again, as stiffly as might be, and I turned towards the door.

"Monsieur!" she called after me. I halted.

"Mademoiselle?"

She stood demurely, with eyes downcast and hands folded. "I shall be so lonely here."

I stood still. I seemed to stiffen. My heart gave a mad throb of hope, then seemed to stop. What did she mean? I faced her fully once more, and, I doubt not, I was very pale. Yet lest vanity should befool me, I dared not act upon suspicions. And so, "True, mademoiselle," said I. "You will be lonely. I regret it."

As silence followed, I turned again to the door, and my hopes sank with each step in that direction.

"Monsieur!"

Her voice arrested me upon the very threshold.

"What shall a poor girl do with this great estate upon her hands? It will go to ruin without a man to govern it."

"You must not attempt the task. You must employ an intendant."

I caught something that sounded oddly like a sob. Could it be? Dieu! could it be, after all? Yet I would not presume. I half turned again, but her voice detained me. It came petulantly now.

"Monsieur de Bardelys, you have kept your promise nobly. Will you ask no payment?"

"No, mademoiselle," I answered very softly; "I can take no payment."

Her eyes were lifted for a second. Their blue depths seemed dim. Then they fell again.

"Oh, why will you not help me?" she burst out, to add more softly: "I shall never be happy without you!"

"You mean?" I gasped, retracing a step, and flinging my hat in a corner.

"That I love you, Marcel – that I want you!"

"And you can forgive – you can forgive?" I cried, as I caught her.

Her answer was a laugh that bespoke her scorn of everything – of everything save us two, of everything save our love. That and the pout of her red lips was her answer. And if the temptation of those lips – But there! I grow indiscreet.

Still holding her, I raised my voice.

"Ganymède!" I called.

"Monseigneur?" came his answer through the open window.

"Bid those knaves dismount and unsaddle."

# Rafael Sabatini

## Captain Blood

*Captain Blood* is the much-loved story of a physician and gentleman turned pirate.

Peter Blood, wrongfully accused and sentenced to death, narrowly escapes his fate and finds himself in the company of buccaneers. Embarking on his new life with remarkable skill and bravery, Blood becomes the 'Robin Hood' of the Spanish seas. This is swashbuckling adventure at its best.

## The Gates of Doom

'Depend above all on Pauncefort', announced King James; 'his loyalty is dependable as steel. He is with us body and soul and to the last penny of his fortune.' So when Pauncefort does indeed face bankruptcy after the collapse of the South Sea Company, the king's supreme confidence now seems rather foolish. And as Pauncefort's thoughts turn to gambling, moneylenders and even marriage to recover his debts, will he be able to remain true to the end? And what part will his friend and confidante, Captain Gaynor, play in his destiny?

'A clever story, well and amusingly told' – *The Times*

# Rafael Sabatini

## The Lost King

*The Lost King* tells the story of Louis XVII – the French royal who officially died at the age of ten but, as legend has it, escaped to foreign lands where he lived to an old age. Sabatini breathes life into these age-old myths, creating a story of passion, revenge and betrayal. He tells of how the young child escaped to Switzerland from where he plotted his triumphant return to claim the throne of France.

'...the hypnotic spell of a novel which for sheer suspense, deserves to be ranked with Sabatini's best' – *New York Times*

## Scaramouche

When a young cleric is wrongfully killed, his friend, André-Louis, vows to avenge his death. André's mission takes him to the very heart of the French Revolution where he finds the only way to survive is to assume a new identity. And so is born Scaramouche – a brave and remarkable hero of the finest order and a classic and much-loved tale in the greatest swashbuckling tradition.

'Mr Sabatini's novel of the French Revolution has all the colour and lively incident which we expect in his work' – *Observer*

# Rafael Sabatini

## The Sea Hawk

Sir Oliver, a typical English gentleman, is accused of murder, kidnapped off the Cornish coast, and dragged into life as a Barbary corsair. However Sir Oliver rises to the challenge and proves a worthy hero for this much-admired novel. Religious conflict, melodrama, romance and intrigue combine to create a masterly and highly successful story, perhaps best-known for its many film adaptations.

## The Shame of Motley

The Court of Pesaro has a certain fool – one Lazzaro Biancomonte of Biancomonte. *The Shame of Motley* is Lazzaro's story, presented with all the vivid colour and dramatic characterisation that has become Sabatini's hallmark.

'Mr Sabatini could not be conventional or commonplace if he tried'
– *Standard*

Made in the USA